THE SHAMER'S SIGNET

LENE KAABERBOL

Henry Holt and Company

New York

Henry Holt and Company, LLC
Publishers since 1866
175 Fifth Avenue
New York, New York 10010
www.henryholtchildrensbooks.com

Library of Congress Cataloging-in-Publication Data
Kaaberbol, Lene.
[Skammertegnet English]
The Shamer's signet / Lene Kaaberbol.—1st American ed.
p.   cm.—(The Shamer chronicles; bk. 2)
Summary: When eleven-year-old Dina, who recently inherited her mother's
gift of perceiving secret shames through eye contact, is kidnapped and
forced to shame enemies of the evil Valdracu, her fifteen-year-old brother
Davin rides to her aid.
ISBN-13: 978-0-8050-8217-3
ISBN-10: 0-8050-8217-4
[1. Fantasy.]   I. Title.
PZ7.K113Sm 2005   [Fic]—dc22   2004052363

First published in the United States in 2005 by Henry Holt and Company, LLC
Originally published in Danish in 2001 by Forlaget Publishers, Copenhagen,
under the title *Skammertegnet*. First English language edition published in Great Britain in
2003 by Hodder Children's
Books, published in agreement with Lene Kaaberbol, represented by the Laura Cecil
Literary Agency, London, in association with ICBS, Copenhagen.
First Henry Holt paperback edition, 2007
Printed in the United States of America on acid-free paper. ∞
1   3   5   7   9   10   8   6   4   2

THE SHAMER'S SIGNET

The Child Peddler

Among heather-grown slopes nested three low stone houses. A narrow cart track, not much more than a path, swerved to pass quite near, but there was little reason to halt here, unless one was very fond of heather, open sky, yew trees, and grazing sheep.

Nevertheless, a peddler's cart stood on the patch of packed dirt between the houses, and in the stonewalled fields the sheep had company—two mules and four horses rested, heads low and tails swishing, dozing in the early evening sun. And now we were making our way down the hill, my mother and I, and Callan Kensie. Most of the sheep stood stock-still, watching us suspiciously, and I could almost feel their puzzlement. Probably they had never seen so many strangers at Harral's Place before.

The sun hung huge and orange just above the ridge. The day had been warm and almost summery, and the air was still pleasant. Next to the peddler's wagon, three men were playing cards, using a beer barrel for a table. A pile of round flatbreads, three mugs of beer, and a fat, darkly gleaming sausage competed for space on the barrel top. It looked like something one might see outside any village inn on a breezy spring evening, until one noticed the leg iron that kept the peddler's ankle chained to his own wagon wheel.

The peddler carved himself a fat slice of sausage and slid the rest of it across the barrel top toward the two men who were supposed to be guarding him.

"Here," he said. "Eat. A good game of cards can make a hole in a man's belly."

"Never mind the belly," grumbled one of the guards. "Losing four copper marks and a perfectly good knife makes a sizable hole in a man's pocket!" But his complaint was good-natured, and he accepted the sausage.

At that moment, one of the mules brayed earsplittingly, and the guards looked up and caught sight of us. They leaped to their feet, and one of them hastily swept the cards off the barrel, as if we had caught them doing something disgraceful. But I knew how they felt. It was hard to act harsh and commanding toward a man once you started drinking his beer. And it was difficult to believe that there was any truth to the accusations that had been made against the cheerful little peddler. We knew him. He had come by our village often enough, and everyone enjoyed his visits. He was never without a joke or a good story, and he had a chuckling laugh and so many crow's feet that one could hardly see his eyes when he smiled. His eyebrows looked like two fat black slugs, except that they moved more quickly—one of them would shoot up questioningly at every other word. No, I thought, he was hardly guilty of anything more serious than cheating a bit on his measures. The boys must have run away, just like he said they had.

"Medama," said one guard, bowing in my mother's direction. He eyed me dubiously—just how polite did one have to be to an eleven-year-old girl? He settled for another bow, slightly less deep. "Medamina." After all, I *was* the Shamer's daughter. The third person in our party, Callan Kensie, received not a bow, but a measured nod, of the kind men give each other when there is respect between them, but not necessarily friendship. "Kensie. I thought you were guarding caravans down in the Lowlands."

Callan returned the man's nod, in exactly the same manner. "Well met, Laclan. But no. I have other duties now."

"So. The Kensie clan takes good care of their Shamer, I see." The guard's eyes rested for a moment on Callan's shoulders, very wide and knotted with the muscles a man gets from wielding a sword every day. Like most people, he avoided looking too hard at my mother. If one did not already know, the Shamer's signet resting on her breast, in clear view, provided ample warning: a heavy round pewter circle, enameled in white and black to look like an eye. I had one almost exactly like it, but with blue instead of black, because I was still only my mother's apprentice. Anyone who saw the signet would look away—or pay the price.

The peddler had also risen. "Well met," he said, grinning. "And none too soon. The company has been pleasant, but I had hoped to reach Baur Laclan before dark."

There was no trace of anxiety in his manner, and I grew even more convinced of his innocence. Not many people await the Shamer's call with such steadiness. He bowed briefly to my mother and then to me. "Well met," he repeated. "But what a pity to send two ladies on such a long journey, and for no reason."

My mother raised her head and glanced briefly at the peddler.

"Let us hope there is no reason," she said, not loudly, nor in any threatening tone of voice. Yet for the first time the grin on the little man's face started slipping, and he raised his hand to his mouth involuntarily, as if to prevent more words from escaping. But he recovered quite quickly.

"May I offer some refreshment after your long ride? Good beer? A bite to eat?"

"Thank you, no," said my mother politely. "I have a duty. That must come first."

She dismounted, graceful still despite the long ride. Falk, our black gelding, nosed her hopefully, wanting to be rid of his bridle, but she handed the reins to Callan. I got down off the small tough Highlander pony I had borrowed—less gracefully, I'm afraid. I get less practice. Callan loosened the girths to allow the horses to breathe freely, but he made no move to unsaddle them. He clearly did not expect a long stay.

"What is your name, peddler?" my mother asked, quietly still, with no hint of anger or threat.

"Hanibal Laclan Castor, at the lady's service," he said, delivering an unexpectedly smooth bow.

My mother pushed back the hood of her cloak and looked at him. "My name is Melussina Tonerre, and I have been tasked to look at you with a Shamer's eyes, and speak to you with a Shamer's voice. *Hanibal Laclan Castor, look at me!*"

The peddler started, as if someone had turned his own long skinner's whip on him. The tendons in his neck stood out tightly, like the strings on a lute. Much against his will, he raised his head to meet my mother's gaze. For a while, the two of them stood locked in complete silence. Sweat beaded the peddler's forehead, but my mother's face remained as expressionless as a mask of stone. All at once, the peddler's legs buckled, and he dropped to his knees in front of her. Still she held his gaze. He knotted his fists so tightly that his nails bit into the palms, and a few drops of blood appeared between the clenched fingers on one hand. But however much he wanted to, he could not look away.

"Release me, Medama," he finally begged, choking. "Be merciful. Let me go!"

"Tell them what you have done," she said. "Tell them, and let them witness it. Then I shall release you."

"Medama . . . I have merely done a bit of business—"

"Tell them. Tell them exactly what you mean by *doing a bit of business*, Hanibal Laclan Castor!" For the first time, emotion crept into my mother's voice: a seething contempt that made the little peddler shrink and become visibly smaller.

"Two boys," the peddler breathed, his voice hardly more than a whisper. "I took two boys into my service. It was an act of human kindness, they were both orphans. . . . No one in the village wanted them. . . . I treated them well, fed them properly, and saw to it that they were decently clothed. They had never been better off in their lives!" The last words came loudly and defiantly, a final defense. But they did not impress my mother.

"Tell us what happened later. How *kindly* you then acted."

"The winter was a hard one. I lost an entire load of seed corn when we were snowlocked at Sagisloc. It sprouted and fermented, corn worth sixty silver marks, completely useless! And the boys . . . one of them was all right, a soft and biddable lad. Not very strong, though. But the other! Trouble, he was, always trouble, from the very day I laid eyes on him. One time he pinched seven needles from my stock and sold them on his own. And spent the profits on cake and hot cider! Gave him a beating for that. Of course I did. But it was useless. He only got worse. Always contrary, always disobedient. If I asked him to unhitch the mules, he would scowl and tell me to do it myself. Send him for firewood? He would be gone for hours, and I would see neither hair nor hide of him until the fire had been long lit and the soup cooked. What was I to do? Sooner or later he'd have scarpered, and there I'd be, with nothing to show for all the money I'd spent on food and clothing for that lout. No doubt he would have taken the other one with him, they were such little pals, the two of them."

The peddler's flow of words came to a halt.

"And then?" My mother's voice prodded him onward. "What did you do then?"

"Then . . . I found them other employment."

"Where?"

"With a real gentleman—cousin to Drakan himself, the Dragon Lord at Dunark. Not such a bad fate, I'd say— serving a lord. If they play their cards right, they may end up with a knighthood! The Dragon Lord looks not on birth and reputation, they say, but on whether a man serves him well and true."

"And the price, peddler. Tell us your reward."

"There were my expenses," the peddler moaned. "Had to get a bit of my own back, didn't I? What's so bad about that?"

"How much, peddler?" The question came like a lash, and the peddler opened his mouth to answer, unable to stop himself.

"Fifteen silver marks for the runt, and twenty-three for the lout. He was tall and strong for his age."

The guards who had drunk his beer and eaten his food now looked as if they regretted it. One of them spat, to clear the taste from his mouth. But my mother had not finished with the man.

"And it was then you discovered that this was a profitable line of *business,* wasn't it? Tell us, so that the witnesses may hear. How many more? How many more children did you sell to Drakan?"

It seemed that for the first time the peddler looked beyond defenses and excuses. His wrinkled face was pale now, the eyes lightless like charcoal. Only now, trapped in the merciless mirror that the Shamer had created for him, did he see himself clearly. His voice cracked.

"Nineteen," he said, hoarse with shame, "including the first two."

"The outcasts. The orphans. The rebels and the crazies, the slow-witted and the crippled. The ones the villages are eager to be rid of. *Do you really think, Hanibal Laclan Castor, that Drakan buys them so that he can make knights out of them?*"

Tears trickled among the crow's feet. "Let me go. Medama, I humbly beg, let me be. . . . I'm so ashamed. By the Holy Saint Magda, I'm so ashamed."

"Witnesses. You have heard this man's confession. Have I done my duty?"

"Shamer, we have heard his words. You have done your duty," said one guard slowly and formally, glancing contemptuously at the weeping man crouched at her feet.

My mother closed her eyes.

"What will ye do to the little bastard?" Callan asked, not even deigning to look at the peddler.

"He is a Laclan," said one of the guards. "Through his grandfather only, but still . . . the Laclan clan must judge him. We'll stay here overnight and bring him to Baur Laclan in the morning."

"To sell people . . . to sell *children* . . ." Callan's voice was thick with disgust. "I hope he hangs!"

"Likely so," said the guard drily. "Helena Laclan is not a soft woman, and she has children of her own. And grandchildren."

Callan tightened the girths and then offered his hand to my mother, who had sunk down on one of the stone walls, looking completely exhausted.

"Medama Tonerre? Will ye ride? The sky is clear and we'll have a full moon to see by. And I've no liking for *his* company." He jerked his head toward the peddler.

Mama raised her head, but politely refrained from looking straight at him. "Yes. Yes, let's ride, Callan." She accepted his hand, but was too proud to let herself be lifted into the saddle. She made it on her own, but we could all see that she was shivering from strain and exhaustion. No doubt it would have been more sensible to stay the night, but I bit my lip and did not speak until we had crossed the first ridge and were out of sight of the guards and their sniffling prisoner.

"Was it bad?" I asked cautiously. She looked as if she was in no fit state to sit a horse.

The same thought had occurred to Callan. "Are ye fit to ride, Medama?" he asked. "We could make camp. . . ."

She shook her head. "I'll be fine. But it's . . . Callan, I see what he sees. When I look into his soul and his memory . . . to me it's not just a number. Nineteen. Nineteen children. I've seen their faces. Every one of them. And now . . . he has *bought* them. Bought them and paid for them, as though they were animals. What do you think he is going to use them for?"

None of us had an answer. But as we followed the track below the heather hills and the darkness grew close around us, I heard Callan mutter once more: "I hope the little bastard hangs."

He didn't. A couple of days later, a sheepish-looking Laclan rider came to tell us that the little peddler had carved through the spoke of the wagon wheel they had chained him to, using the knife he had won at cards. He had run off, and Laclan had declared him an outlaw in the Highlands, denying him his name and his clan rights from now on till the end of time. Anyone who saw him could now kill him freely, without fearing Laclan's wrath. But no one had seen him since.

The Sword

Carefully, I freed my new sword from its hiding place in the thatched roof of the sheep shed. It was not what you'd call shiny bright—not yet. A blackish gray color, it was, thick and heavy, and without much edge or point. It was little more than a flat iron bar at the moment. But Callan had promised to help me file and sharpen it, and in my mind I could see it already, the way it would be: a slim, bright weapon, sharp and deadly. A weapon suitable for a man.

It had cost me two of my good shirts—I now had only one left—and all of the seven coppers I had earned last summer, helping out at the mill in Birches. It was well worth the price, I thought. As long as my mother didn't find out about the shirts. Or at least not right away . . .

"Davin, will you please take the scraps out for the goats?"

I don't know how she does it. I really don't. But anytime I'm about to do something remotely fun or exciting, every time I'm about to do something she might not like, she can sense it from a distance of at least three miles, and instantly sticks me with some boring task I have to do instead. Feed the goats. Dina could feed the goats. *Melli* could feed the goats, and she was only five. She didn't need me for that. I was sixteen—nearly, anyway—and I was pretty sure I was growing a beard. When I felt my upper lip, there was something there, not bristles exactly, not yet, but *something*. Feed the goats! Not exactly a manly task. And I had more important things to do.

In a couple of quick moves, I was around the corner and over the fence. I trotted up the hill as fast as I could without getting completely winded. Maybe I could convince myself I hadn't really heard her. Maybe I could make her think I had already left. Not very likely, mind you—not with a mother who could make hardened murderers weep and confess with a single glance—but I could try, couldn't I? And as I ran across the High Field, very close to the sky and far, far away from goats and scraps and mothers with Shamer's eyes, I felt so light and free inside I could almost fly.

"There ye are, lad. We'd about given up on ye."

Callan and Kinni and Black-Arse were waiting for me outside Callan's tiny croft. It's a strange thing, that croft. Callan is as tall as a house and as wide as an oak tree. When you see him outside, it seems as if he can't possibly fit inside. But he can. He and his old gran both.

"Ah, likely his ma wouldn't let her little boy come," said Kinni.

I got fed up with Kinni sometimes. Most times, in fact. He was always going on at me about my mother, but I'd noticed that he lowered his eyes and called her "Medama Tonerre" just like everyone else—when she was around, at least. Kinni's father was a merchant, and he *paid* Callan to teach him how to use a sword.

I liked Black-Arse better. Of course, that was not his real name. Really he was Allin, but no one ever called him that anymore. He loved anything that could go bang. One time he had got hold of some niter and a jar of petroleum, and *boom!* Suddenly Debbi Herbs had lost an outhouse. When she saw Allin running for dear life with a huge black spot on his singed trousers, she screamed at him: "Come back here, ye black-arsed bastard, and I'll give ye what for!" And ever since, everybody has been calling him Black-Arse.

Black-Arse was the closest thing I had to a best friend here. If I had been born up here, we definitely would have been friends. But to Black-Arse and everyone else, I was still "the Shamer's boy from the Lowlands," and although everyone had been really helpful and nice and polite, they always somehow let you know that you were a stranger. A Highlander didn't completely trust anybody he hadn't known since he was in swaddling bands. The longer we stayed here, the more obvious it became to me that in their eyes, we simply were not clan, and never would be. And even though Black-Arse *liked* me much better, it was Kinni he would turn to if he was in trouble. Because Kinni was his great-great-cousin, and I was just a Lowlander. If I lived here for fifteen years, I would still be just a Lowlander. Sometimes it made me so mad I wanted to say the hell with it, the hell with *them*, and go back to Birches where I might still be the Shamer's boy, but at least they had all known me almost since I was born. Sometimes I got so homesick for Birches that I would be about ready to cry. And that was just too bad, because we couldn't go back. Cherry Tree Cottage, where we used to live, was a burned-out ruin, and Drakan's men were still looking for my mother and my sister. And for Nico, who caused it all, in a way.

Every time we practiced, Callan found a new place for us. He was always saying that a good caravan guard must be able to fight anytime and anywhere—in the mud, on a mountainside, in a forest, or in a bog. Robbers lie in ambush where they choose. They don't wait politely until you've reached firm, even ground.

On this particular day he brought us to a narrow dried-out gorge that had once been a riverbed. The bottom of it was full of round rocks and boulders, and the footing was terrible. If you forgot to watch your feet, down you went, and falling was a painful business on those rocks. But if you forgot to watch your opponent, it hurt even worse. Callan hit you *hard* for that. Most practice days, I took away quite a collection of bruises. Kinni sometimes complained, but Callan took no notice.

"Which would ye rather—bruises now or sword cuts later? If ye'll not learn that block, ye'll likely lose an arm the first time ye're in a real fight."

I listened, and kept my mouth shut. Bad enough to be a Lowlander—I had no intention of being a crybaby on top of it.

We trained until twilight. Some of the time we used heavy sticks, but in the end Callan let us use the swords, and the gorge echoed with a wonderful ringing sound every time the blades met. It sounded almost like bells, I thought. I sweated and stumbled and recovered, and not once did I think of my mother and her eyes, or of the stupid goats and their scraps. I just felt happy and warm all over, especially when Callan slapped my shoulder and said, "Well done, lad. Ye have the knack."

The best thing about it was that I knew he was right. Even though I hadn't been training long, I was already better than Kinni and Black-Arse. It was as if my arms and legs knew things that I didn't: Hold the sword *so* to block that blow. Swing it just *so* or you'll lose your balance. I loved my body at times like that, my clever body with its balance and strength and quickness.

Suddenly, a voice cut through the twilight: "Davin! Your mother is looking for you!"

For a moment, my body was not clever at all, but just

an awkward collection of limbs. Kinni took advantage and slugged me on the shoulder, and I lost all feeling in my right arm. My sword fell to the rocks with a dull clank.

"Ye're dead," said Kinni triumphantly and prodded my chest with his sword. And all the joy and warmth and excitement certainly died.

"Running her errands again, Nico?" I rubbed my right arm sourly. "Haven't you got better things to do?"

Nico stood at the edge of the gorge, staring down at me. His blue eyes were exceedingly cold, and he looked very much the noble, despite his commoner's clothes.

"No, Davin, I haven't, actually. You forget who your mother is. If not for her strength and courage, they would have flung my body on some middens long ago to feed the crows. I would have lost my head for three murders done by someone else. I owe her *everything*. And you owe her at least the courtesy to tell her how you spend your time. She worries about you."

Kinni giggled. "Davin-baby," he whispered, quietly, so Nico wouldn't hear him, "Mama Shamer is so *worried* about her little boy."

Angrily, I picked up my sword. I felt like clouting Kinni over the head with it. But I felt even more like flinging it at Nico and his stupid superior face. Who did he think he was, to preach about what I owed my mother? So I wanted to learn how to use a sword. What was wrong with that? What was wrong with learning how to fight, so that one day I'd be able to protect my mother against Drakan and all the other enemies *Nico* had made for her?

"Get along with ye, Davin," said Callan. "We're about done for the day. See ye in the morning, if ye still have a mind to join the hunt."

I nodded. I had been looking forward to that hunting trip. Callan had lent me one of his bows, and I was getting quite good at hitting what I aimed at. But what if Nico told Mama about it, and she said I couldn't go?

I climbed the edge of the gorge and started walking rapidly, hoping that Nico would leave me alone. No such luck. He waited until we were clear of the forest and could see the Dance, the great circle of standing stones on the hill just above our new cottage. Then he spoke his mind.

"Why don't you tell her, Davin? You just disappear, and she has no idea where you go."

"If she really wants to know, all she has to do is look at me. Then I'll have to tell her, won't I? Whether I want to or not."

Nico seized me by the arm and forced me to stop. The twilight mist had made the air clammy and beads of moisture glistened in his dark beard.

"Why are you being so stupid? Don't you see that that is the last thing she wants to do?"

What did he mean? I didn't get it. But I was determined not to let my puzzlement show.

"Don't call me stupid," I snarled. "At least I *do* something. You just sit around, waiting for them to come and get you!"

Nico clenched his fists, and his eyes flashed beneath his dark brows. I almost wished he would go ahead and slug me so that we would have an excuse to fight. But he didn't. Of course he didn't—Nico prefers cutting people up with words.

"If you would get your nose out of your own backside for a moment, you might discover that she is trying to let you grow up. Has she asked why you have to wash that same poor shirt every week when you ought to have two other perfectly good ones to wear? And incidentally, you've been had. That thing is little more than a bar of pig iron. You'll never get a proper blade from *that*."

"If you're so smart, why don't you help me? You could train me much better than Callan can." Nico was the son of a castellan and had had the best fencing masters his father's purse could hire.

It took a while before he answered.

"If I promise to help you," he finally said, "will you then tell your mother the whole thing?"

"It's no business of hers. Does she have to know every-thing?"

"Why not? Are you ashamed of what you are doing?"

"No!" But I knew Mama wouldn't like it. "Can't I keep one little thing to myself? Nico, you could help me. You know you could."

He shook his head. "I don't care for swords," he said. "And your mother wouldn't like it."

"You and your fancy likes and dislikes! If it hadn't been for you, we wouldn't have lost Cherry Tree Cottage. If only you had had the *guts* to strike when you had the chance, then—then—" I couldn't finish. Nico was staring at me, and his face was deathly pale. He knew I was right. Last autumn he had had the chance to kill Drakan. Drakan who had murdered his father, his brother's widow, and his tiny nephew. But he had used the flat side of the blade instead of the edge. And a few days later, Drakan and his men had burned down our cottage and killed almost all our animals.

Nico spun on his heel and stalked off without a word. I knew I had wounded him as surely as if I had stuck a knife in him. It would have been easier for him if I had just lost my temper and slugged him. And easier for me too, I think. I felt bad about that white face, knowing it was my fault. But I simply did *not* understand him. I couldn't for the life of me understand why he hadn't chopped the bastard's head off. If it had been me, if Drakan ever again caused any kind of harm to Mama or the girls . . . that was why I spent so much time practicing. Because I wanted to defend them. Because I wanted to kill Drakan.

Mama and the girls were already having dinner when I walked in. Dina threw me a furious look across the kitchen table. After what happened last year, she had become a bit of a mother hen where Mama was concerned. But then, Dina had been there, in Dunark, in the middle of the whole bloody business. A dragon had tried to bite her arm off. That was another reason I wanted to learn how to use a sword. The next time some monster wanted to take a bite out of my sister, it would be me doing the dragon slaying, not Nico.

I took my bowl down from the shelf and pretended not to notice Dina's furious looks. She has Shamer's eyes just like Mama, even though she is still only eleven, and when she is angry, looking at her is a really bad idea. That glare—it's a bit like being kicked by a dray horse. Rose, Dina's friend from Dunark, who lives with us now, ladled soup into my bowl with the big ladle she has carved for us herself. She knows how to use a knife. Actually, she stabbed Drakan in the leg last year. The only ones who *hadn't* fought Drakan in some way happened to be five-year-old Melli . . . and me.

"Why is Davin so late?" asked Melli, in her most innocent-sounding voice. "Where have you been, Davin?"

"Out," I said sourly.

Mama didn't say anything. Dina didn't say anything. The silence was loud enough to crack an eardrum. I blew on my soup to cool it, and carefully did not look at either of them.

Pheasants on the Slope

When we got up the next morning, Davin had vanished. Again. Before breakfast, even. I didn't eat much either. I was so furious with my brother that I could barely swallow my food. How *could* he behave like that, and at such a time too, with Mama worried sick over that business with the child peddler. Didn't she have enough to think about?

"Eat your porridge, Dina," said Mama absentmindedly, setting aside a bowl for Davin and covering it with a clean dishcloth.

"I'm not hungry," I muttered.

"Oh? Is there anything wrong with the porridge?"

I shook my head. "It's not the porridge, I'm just not—"

"Well, stop moping and eat it, then! Or feed it to the chickens, I really don't care!"

Rose looked up in surprise. Mama rarely raised her voice over little things like that, but here she was, yelling at me, as if the whole thing were *my* fault. The unfairness of it brought tears to my eyes. I pushed back my chair with a jerk and went outside and did exactly what she had told me to do. The chickens cackled around my feet, jostling to get their share of this unexpected tidbit. The early morning sun played along their backs, raising golden gleams. The chickens we had now were all much bigger than the ones we had kept at Cherry Tree Cottage, and they were a beautiful roan color, almost like copper. Apparently, that was what Highland hens looked like—at any rate, all the other chickens in the vicinity looked exactly the same.

I heard the door open. That would be Rose, I thought, coming to share my troubles. But it was Mama. Without saying anything, she put her arms around me from behind and rested her cheek on my hair, and for a while we just stood like that, watching the chickens pecking and scrabbling and fighting over the remnants of the porridge.

"Hmm . . . well, at least *they* like my cooking," said Mama, but this time it was a joke. This time she said it to make me smile.

"Davin is *stupid*," I said viciously. "Why has he become so—so—" I couldn't even think of a word to describe him.

"He is not stupid," said Mama, sighing, and I felt her breath against my neck. "He is just trying to figure out how to be a man. I think it's best if we can leave him alone for a while. I think we need to give him . . . a little growing space perhaps."

I didn't feel like giving him anything at all right now—unless it was a well-placed kick.

"He hardly ever looks at me," I said, and suddenly I was crying, without wanting to and without being able to stop myself. When there are only four people in the whole world who are willing to look you in the eye, losing one of them really hurts.

"Oh, sweetie," Mama whispered and tightened her arms around me. "Sweetie, I'm so sorry. I hadn't even noticed. I suppose I've been too busy trying not to mind that he'll no longer look at *me*."

"Why does he do it?" I snuffled. "Why does he turn away from us like that?"

Mama didn't answer right away. "I'm not entirely sure what's going on with him," she finally said. "But Davin . . . once he was just a boy, and he knew how to do that. Now he has to become a man, and I'm not quite sure he knows what that is supposed to mean. And it's hardly something you and I can teach him. He'll learn, though. And when he does, he'll come back to us."

"Are you sure?" My voice shook, and I knew I sounded like a little kid, hardly older than Melli. Because what if he didn't? I knew very few grown men who would look a Shamer in the eye. Nico tried, but it hurt him; he felt guilty about so many things. The only one who did it unflinchingly was Drakan, and that was because he had no more shame than an animal.

"Of course he will," said Mama. "If our Davin does not

become the kind of man who can look us in the eye, then we've done a poor job of raising him, haven't we?"

Again, she meant for me to smile. But I couldn't do it.

At that moment, there was a warning *wroof!* from Beastie, our big gray wolfhound. Mama let go of me.

"Go and wipe your face, sweetie," she said. "We have company."

The visitor was a Laclan man, a slim, dark-haired gentleman with very fancy manners. He was dressed fancily, too. His shirt was elaborately embroidered, and instead of a common leather belt he wore a slim silver chain around his waist. A wool cloak bordered with the red and yellow Laclan colors was slung dashingly over one shoulder. He looked quite out of place in our lowly farmyard, among the squawking chickens.

"Have you found the child peddler?" The question burst out of me as soon as I saw the Laclan colors.

He almost looked at me, but caught himself in time. "No, Medamina," he said politely. "He is still on the loose. In all probability he has escaped into the Lowlands. No, unfortunately my errand is a different one. We have another task for the Shamer, if Medama is willing."

I could see the tension hardening Mama's shoulders immediately. The business with the child peddler had been a strain on her; for almost two weeks, she had had to dose herself with an infusion of hops and allheal to be able to sleep at night.

"So soon?" I said with some bitterness. "Are there so many evildoers in the Laclan clan?"

"Dina!" Mama's voice was sharp and reproachful, and I did actually regret the words as soon as I had said them. Highlanders are easily angered when the honor of the clan is at stake. But the man in the dashing Laclan cloak merely smiled.

"They say trouble breeds trouble. But this time, the case is fortunately less serious. Merely a matter of some missing sheep."

That did not sound too horrible, and some of the tension left my mother's shoulders. She still looked tired, however.

"Mama," I said, "couldn't I do it?" I could hardly bear to see her so pale and worried. "If it's only some missing sheep . . ." I had been my mother's apprentice for less than seven months, but such a minor task should be well within my powers.

The Laclan man opened his mouth to protest and then thought better of it. It was obvious, however, that he did not want to have to make do with the Shamer's eleven-year-old daughter.

Mama caught his disconcerted look and smiled slightly.

"We can both go, Dina. If you need me, I'll be there.

Rose, would you take Melli down to Maudi's? She'll be glad to see you both. And she is so proud of the spoons you carved her—if you make her a few more, she'll probably offer you one of those puppies you've been sighing over."

Rose flashed her a smile, and blushed a bit. She was not much accustomed to praise. Back in Swill Town, the meanest and dirtiest part of Dunark Town, too many people had called her a bastard and a whore's brat, her own brother included.

"What would Beastie do if I brought one of those home?" she said.

"Beastie is a sensible old dog," Mama said. "He knows that one must be patient with the young."

Somehow, I don't think Mama was thinking only of puppies when she said that.

We have only one horse, our black gelding Falk that Maudi Kensie gave to us when we lost Blaze in Dunark last year. Mama asked Debbi Herbs if we could borrow her small, rough-coated gray pony, and Debbi said we could. But that was not the end of the difficulties. Mama hardly ever went anywhere without Callan to guard her, and he was nowhere to be found. "Out hunting." That was all his old gran knew of his whereabouts. "I shall protect Medama," said the Laclan man. "I'll gladly accompany Medama and her daughter on the return journey as well."

Mama hesitated for a moment. Then she nodded.

"Rose, tell Maudi that we have gone with Ivain Laclan to Hebrach's Mill. We should be back again before nightfall."

And after that, we were finally able to ride off in the direction of Hebrach's Mill, to see a man who might have stolen three sheep from his neighbor.

It had rained in the night, but now the sun had come out, and the day was warm and mild. When we reached the stand of birches at the foot of Ram Hill, Ivain courteously held back the wet branches so that Mama and I could pass without having our cloaks spattered. He really was very polite, with manners much more polished than most people I knew. Callan, for instance, would assume that we were perfectly capable of ducking a wet branch. He would have been waiting for us at the top of the hill instead, having scouted ahead to make sure no enemies were lurking behind the rise.

"He seems very . . . you know . . . courtly or something," I whispered to my mother. I had never before met a Highlander who shaved off most of his beard and left only one neat little triangle, almost as if he had wiped his chin with a coal-blackened finger. "The way he talks, too."

Mama smiled. "Oh, come on. You know by now that there are plenty of Highlanders who do not dress in hides and speak in monosyllabic grunts."

"Callan does—just about," I mumbled.

"He does not!" she said, but she couldn't help smiling, for Callan could be very much the Highlander when the mood took him.

"Medamina," called Ivain, by now nearly ten lengths ahead of us, "is the pony capable of a slightly speedier gait? I did promise to have the ladies home by nightfall."

"Oh, he's capable, all right," I called back. "Willing, now that's another matter." Debbi's gray would keep going all day at his own pace without balking, but if you tried to hurry him he sometimes got stubborn. Still, I tightened my legs around him, and although he flicked his ears and swished his tail in annoyance, he agreed to a lumbering canter until we had caught up to Ivain and his big bay stallion.

We went more or less due east, as the sun rose higher and higher in the sky. For once, a day without rain, fog, or lashing winds, I thought, and began to forget about Davin and my earlier bad mood. Debbi's gray might be no fairy-tale palfrey, but it was pleasant to be out riding on a beautiful spring morning, especially knowing that it would have been laundry day at home.

I had never been to Hebrach's Mill, but it seemed my mother had, for when Ivain wanted to pass to the east of a rocky ridge, she reined in Falk and brought him to a halt.

"Shouldn't we be on the west side of Kemmer's Ridge?" she asked.

"The Kemmer ford is almost impassable at the moment, due to the rain and the last of the melt water," said Ivain. "I will not risk the ladies to it. This way is longer, but the crossing is much safer."

Here he goes again, I thought, with his talk of "ladies." Men could drown too, couldn't they? But Mama merely nodded and let him have his way.

It was a beautiful place. The trail followed the bank of the Kemmermere, a narrow, mirror-smooth lake. On both sides of it, steep slopes rose, covered with silver birches. The water was so still that gray rock, pale green leaves, and black-and-white birches were all mirrored to perfection on the dark surface. A moorhen sailed by, leaving a wake that caused the reflection to wobble and break, but it soon steadied again, so sharp and precise that it was hard to tell the difference between landscape and waterscape. As I looked at the image in the water, I suddenly caught a glimpse of something—a large animal, or perhaps a man? I looked up, scanning the slope above us. I couldn't see anything now, but there had been something, I was sure of it. I reined in the gray pony.

"There's something up there," I said, pointing. "On the slope."

"Yes, I saw it," said Ivain. "It was just a pheasant."

That's when I knew that things were really wrong. Whatever it had been up there, it certainly was *not* a pheasant. And suddenly it felt very dangerous to be riding here without Callan, along a different road than usual, and with only a stranger to guide and guard us.

"Come along now, ladies," called Ivain encouragingly. "The sun is speeding, and the sheep rustler awaits us!"

But I did not prod the pony onward, and Mama and Falk could not easily get by me on the narrow trail.

"Come on, Dina. Ride."

"Let's go back," I said to my mother in a low voice. "That was no pheasant."

A year ago she would probably just have said "Nonsense!" and ridden on. Not anymore. Now we had learned to be careful. Without saying a word, Mama turned Falk around and set off at a gallop, back the way we had come. The pony did not need much encouragement to follow— he knew very well which way was home.

I looked over my shoulder just as Ivain was discovering that he no longer had two obedient "ladies" on his tail. He did not call "Stop!" or "Wait!" or anything else you might expect. For a brief moment he simply looked furious. Then he put two fingers to his mouth and gave a piercing whistle.

The shrubbery on the slope came alive with movement and noises, and with shouts that definitely did not come from any kind of pheasant.

"*Ride!*" yelled my mother. "As fast as you can!"

Falk sprang forward with a great deal of will and speed, and the gray pony followed as best he could, but his sturdy legs were much shorter than those of Ivain's bay stallion. I heard hoofbeats behind me, much too close, and suddenly the stallion was beside us, shoving against Debbi's gray so that he stumbled and I nearly came off. Ivain seized my reins and forced both horses around with their noses up against the slope and their rumps uncomfortably close to the lake bank.

"Hold it, Shamer!" he shouted at Mama. "We have your daughter!"

Mama jerked back on the reins so abruptly that Falk half-reared on his haunches. She turned in the saddle to look straight at Ivain, and her eyes were dark with fury.

"What kind of a man are you—" she began in that voice, the Shamer's voice, which cuts right to the soul.

"*Shoot,* damn it!" yelled someone from the shrubbery, and suddenly something long and dark was in the air, and there was a whirring sound and then a sickening thud. Mama collapsed across Falk's neck, and the long dark thing was stuck in her shoulder.

They had shot my mother.

They had shot my mother.

At first, that was all I could think of. Falk took a few uncertain steps forward, then came to a halt again. One of the ambushers emerged from the shrubbery and was sliding the last few yards down to the path. He started walking toward our black gelding.

I turned to Ivain. Mama's eyes had struck home, and he was looking somewhat dazed. It was up to me to finish it.

"What kind of man are you to hurt an unarmed woman and her child?" I hissed, and although I was both furious and half out of my mind with fear, I got the voice right, and I clawed at him with my eyes, so that he shrank back and shielded his face as if I were spitting acid. I drew my meat knife from my belt and sliced through the reins of the bay with two quick cuts, just below the bit. Then I hit the horse across the muzzle as hard as I could. Startled, it tried to back up, put one hoof over the edge and had to scramble to stay on the path. Ivain caught at his reins, but that did no good, of course. Just as the bay was regaining its footing, I pricked its quarters with my knife, and the stallion decided that enough was enough. It leaped forward and disappeared down the trail at a panicked gallop, and there was nothing Ivain could do to stop it. Quickly, I turned Debbi's gray and rode him straight at the man approaching my mother. He spun around. His mouth became a dark O of astonishment, and then the gray pony's shoulder struck him and knocked him off the path. For a moment, he seemed to hang in the air, his arms windmilling in a desperate effort to regain his balance. I did not see him fall—I just heard the splash.

"Mama . . . Mama, are you—can you—"

Somehow, she was still in the saddle.

"Ride!" she hissed through clenched teeth. "Falk will follow."

I edged Debbi's gray past our black gelding. The path was much too narrow for us to ride side by side, so I had to trust that Falk would follow his instincts and his herdmate. The last two ambushers had reached the path now, but they had no horses and even my gray pony would be able to outrun them. I rode. And Falk followed.

The Willow Place

Away! That was my only thought at first. Far away, and quickly. But I soon realized that my mother would not be able to travel very far. If we simply followed the path until her strength failed, they would catch us anyway. We had a lead, but they probably had horses waiting somewhere, and once they got themselves mounted, they would be hot on our trail. We had to find somewhere to hide, and preferably a place that would provide some shelter against the chill and dampness of the night. If only this had happened at Birches, or at least a little closer to Baur Kensie where I was beginning to know my way around. I had no idea where to go. And horses are hard to hide. They are too big, and it is difficult to get them to be still. Perhaps it would be better to find one place for them and another for Mama and me? But the thought of parting company with them was frightening. If I lost them, I'd never be able to get Mama home.

A small creek crossed the path and tumbled on down toward the lake. Instead of crossing it, I persuaded the gray to wade along it, upstream. The bottom was rocky and difficult, but this was the sort of thing the gray pony was good at: he was no racer, but he knew how to watch his footing.

"Mama?"

"Hush," she whispered. "Just ride." She had tucked her right hand into her belt and was clutching Falk's mane with her left, so as not to fall. The arrow was sticking out from her right shoulder like a quill on a porcupine.

"Shouldn't we . . . draw the arrow?" I said it hesitantly, knowing that "we" meant *me,* and I was not at all sure I had the courage or the strength.

She shook her head faintly.

"No. It'll bleed too much. Later."

We splashed onward up the creek. The banks had become steeper and taller, and branches curved and tangled overhead so that it was like walking through a tunnel. And then there was suddenly no way forward. A fallen tree blocked the creek, and although a person could climb under it—at least a person who did not have a yard-long arrow sticking out of her—there was absolutely no way we would be able to get the horses past it.

I stared at the fallen birch tree and felt the tears burning hotly on my cheeks, from fear and utter despair. We were trapped. There was no way up the banks, they were much too steep. There was no way forward. And if we went back, we would be heading straight for Ivain and his men.

"Haul it," said Mama. "Haul it out of the way."

Haul it? There was no way I'd be able to move an entire birch tree. And then I saw what she meant. Debbi's gray was not, after all, chiefly a riding horse. He was a tough little worker who had hauled plenty of timber in his day. And fortunately Callan's lessons on how to survive in the Highlands had not been totally wasted on me. "Rope, blade, and tinderbox," he would preach. "*Never* set out without rope, blade, and tinderbox."

I slid off the pony's back, got out my coil of rope, and got a loop of it around one end of the tree. The other end I attached to the saddle. But what was the command the Highlanders used for this?

"Halla-halla," Mama whispered. I nodded, and swallowed. Would Debbi's pony obey someone who had never done this before?

"Halla-halla-halla," I said loudly and firmly, and followed it up by clicking my tongue a couple of times just to be on the safe side. And Debbi's gray may have looked like a rather plain and rough-coated little gelding, but in reality he was a treasure, a rare treasure on four legs. He set his hooves firmly in the bottom of the creek and hauled with every ounce. And slowly, slowly and draggingly, with a lot of snapping and cracking and clattering, one end of the tree came free of the bank, and the trunk settled lengthways in the creek instead of crosswise.

"Good boy. *Good* boy," I said, and patted the rough gray neck. "And *halt!*" And my gray pony halted and stood there, calm and solid, not knowing that he had just saved our lives.

I carefully led Falk past the tree and commanded him to halt also. And then I got a great idea. I looped the rope around the saddle horn once more and got Debbi's gray to haul the tree back to its crosswise position. It felt wonderful. It felt like closing a door behind us. *If* they guessed that we had ridden up the creek, *if* they got as far as the tree . . . then they would think they had been mistaken. And even if they were clever enough to guess what had really happened, they might not be able to do anything about it, because I very much doubted that any of them would be riding a tough little Highland workhorse who thought nothing of hauling timber from sunup to sundown.

"Good idea," said Mama in the hoarse, weak whisper that seemed to be all the voice she had left now. I could see we were running out of time. I had to find some kind of hiding place soon, some place where I could get her off the horse and get her to lie down. I coiled the rope again and got back on the gray, and we rode on, farther up the creek, slowly, so that Mama would be able to hold on just a little longer.

The banks of the creek were much lower here, and the water flowed more slowly. A narrow trail wandered along the bank, probably made by passing deer. I urged the gray pony up the bank, got off, and went back to support Mama in the saddle as Falk made the climb. For a while we followed the trail.

Then I saw the willow.

It was huge. A green waterfall of leaves. Once it had grown at the top of the bank, but then some storm had half-uprooted it—one could still see the yawning hole where its old roots had been torn from the ground. But the tree had survived and had continued to grow, almost vertically, and had created its own little spur of land down in the bed of the creek.

I got off and once more commanded Falk and the gray to halt. Carefully, I climbed down the willow's trunk. It was like passing a curtain made from slim green and yellow leaves. And once past the curtain, there was a small sandy island to stand on, a hidden island completely shielded by the dense foliage. A bower. A tree house. The perfect hideaway.

"We'll have to go back to where we can get down into the creek again," I told Mama. "But it's worth it—even the horses will fit inside!"

Mama only nodded, a very faint nod. She was deathly pale now and blue around the lips, like a child who has stayed too long in the water. Blood from the wound had soaked her shirt, but there was less of it than I would have imagined, so Mama had probably been right to leave the arrow where it was. I tried to push my fears for her aside. Once we were down there in the willow place, sheltered and safe, then I would be able to tend to her. Not before.

It felt frightening and wrong to turn back and ride in the direction of Ivain and his men. Luckily we did not have far to go. I got the horses down the bank once more, and then we rode up the creek again until we reached the willow. I got off—by now my boots were totally soaked— and led the pony through the curtain of leaves. He went calmly and willingly past that obstacle as well. I tied him to a solid branch and returned for Falk. He balked at first, tossing his head in alarm; I could see how his every jittery move hurt my mother, and I felt like screaming at him to behave, but it would have done no good. Only quiet words and soothing touches would persuade him. And finally he came, perhaps because he caught the pony's scent and knew that his herdmate waited in there behind all that frightening green stuff.

I helped Mama down off his back and got her to sit on a pile of old willow twigs I had hastily gathered. I would have to get us a drier bed eventually, but there were more urgent things to be done right now. I unhooked my tin cup from my belt and got Mama a drink of water.

"I have to go back there and wipe our tracks," I said. "If they find our trail, and the hoof marks suddenly stop right by the willow . . . well, it won't be too hard for them to guess the rest."

Mama sipped the cool, clear water. "Go," she said. "I'll wait here."

She meant that bit as a joke. But her smile turned into a grimace of pain, and I had to fight back the tears. Again.

Once I had done what I could to erase our tracks, I gathered some pine boughs to make a sort of bed for us. And then there was no avoiding it anymore. We had to do something about the arrow. It had not gone completely through the shoulder, but I could feel the point like a hard lump beneath the skin, just below her collarbone.

"What should I do?" I asked. "Should I pull it out?"

Mama shook her head. "Pulling won't do it," she said. "It needs to be pushed. It has to come out here in front. And you're just not strong enough."

"But . . . we can't just leave it. You won't even be able to lie down!"

"Use your knife. Cut off the shaft."

I did what she said. It wasn't easy. I could see just how badly I hurt her every time I even touched the damned arrow. When I was done, tears were streaming down her face. It was horrible. It's horrible to see your mother cry like that. And afterward she lay there so pale and quiet, I was afraid she had begun to die.

Even though it was dangerous I lit a tiny fire—just enough to heat a cup of water. There were enough twigs and dry leaves around. And that was another good thing about our hideout: there was no shortage of willow bark, and willow-bark tea is a good remedy for pain and fever and infection. When she had finished the tea, I helped her to lie down and wrapped her in my cloak as well as her own. She ate a little bread. I ate a bit more, along with some of the cheese we had in our saddlebags. The bread felt lumpy and strange in my mouth, as if eating had suddenly become an alien practice. But I did feel a bit steadier with a meal inside me, despite everything that had happened.

Sometime in the afternoon, I heard voices, and I leaped up and went to stand next to the horses to keep them quiet. Mama was asleep, and I didn't want to wake her. They either found us, or they didn't. We could not run any farther, and there was nothing to do except wait.

The voices came closer, and there was the sound of hooves clip-clopping along the stony bank. Falk's nostrils twitched, and I put a warning hand on his muzzle. The pony raised his head and snorted quietly, but otherwise stayed his usual unexcitable self. The hoofbeats never paused, and the voices eventually faded. I started to breathe again.

We stayed in the willow place all day, and all night, too. I did not dare to leave our shelter as long as Ivain's men might still be near. Once the dappled sunlight fled, the creek became cold and damp, and I lay down next to Mama and put my arms carefully around her, hoping to warm us both a bit. She breathed more easily after the willow-bark tea, but she was still frighteningly pale. And there had to be a limit to how long one could leave an arrow like that before infection set in.

It was a very long night. I made the tea for Mama three more times, and once I woke at the sound of distant voices, but fortunately they never came close. Finally the morning sun came back, filtering through the curtain of leaves. I sat for a while watching the shimmer of sun spots and shadows, but I knew I couldn't stay here. I knew that I had to leave Mama and go for help. We could not sit around together, waiting for the right people to find us before the wrong ones did, nor could Mama ride any farther. But taking the gray pony and leaving Falk would not do. Falk would become lonely and restless and might begin to whinny. No horse likes to be alone, but Falk was unusually sociable. It would probably be best to take both horses. I could ride Falk and lead the pony. Of the two, he was the one least likely to give trouble.

"Mama?"

She had been silent for a long time, and I was afraid she might be unconscious. But she opened her eyes when she heard my voice.

"I have to go for help," I said. "I've made two cups of willow-bark tea. Drink one of them while it's hot."

It felt awkward to be saying things like that—as if I were the mother, and Mama the child. But she merely nodded.

"Be careful, sweetie," she said.

I stayed until I was sure that she was able to drink the tea by herself. Then I set out the bread and the cheese next to the second cup of tea, saddled Falk and the pony, and led them out through the leafy curtain. I let them drink a bit from the creek, but not enough to bloat their bellies. We had some way to go, and I wanted them to be able to run if they had to. Then I got up on Falk and made for the ford, leading the gray behind me.

Two People in This World

I had shot my first deer ever, a fine buck, and I felt all warm inside with happiness and pride. Black-Arse and Callan had come home with me—they had to, there was no way I could carry that buck by myself. But as soon as we entered the kitchen, I knew the house was empty. On the table was a bowl covered with a dishcloth; Mama had set aside some of the morning porridge for me, and I felt a pang of contrition mixed with all the pride and joy.

There was a note written in Dina's careful hand.

"Mama and Dina have gone to Hebrach's Mill with someone called Ivain Laclan," I said, once I'd managed to spell my way through the message. Reading is not my strongest suit. Dina is much better at it, for all that she is four years younger than me. She has more patience. "A matter of some stolen sheep, it seems."

"Without me?" Callan said, looking ill at ease. He was very serious about guarding my mother.

"They didn't know where to find us. But Laclan has promised to see them home again."

Callan made a growling sound. He didn't like it, that was obvious, but right now there was nothing he could do about it.

"I had better go fetch Rose and Melli from Maudi's," I said. "That is, if they want to come home."

They didn't. Rose was carving spoons for Maudi, and Melli was playing with the puppies.

"I shot a deer today," I told Rose, just to hear the sound of it. "A buck."

"That's nice," she muttered absentmindedly and kept carving. She would have said the same thing if I had brought home a grouse or a rabbit. Rose doesn't know a whole lot about hunting. I watched her for a bit while she worked. For once, her flaxen braids hung totally still, and there was a frown of concentration on her face. Somehow, she had made the handle of the spoon into a dog, a hunting hound with a pointed nose and long floppy ears.

"I think I'll go see if Nico's in," I said.

"Mmmh . . ." She was making a lot of little scratches now, giving the dog fur. She still used the old half-rusted knife she had brought with her from Dunark. If I was ever able to afford it, I would buy her a new one, I thought, a really good one. Although a knife that had once stabbed Drakan in the leg could not be half bad. . . .

Nico and Master Maunus had moved into one wing of

Maudi Kensie's farmhouse last autumn, when we first came here. In the beginning we lived there too, until we had the cottage roofed. Kensie would readily have helped Nico and Maunus build a cottage too, but although Master Maunus constantly complained about having to live under his mother's roof—"A man my age!"—he showed no signs of wanting to move. Perhaps Maudi's suited him, despite his complaints. Or maybe it was because he still dreamed of returning to Dunark someday.

He and Nico were in the middle of a fight. Nothing unusual about that—as far as I could tell, that was their normal way of talking to each other. Dina said they cared for each other like father and son, but they could have fooled me.

"Why do you always have to play the imbecile?" shouted Master Maunus. "You *know* I'm right!"

"I know nothing of the sort," said Nico more quietly, but with just as much passion.

"Fine! Excellent! Play the simple shepherd, then—for however long Drakan will let you."

"There's nothing wrong with being a shepherd!"

"No. If that is what one was born to do, one may be well content with that. But you have an obligation, Mesire, to the town and the castle of Dunark."

"A town that doesn't care two hoots about me! If Drakan is what they want for a lord, they can have him—as long as they leave me in peace!"

I stood uncertainly on the doorstep. Should I clear my throat, greet them, or just quietly leave? I had just decided on the latter when they both caught sight of me at the same time.

"Oh, it's you, Davin," said Master Maunus. "How are you?"

"Fine, thank you. I just shot a deer." But coming on top of all that stuff about Drakan and Dunark, my triumph sounded small and childish.

"Good, good," muttered Maunus, almost as absently as Rose. Nico was the one who asked the right question.

"A clean shot?"

"Straight through the heart." Callan hadn't even had to use his hunting knife. The buck was dead when we reached it.

Nico said nothing more. He just nodded. And that was better than a lot of grand praise. There are a lot of things I don't understand about Nico. And sometimes I think he interferes in things that are none of his business. But there are times when he gets it just right. Times that make me wish he and I were better friends.

"Is your mother back yet?" he asked.

I shook my head. "Not yet."

"I wish I could have gone with her myself, but . . ."

He didn't finish the sentence, but I could figure the rest out for myself. For Nico to set himself up as my mother's guard would have been just plain stupid. If there was one thing that kept Drakan sleepless at night, it must be the thought that Nico was alive and might one day return to Dunark. Drakan had offered a reward—a hundred gold marks, a colossal fortune—to the man who brought him Nico's head, and not necessarily attached to his body. As a bodyguard, Nico would be inviting trouble rather than preventing it.

"Why did she go without Callan?" asked Master Maunus.

"We were out hunting," I said, feeling a little guilty even though it wasn't really my fault. I had had nothing to do with planning the hunt; Callan had just allowed me to tag along.

"She really shouldn't go anywhere without Callan," said Nico. "Drakan is unlikely to have forgotten her yet."

"Ivain Laclan is reputed to be a capable man," said Master Maunus. "His protection may be quite as good as Callan's, particularly in Laclan territory."

"I'll let you know when she gets back," I said.

All afternoon I was hard at work putting a better fence around my mother's herb garden; maybe this one would keep the goats out. She had put her garden in a spot that was as sheltered and sunny as possible, but even I could see that her herbs did not do nearly as well up here as they had in Birches. Starting over the way we had had taken a lot of effort and hard work. I knew I should help out more than I did, but learning the sword was important too, I felt. What was the use of slaving away to build a cottage and sheep pens and herb gardens if Drakan came to burn the whole thing down again and no one could stop him?

Dusk fell, and Mama and Dina still weren't back. I went down to Maudi's to have supper with her and the girls.

"When is Mama coming home?" Melli asked, her lap full of puppy. "She promised to be home before dark, and it's dark now!"

"Maybe they've decided to stay the night in Hebrach's Mill," I said, trying not to notice the small worm of unease gnawing away at my innards. Melli was always upset when Mama had to stay out overnight, and after Dunark it had become even worse. Mama usually did everything she could not to stay away a moment longer than necessary.

Melli clutched the puppy so tightly that it began to whine and wiggle, trying to get down.

"Melli, be careful. Don't hurt it."

Melli looked as if she didn't even hear me. Tears were streaming down her tanned and chubby cheeks.

"What if Mama never comes back?" she said.

I calmed her as best I could and told three of her favorite bedtime stories. "Of course Mama will come home," I said. Of course she will.

Shortly past noon the next day, Dina came riding over the hill on Falk, leading Debbi Herb's gray pony. Her face was chalky pale with fear and weariness, and it hurt to even glance at her.

"Mama has been shot," she said in a voice flat and hoarse with exhaustion. "Hurry. I'm so afraid she'll die."

Nine days went by before we knew that Mama would live. Sitting by her bed those nine days, just waiting . . . there are no words for how I felt. But as I sat there, watching over her, I knew that there were now two people in the world that I wanted to kill: Drakan—and Ivain Laclan.

The White Doe

"Ivain Laclan," I said.

Callan didn't even look at me. He just swung the ax in a precise and practiced arc, and the log split and sprang apart in two neat pieces. Callan bent, took a new log, and set it on the block.

"What about him?" he asked.

"He led my mother into an ambush. He tried to kill her."

The afternoon sun flashed briefly along the edge of Callan's ax. *Clack!* Two more pieces fell to the ground. I looked at Callan's bent back in irritation. Couldn't he put down that ax for a moment and talk to me? What I had to say was important. A matter of life and death, in fact.

"Callan. We have to do something!"

Clack! The ax flashed yet again.

"We've sent a message to Helena Laclan."

"So? She is his grandmother. Do you really think she will punish him as he deserves? I want that . . . that traitor *dead,* Callan!"

Finally, he straightened his back and looked at me. "Whatever Ivain Laclan has done, and whatever punishment he deserves, it is a Laclan matter." His eyes were granite gray under the red brows. "Ye have to understand that, lad."

What he meant was that clan rights were sacred. Under clan law, only Laclan judges could condemn a Laclan man. But back home in our new cottage my mother lay on her bed, still so weak that Dina had to hold the cup for her every time she needed to drink. And Ivain Laclan was the cause of that.

I slowly shook my head. "No, Callan. I don't understand it at all."

I turned abruptly and left him there. I could feel his gaze on the back of my neck all the way up the hill. But just as I reached the ridge, there was another sharp *clack!* from below. I bit my lip. So what? I thought furiously. So what if he doesn't care? Let him go on splitting stupid logs. I would simply have to take care of the business myself.

It was very early, and the sun had barely touched the sky. The huge stones of the Dance looked like sleeping giants, tall and black, with just a faint gilding at the top, as if dawn wanted to crown them. In the cottage they were all still asleep, Mama, Melli, Dina, and Rose. Beastie had risen from his wicker basket by the door as I slipped through the kitchen, stretching himself and wagging his tail, but I made him lie down again. It would have been nice to have him with me, but someone needed to stay and look after Mama and the girls.

I crossed the yard. The dew was heavy on the grass, and my ankles were soaked in seconds. There was no gravel and cobbling here the way there had been at Cherry Tree Cottage. The yard was really just the dirt and grass that happened to be between the cottage and stable.

Falk put his head over the edge of his stall and nickered sleepily. Bits of straw were caught in his forelock, and he had obviously been snoozing cozily in his bedding until I came in to disturb him. I gave him a few fistfuls of oats, and he ate them greedily while I brushed him and picked his hooves. Luckily he was used to being saddled at odd hours and made no fuss about it. I left him in his stall for a moment and went to get my sword.

Hearing me outside the shed, the sheep bleated, wanting to be let out, but I pretended not to hear. The sword was in its usual hiding place, buried in the thatch an arm's length from the south gable. I drew it. For a moment, doubts seized me. It was as if Nico were standing right next to me, making his down-putting remark once more: *That thing is little more than a bar of pig iron. You'll never get a proper blade from* that. But I had spent hours and hours this week sharpening it and polishing it, and the edge was now keen enough to break the skin if one didn't handle it carefully. It might not be the handsomest sword in the world, but it would do. It had to. I had no other weapon.

Falk's hooves made a clear track in the dewy grass as I rode him up the hill. But when I looked back, the cottage was still wrapped in sleep, with shuttered windows and closed doors.

It took me nearly two days to get to Baur Laclan, mostly because I got lost three times. I spent the night in a lean-to, surrounded by timid sheep. Every time Falk twitched his tail, they scattered in terror, bleating loudly, and I did not get much sleep. For breakfast I had the last of the bread I had brought. Falk had to make do with grass.

On the afternoon of the second day I finally reached the crest of the last hill. Below me lay the town, its rooftops a mixture of turf and slate, some walls stone gray, others a reddish ocher. It was so much bigger than I had expected—totally different from Baur Kensie, which was really just a village, and an unusually scattered village at that. Baur Laclan resembled the Lowland towns, with streets and squares, some of them even cobbled; a lot of the houses still looked like Highland crofts, low and wide, with turfed roofs, but here and there a clansman or a settler had built in the Lowland manner, with two floors and a gallery. And whereas Maudi's farmhouse looked much like everybody else's, Helena Laclan's home was much more impressive: tall granite walls and towers with archers' slits protected her against unwelcome visitors.

Falk was tired, and so was I. I stared at the town, feeling my heart sink. I had thought it would be . . . not easy, exactly, but . . . well, simple. In my imagination, it had looked like this: I would ride into town, cast my challenge in Ivain Laclan's face, and we would fight. And if I was as good as Callan said I was, then I would probably win. I might get hurt, and that was all right with me, as long as it left me uncrippled once the wounds healed. That I might also be killed had occurred to me, but I didn't think about it much. It was well worth the risk, I thought. At least everyone would know that one did not just shoot my mother and walk away unpunished.

That was how I had imagined it.

The thought that I might have trouble *finding* Ivain had not entered my mind.

Falk deserved a nice stall and a good feed, but I had no money. I couldn't just tie him to a tree and collect him later. There were wolves in the Highlands, even though they did not often come this close to human habitation; or someone might steal him—he had the brand of the Kensie clan on his haunch, and no clansman would touch him, but Baur Laclan was on the caravan road, and not all travelers were as law-abiding as the Highlanders. Besides, my own belly rumbled with hunger, and I was so tired my eyes stung. It might not be the brightest idea in the world to go into one's first serious sword fight in that condition.

Falk sighed deeply and shook his head, making bits of foam fly from his mouth. I had to make up my mind. Why was everything suddenly so complicated? In the sagas the hero simply rode up to the dragon and chopped off its head, and that was that. Nothing was said about how he got fodder for his horse.

Falk got tired of waiting. Without any signal from me, he headed down the hill in a resolute manner. It suddenly struck me that he might actually know more than I did—after all, he had been to Baur Laclan before. Perhaps I should simply leave things up to him.

The clatter of Falk's hooves echoed between the walls of the first houses we came to, and sent a couple of chickens scrambling out of our way, squawking and cackling. From a narrow, fenced-off alley came a furious barking, and a small rough-coated gray dog thrust its head through the fence, snapping at Falk's hocks. For once, Falk was completely uninterested in skittishness. He turned into another alley and from there through a gateway into a cobbled yard. He headed straight for the water trough in the middle and sunk his muzzle deep into the water. I looked around. Two stories on all sides of that ocher-colored wattle and daub. And above the door of one wing hung a cast-iron sign with THE WHITE DOE in big letters, and a painting of a deer, white on blue. Falk had found us an inn. But what did one do when one had no money to pay the innkeeper?

A small, balding man with bushy black eyebrows emerged from the stables—the ostler, probably, who looked after the horses. A couple of straws decorated the back of his worn woolen waistcoat; it looked as if I had woken him from his afternoon nap.

"How may I serve—" he began. Then he noticed that the customer was only a boy with a tired mud-spattered horse, and changed his tune. "What d'ye want?"

"I . . . erh, is there any work to be had? Just so I can pay for a good feed for my horse and a night in the stable for both of us?"

He looked at me. Then he looked at Falk. And then at me again.

"What are ye doin' with one of Maudi Kensie's horses?" he asked.

I could feel my cheeks burn, as if I actually were the horse thief he took me for.

"It belongs to my mother now," I said.

"Oh," he growled, "ye're the Shamer's boy. Why didn't ye say so at once? Put the horse in the corner stall there, and then we'll see about the rest."

The Shamer's boy. I had ridden for two days with the sword on my back, ready to risk my life, ready to fight like a man, but in his eyes, I was obviously still Mama's little boy. He sounded just like Kinni, damn him. I suppose it was better than being taken for a horse thief. But not much.

"I don't want any handouts," I said angrily. "I'll work for my keep!"

"Oh, aye," he said. "That ye will. No need to crow at me, cockerel."

Two hours later I was thoroughly regretting my words. "Aye, well, ye might just clean the henhouse for us" was the way the innkeeper had casually put it. He did not mention that the henhouse was the size of our cottage, or that it had three separate coops, each with a highly belligerent cock lording it over more than a score of heavy, copper-colored laying hens . . . or the fact that it had been at least five years since anyone had made any effort to clean the place. Five years' worth of chicken shit, ranging from the ancient and hardened, practically fossilized layers to oozingly liquid-fresh spatters. Phew, what a stench! The air was thick with dust, and with bits of straw, down, and feathers, not to mention mites and fleas. I had to take off my shirt and tie it around my nose and mouth to be able to stand it. And when I got to the third flock and wanted to chase them out into their run, the cock went for me, clawing three long bleeding scratches across my chest.

"I hope you end up in the soup pot," I cursed, finally managing to get the contrary creature out the hatch with the aid of the broom I had borrowed.

It was a long and weary while before I was able to wheel away the last barrowful of muck and put fresh golden straw into clean nesting boxes. Darkness was falling, and the hens were crowding anxiously around the closed hatches. The ostler with the bushy eyebrows poked his head through the door to inspect.

"Hmm," he growled. "Well, ye seem to be doin' a proper job of it. Good for ye."

"Is there somewhere I can wash?" I asked. "And wash my shirt?"

"Scrub off the worst of it by the pump," the ostler said. "If one of the guests has ordered a bath ye can use the tub when he's done, but I can't see Master firin' the kettle just for you."

I stuck my head under the pump and scrubbed till it hurt. I felt as if I were positively crawling with lice and fleas. I knew most of it was only in my imagination, but I had *seen* the bugs leaping in the filthy old bedding, and it felt as if they had all leaped onto me.

"Here," said the ostler, handing me a gritty gray sliver of soap. "The baths are over there, down them steps. If ye hurry, the water'll still be hot."

I hurried. The water in the stone tub was more luke-warm than hot, but it was much nicer than the cold pump. When I had finished scrubbing myself, I started on the shirt and kept at it until it was once more reasonably white and certainly smelled a whole lot better.

I got out of the tub and wrung the water from my hair. I had told Mama to stop cutting it last year, and it was now long enough to be gathered into a ponytail like the one Callan wore. I was tying the leather thong around it when I suddenly heard a chorus of suppressed giggles.

I spun around. In the doorway were two girls, fifteen or sixteen years old, wearing white caps and aprons. One of them had the hem pressed to her lips in an attempt to smother her laughter. I grabbed my shirt and held it so that it covered my crotch. What were they laughing at? Was there anything wrong with me, or was it just because I was naked?

"Mistress says to say that there's food for ye in the kitchen," said one of them and let go of her apron so that I could see her face. Her teeth were a bit rabbitty, but apart from that she was quite pretty. I could see that the laughter was still bubbling inside her, though.

"Thank you," I said. "I'll be there in a minute."

"Ye might want to get dressed first," she said. Her companion practically squealed with laughter, and as they both retreated down the passage, giggles kept floating back to me. It was a relief when they were finally gone. I looked down at my body. Was I really that comical? I thought I looked fairly ordinary. A bit on the skinny side still, perhaps, but my shoulders had become a little more impressive these last six months. And as for the rest— when I and Black-Arse and Kinni went swimming, nobody laughed. Silly geese. I tried to forget about them, but suddenly I didn't feel like sitting about in my bare chest and woolen waistcoat the way I usually did while my shirt dried. I wrung the shirt as best I could, but it was still very wet. And then I suddenly thought that it was stupid of me to pay so much attention to a couple of giggly girls when I had come to this town to fight a man, life or death. I left the shirt to dry and put on just the waistcoat.

The innkeeper's wife gave me a bowl of broth thick with meat and split peas, and as much bread as I could eat.

"There's a mug of beer for ye when ye've eaten," she said. "But just one. The water is good here, ye can drink yer fill of that."

"Thank you, Mistress," I said, blowing on the soup. It was steaming hot, and I was so hungry that I could barely wait for it to cool.

Later, as I sat enjoying my beer, I asked casually: "Does Mistress know where I might find Ivain Laclan?"

"Ivain? He lives up at the castle, or he does when he's here. The man does a lot of travelin'. Why? What d'ye want of him?"

I took another swallow of cool beer, then wiped the froth off my lip. "Oh, nothing much," I answered, not looking at her. "It's just that I have a message for him from my mother."

Ring of Iron

They let me sleep in the barn, and I lay comfortably nested in last year's hay, with my blanket under me and my cloak on top. Despite my tiredness, I found it hard to sleep. I think it is easier to do something dangerous if you can do it right away and not have to think about it so much. Callan's many warnings tumbled through my mind—"Look at the *sword*, lad, not his silly face!"—and for the first time I considered what it would feel like to push the sword into a man's body and see him fall and become limp and cold, like a pig one had butchered. And what if it turned out *I* was to be the butchered pig?

When I finally did sleep, I dreamed that my sword had suddenly become so heavy that I couldn't lift it, and a man in shirtsleeves and a butcher's apron was circling me, cutting me here and there, so that the blood streamed down my arms, legs, and stomach. I tried to defend myself, but my sword felt chained to the ground, and my opponent laughed and made a deep cut in my neck. Falling, I saw a whole flock of white-capped maids descending on me, giggling and squealing and brandishing butcher's knives. "Hurry, hurry!" they cried. "He'll make sweet ham, will that one."

I woke up with a start at the crack of dawn, as one of the innkeeper's cocks started crowing like a bird possessed. Probably the one that had scratched my chest yesterday, I thought sourly. I tried to roll over and go back to sleep; I felt far from rested. But of course the other two soon joined the fanfare, and then I suddenly remembered what I was doing here, sleeping on top of a haystack in an unfamiliar town. The last vestige of sleepiness vanished like mist, and my stomach turned cold and strange. But then I reminded myself of what my mother had looked like with that awful wound in her shoulder, and the anger made me much warmer.

I washed at the pump, then put on my shirt—still a bit damp, but at least it looked better. I brushed the hay off my cloak and walked out of the inn's courtyard and into the cobbled street, striding toward the castle were Ivain Laclan lived.

"What d'ye want?" asked the gate guard sullenly. "Ye're up awful early."

"I need a word with Ivain Laclan. Is he here?"

"Aye, he might be. But he'll not like bein' woken at this hour."

I was tired of waiting. I wanted to get it over with.

"Tell me where to find him, and I'll go wake him myself."

He looked at me for a bit. Then he shook his head.

"If ye like," he said. "But don't say I didn't warn ye. He has a temper on him, does Ivain." He stepped aside and pointed across the courtyard. "Up them steps to the second floor, and then right. He still sleeps in the Armsmen's Hall when he's here."

I nodded, thanked him, and crossed the courtyard with what I hoped were firm steps.

The Armsmen's Hall was a long, high-ceilinged room lined with alcoves along one wall. Loud snoring in many different keys rumbled behind the curtains, and clothes—breeches, shirts, and cloaks, most of them in Laclan colors—were strewn across the room. I jerked back the curtain of the nearest alcove. Inside sprawled a big hairy-chested brute of a man with his mouth open and his arms flung wide, as if he had just toppled backward into the bedding. The morning light made no impression on him; he snored on regardless. I hesitated. I had no idea whether this could be Ivain or not. I realized that I had only the vaguest notion of what the man looked like. And it didn't seem like the best of ideas to prod a total stranger awake with my sword in order to challenge him to a duel.

"Ivain," I said tentatively. He gave no sign of having heard. "Ivain Laclan!"

It was hopeless. Either it wasn't him, or stronger

measures were called for. And I was getting sick and tired of all the stupid little hitches my simple plan had suffered. Somewhere in this room was Ivain Laclan, if the guard at the gate could be trusted—and I would see to it that he woke up!

I seized an empty chamber pot, leaped onto a table, and started to bang the pot with my sword. It made a beautiful racket.

"Ivain Laclan! Ivain Laclan!" I yelled at the top of my lungs. And now the alcoves came alive, as sleep-sodden, cursing men toppled out of the bedclothes and went for their weapons.

"Stop that infernal noise," roared one of them. "What's wrong? And who the hell are *you*?"

I stopped beating on the tin pot. "Are you Ivain Laclan?" I asked.

"Aye. And who are you?"

I measured him with my eyes. He was not quite as big as Callan—luckily—but he was taller than I, and his bare chest and arms looked muscular and strong. But Callan had taught me that skill and will were more important than brawn.

"I am Davin Tonerre," I said, and went on to deliver the little speech I had rehearsed all the way from Baur Kensie. "And as you are a traitor and an honorless man and have done great harm to my mother, I challenge you to fight me, man to man!"

A heavy silence fell.

Ivain Laclan looked at me, cold-eyed and annoyed.

"Take that back, boy," he said.

I shook my head. "Every word is true," I said. "And no man shoots my mother and walks away unpunished!"

"I've heard those lies before," Ivain said slowly. "From the Kensie messenger. Why Kensie is suddenly so eager to do us insult, I don't know. But every word of it is a lie, a damned lie. I've never hit a woman in my life, let alone shot one! Take it back, cockerel, unless ye want to meet me in the Ring of Iron."

I had not really expected him to confess to his crimes, but there was something about the way in which he stood there, denying it so coldly, that made me still more furious.

"I would not meet you anywhere else, traitor!" I snarled. "And may only one of us leave the Ring alive!"

Often, the Ring of Iron is merely a circle scratched in the dirt; or, if there are men enough and weapons enough, a ring of swords stuck firm in the earth, with a rope linking the hilts. But Baur Laclan had fancy Ring of Iron posts shaped like swords, with a span of heavy rust-colored chain between each post. Scratched line or forged chain, it made no difference: once two men stepped into the Ring they were in a different world. No one could aid, and no one could hinder. And as long as they had stepped in willingly and lawfully, no man could afterward avenge whatever had been done within the Ring. In this way two men could fight and even kill each other without involving the rest of either's clan in a feud. And a quarrel that might have cost many lives would take at the most one or two.

Ivain Laclan's cold steel-gray eyes followed me every second from the moment we stepped into the Ring, even though the signal had not yet been given. My stomach felt like a small hard lump, but I only needed to think of my mother to bring back the fury, and the heat of my rage felt good.

It was still very early, and the morning was so chill that my breath plumed in the air in front of my face. Despite the cold, Ivain was stripped to the waist, and I too had taken off my shirt. That seemed to be the way it was done. I swung my sword in one of the patterns Callan had taught me, trying to limber up a bit. Ivain merely stood there, watching me. Perhaps he thought that warm-ups were unnecessary before taking on a "cockerel" like me. Around us, outside the Ring, stood about thirty silent onlookers, all Laclans. They made me appreciate the chain—I'm sure they felt no urge to come to *my* aid, and that rusty chain ensured that they would at least not help Ivain either.

Helena Laclan had come down into the courtyard too, supporting herself with a long black staff. Her hair was white as ash and her back bent by age, but her voice cut through the silence like a knife.

"For the last time, then, I ask you: is there no other way to settle your dispute?"

"Only if he swallows his damned lies!" snarled Ivain.

I only shook my head.

"You, Ivain Laclan, are you here of your own will and calling?"

"Aye."

"And you will not turn back from this?"

"No."

"You, Davin Tonerre, are you here of your own will and calling?"

"Yes." My voice sounded nearly normal.

"And you will not turn back from this?"

"No!"

"Then let the Ring be closed. What starts here, ends here. No aid, no hindrance, no revenge."

She made a tiny break, as if to give us one last time to turn back. It sounded as if all of Baur Laclan held its breath the while. Neither Ivain nor I said anything.

"Then let the fight begin," said Helena Laclan, and thumped the heel of her staff against the flagstones with a sharp crack.

Ivain raised his sword for the first time, and I could see at once that he was trained in its use. I had expected nothing else. My legs found the position without my even thinking about it—the one Callan had pounded into us until we could barely stand: "Right foot forward, lad! *Raise* that arm!" I could hear his voice in my head. I thought I was ready. I felt ready. But when Ivain launched his first attack, I barely managed to raise my sword in time to parry a slash that would have severed my arm from my shoulder. The blades rang, and my hand and wrist prickled and numbed from the force of it. That blow had been *hard,* much harder than anything Kinni and Black-Arse were capable of, and at least as hard as the ones Callan had landed on me in practice. And that was only his opening move. Where would his sword fall next? "*No* strike is the final one, until it is," muttered Callan-in-my-head. "Think on. Think of the next, and the next after that."

Not that I really had time to think, at least not with my head. I had to leave that to my body. Ivain pounded away at my parries with a hail of blows to the shoulder, to the head, to the chest; had there been time, I would have been scared, for this was nothing like practice. I could forget all about trying to attack, unless I was ready to lose an arm, or worse. How could he be so fast? How could he keep on hitting me so hard? He came at me with feints and thrusts I'd never even seen before, and how I ever managed to prevent him from taking off my head is a mystery to me still.

A heavy gray feeling of despair spread through me. It was the dream all over again—my arms hurt enough to make me want to scream, and the sword seemed to weigh a ton. Ivain's ice-gray eyes did not leave me for a second, and the message in them was clear: I was just a beast that needed slaughtering, the quicker the better. And me—me with my dreams of avenging my mother's hurts and making the traitor pay—I could do nothing except retreat and parry, parry and retreat, until I felt the heavy coldness of the chain against the back of my thigh.

I saw him smile faintly, and I knew he thought he had me now. The next blow would be the last one. I even knew which one he'd choose—not a slash I might be able to parry, but a lunge, straight for the heart. Three times he had used that move, and three times I had leaped back out of reach. Now I could back no farther.

The blade I was watching thrust at me like a spear. I dropped to my haunches and felt the steel brush the top of my head. And as it was still dawning on Ivain that he had not killed me after all, I straightened my legs and butted him in the midriff with every ounce of strength I possessed.

"Huff!"

All breath was knocked out of him and he tumbled back, sitting down abruptly. His sword went flying off to one side.

It was my turn now. He was the beast, the beast brought to slaughter. I raised my sword to slice at his neck.

And I couldn't. His eyes rested on me still, not quite so cold now, and I knew he was afraid. Right now he was a human being, a living, breathing man. And if I swung my sword, in a minute he would be nothing. Dead. A body without life.

I lowered my sword. I felt like crying. My mother had nearly *died* because of this man, I had come here to kill him, and now that I had the chance . . . Was I to be like Nico, a weakling who lacked the guts to strike when the moment came? So that Ivain, like Drakan, could live on and do harm to more people? No. He deserved to die. I raised my sword once more and swung it in a sweeping arc, straight for his neck.

Iron hit steel. Ivain's sword was once more in his hand. But he was still crouched on the ground, the moment was still mine. I struck once more, with all the strength I had.

Claaang. A weird, cracked sound, not at all the usual crisp ring of blade against blade. The sword was suddenly lighter in my hand. And as I raised it for one more stroke, I saw why: the blade had broken off, a hand's breadth below the hilt.

I no longer had a sword.

Ivain slowly got to his feet. There was a big angry red bruise on his chest where I had butted him, and his breathing still sounded strained. But he had a blade, and I didn't. He looked at me in a measuring fashion.

"Well, lad," he said, "time for you to say ye're sorry."

I just stared at him.

"Ye called me a traitor. Accused me of hurtin' a woman. Take it back now."

I couldn't.

"Take it back." He raised his sword.

I shook my head. I wanted to close my eyes, but didn't. Then he swung the blade.

He hit me on the shoulder, so hard that I tumbled to my knees, and the hilt of my broken sword dropped to the flagstones with a clang. I looked down. Callan says that if a blade is sharp enough, you won't know that you have lost an arm until you see it lying on the ground next to you. There was no arm. Not even a bit of blood. Slowly I realized that Ivain had hit me with the flat of the blade, not the edge. I looked up at him. His eyes were as cold now as they had ever been.

"Take it back," he repeated.

I looked at him in silence. Then I shook my head once more.

This time he went for the other shoulder. The arm became numb all over, and I couldn't raise it to save my life. But still he used the flat.

"Admit that ye lied."

"I did *not* lie!" I said angrily. And his sword went whistling through the air once more, this time hitting me in the back so that I was knocked sprawling.

That was how it went. I didn't understand why he was so intent on making me "swallow my damn lies." Maybe so that no one would later be able to accuse him. But I couldn't do it. I could not say the words. He could kill me if he wanted to, but I'd be damned if I was going to let him walk away from the Ring a free and "innocent" man because of me. So the blows kept coming. He mostly went for my shoulders, but my back and my legs suffered too. Once, he hit me on the side of the head so that everything went black for a moment, and blood started to trickle down my cheek. I fell, and fell again. Usually he let me get halfway to my feet before hitting me once more. Finally, I just crouched there on my hands and knees, utterly unable to stand up one more time.

He set his foot against my shoulder and pushed, flipping me onto my back. He stood over me, one foot on either side of my body, and there was a strange look of desperation on his face as he set the point of his blade against my throat.

"D'ye *want* to die, boy? Bein' this stubborn can kill a man!"

There was blood in my mouth, and I could no longer see very well. I didn't have one or two places that hurt; the whole of my body was one big pounding pain.

"For the last time," he said, his voice hoarse, "take back yer lies!"

"Burn in hell," I muttered, and closed my eyes. I could feel the pressure of the cool steel against my throat, and I knew that this time he meant to end it. For a moment I thought of Mama and Melli and Dina and felt a strange urge to apologize. But mostly I thought of the pain, and of the fact that that, at least, would soon stop.

"Stop that! Leave him alone, you brute!"

My eyes snapped open, for there were only two people I knew of who could sound like that. For a moment I thought that Ivain had hit me too hard on the head, because it seemed to me that my little sister Dina was dragging on Ivain's arm, all the while yelling at him in a voice that could skin a mule. In the middle of the Ring of Iron, too. Ivain backed from her, holding his temples as if she had hit him over the head with a fencing post. That is the effect my sister has on most people.

"Dina . . ."

She whirled, and her eyes hit me with the force of a whip.

"And you. You *idiot*."

"Dina, leave. Get out of the Ring!"

"So that you can let this brute kill you? No way. What the *hell* do you think you're doing?"

It sounded odd; Dina hardly ever swears.

"You think he should just get away with it?" I said indignantly.

"With what?"

"Shooting Mama!"

"What? Who?"

What did she mean, who? "Him." I couldn't even raise my arm to point. "Ivain Laclan."

"That?" She looked at my opponent, and then back at me. "That's not Ivain Laclan."

Bad Blood

Davin looked terrible. That great brute of a Laclan had beaten him so badly, he could barely move. Blood was streaming down one cheek, and his nose looked like a pig's snout. His upper body was covered in swollen red welts, like the marks of a whip, only wider, and some of them were bleeding where the edge of the sword had broken through the skin. I hardly knew who made me more furious, Davin or the brute.

"And who the hell are *you*?" asked the brute.

"Dina Tonerre," I said. "This idiot's sister."

It's not that I didn't feel sorry for Davin. I mean, anybody could see the shape he was in. But mostly I was angry. What on earth did he think he was doing, sneaking off like that, not a word to anybody, like a thief in the middle of the night? Coming here to wave his stupid sword about and play the hero. Almost getting *killed*. That he was also waving his sword at the wrong man, that was really just the final touch to his perfect idiocy.

Davin tried to sit up, but his abused arms were nearly useless. I knelt down next to him and supported him, so that he could sit more or less upright, bleeding onto my skirt.

"Dina, leave the Ring!" he repeated. He would have pushed me away if he had been able. It seemed to be a big thing with him, that ring. I really couldn't see why. It was just a stupid chain, anybody could step across it, and I couldn't for the life of me understand why no one had done so. How could they let it get this far? How could they stand there watching a grown man beat a boy to within an inch of his life? I dabbed at his cheek with the edge of my apron. It was a nasty cut and would probably need stitching.

"Medamina Tonerre," said a white-haired old woman who had to be Helena Laclan. "Tell me why you think this is not my grandson Ivain?"

I looked up at her and then at the brute. That brawny bully had nothing in common with the delicately mannered gentleman who had led us into ambush.

"They don't even look like each other," I said, dabbing away.

"Medamina, this *is* Ivain."

Surprised, I looked her in the eye for a moment. And I could see, in the instant before she looked away, that she spoke the truth. The brute who had been beating on Davin really *was* Ivain Laclan.

But who then was the traitor?

It was my turn to feel stupid. I knew he had lied to us about everything else; he had led us into ambush with a lie. Why not lie about his name?

"Medama Laclan," I slowly said. "Two weeks ago, a man came to my mother's house claiming that his name was Ivain Laclan, and that the Laclan clan had need of a Shamer. My mother and I followed this man into an ambush that nearly cost her her life."

"And this isn't him?" said Davin hoarsely. "Dina, you idiot! Do you realize I nearly killed him, and now you're saying *he is the wrong man?*"

"Me? Are you calling *me* an idiot? Did I tell you to go gallivanting across the countryside, waving that miserable piece of iron you call a sword? And it seemed to me he was doing the killing, if anybody was!"

"Whoa," said the brute. "Settle down. Or would the pair of ye like to borrow the Ring for a bit? Listen, boy, does this mean I can *now* get ye to take back those words?"

"I suppose so," said Davin. And then, as if it nearly choked him: "Sorry."

"Well, thank God for that," said the man. "I was afraid I'd have to fight yer sister as well. And *she's* enough to scare any man!" He laughed noisily, and laughter also broke out among the onlookers. I could see Davin cringe at it, like a horse afraid of being whipped. This is the strange thing about Davin; he would rather fight, he would rather be beaten—sometimes I think he would rather die—than be laughed at.

"Does it hurt?" I asked.

"Dina," he said slowly and distinctly, despite his swollen lip, "go *away*." And then he closed his eyes and refused to look at me anymore.

Helena Laclan let us borrow a room for Davin, and although my stubborn older brother claimed he was perfectly capable of walking, in the end it was Callan who carried him up the stairs.

"We have a herbwife, but I'm afraid she's gone to a birthing," said Helena Laclan. She was really very helpful and courteous, considering that the Tonerre family had nearly managed to kill her grandson by mistake.

"I can look after him myself," I said. "My mother has taught me herbs and healing. But if I could have some rags and two buckets of water, one cold, one hot?"

Buckets and rags arrived; but my stupid brother wouldn't let me see to him.

"Callan," he begged, "get her out of here. Make her leave!"

"I'm right here, Davin," I said angrily. "Don't call me 'her.' I'm not a cat or a cow!"

Callan took me by the elbow, politely but firmly, and unless I wanted to use the Shamer's Gift on him, there was nothing for it but to let him lead me into the passage outside.

"Medamina," he began, then gave up the rigid formality in exasperation. "Dina, I think ye'd better let the lad alone."

"But he is hurt!"

Callan nodded. "Aye. He got a thorough hiding. But, Dina, the beating's not the worst of it, not for Davin. Losin' was worse. And havin' his sister break into the Ring to save him like he was some little mother's boy."

Why was everything I did suddenly wrong where Davin was concerned? Last year he had just been my brother. Now he had turned into some alien creature; we still spoke the same language, just about, but beyond that he made it crystal clear that I didn't understand a thing.

"Was I supposed to just stand there and watch Ivain beating him? He was about to kill him, Callan! What should I have done, just let him get on with it?" My voice rose, and then cracked.

Callan slowly shook his head. "I did not say that. I'm just sayin' it's best if ye leave the lad alone right now. I'll look after him."

Like the greater part of humanity, Callan avoided looking me in the eye. Fortunately so—it meant he wouldn't see the tears. And I made sure I had control of my voice again before I spoke.

"Use the hot water for cleaning the cuts. Soak the rags in cold water and use them to wrap his arms and his shoulders." I pushed the pile of rags into his hands. "Change them as soon as they lose their chill. But keep the rest of him warm, and do *not* let him sleep. He has had a blow to the head and it"—my voice betrayed me and I had to swallow—"it can be dangerous if he slips from sleep to unconsciousness."

Callan nodded. "Not the first time I've cared for a lad who's taken more of a beating than was good for him," he said. "Never ye fear, ye can leave him to me."

More than was good for him? Surely no kind of beating was good for anyone. But I didn't say so. No doubt it was just one more thing I didn't understand.

"I'll go and see if I can find some plantain to put on those cuts. They'll sting less."

Callan did not look too pleased. "Get one of Helena Laclan's men to go with you," he said. "I'd not have ye wanderin' about on yer own."

I had planned to leave right way, but Helena Laclan wanted to see me.

"Be seated, Medamina," she said, waving a hand at a tall-backed wooden chair. "After such a tumultuous morning, I think we could both do with a hearty breakfast."

"Thank you," I said. Yesterday, Callan and I had arrived at Baur Laclan shortly before nightfall, after a hard day's ride. We had asked around, and Callan had even told the children in the street that there would be a copper penny for the lad or lass who found us Davin. But no one we talked to had seen him, and finally we had had to give up the search until morning. A friend of Callan's, a caravan guard he had served with, gave us a bed for the night. Very early the next morning we were awakened by a pounding on the door. On the doorstep stood a snotty-nosed urchin hardly more than six years old.

"Gie's the penny," he said.

"Why would I give ye a penny, boy?" asked Callan, grouchy at being hauled from his bed so early.

"That Davin ye're after? He's in the Iron Ring with Ivain. Up at the castle. Now, gie's the penny."

He got his penny, and we got busy. Breakfast had been the last thing on my mind then, and now, hours later, Helena Laclan's newly baked bread looked very tempting.

"Honey?" she offered. "Or cheese?"

"Honey, please." Oh yes, honey, please. When something bad has happened, or if I'm in a bad mood, honey tastes even better than it usually does. I don't have quite the sweet tooth my little sister, Melli, does, but right now the rich golden honey was exactly what I needed. I gratefully bit into the honeyed bread, and for a while Helena Laclan just left me to my munching.

"Does the food please you, Medamina?" she asked, smiling faintly.

"Mmmmh," I said, my mouth full. "But Medama, please call me Dina. I'm not that . . . comfortable with titles."

"Dina, then. But you will have to get used to titles. With eyes like yours, people need to show their respect. It marks a fitting distance and makes them less afraid."

I glanced up but did not try to catch her eye. Was *she* afraid? Helena Laclan, more than seventy years old and head of the powerful Laclan clan—no, she could not possibly be afraid of me. Could she?

"Medama—"

"If I am to call you Dina, you must call me Helena."

That struck me dumb. Sitting there with her white hair like a braided crown, dressed in a fine gray woolen robe with red-and-yellow borders, she did not look like the kind of person I could be on such familiar terms with. I totally forgot what I had meant to say.

"How is your mother?" asked Helena Laclan, probably to put me at my ease again.

"Better. But she's still very weak." Rose had had to stay at Baur Kensie to help Maudi look after her. It didn't please her. She wanted to come along with me and Callan when we realized why Davin had suddenly taken off and why he had taken that damn iron bar with him. But Davin was my brother. And sometimes, Shamer's eyes were a better weapon than Rose's small knife.

"There's a thought in my mind," said Helena Laclan,

blowing on her thyme tea. "Why, do you think, did the traitor pick Ivain's name? Why a Laclan?"

"Maybe he thought we would be less suspicious of a Laclan."

"That may be." She sipped her tea. "But the reason could be more dangerous. What if he meant to cause bad blood between the clans?"

The thought had not occurred to me.

"What would Kensie have done if we had killed their Shamer?" She drew her forefinger across the steam from the teacup so that it whirled and danced like a tiny elf-maid.

"But Callan . . . Davin said that Callan refused to do anything because Ivain is a Laclan and he would not meddle in Laclan matters. I suppose that was why Davin felt he had to come here on his own." What Davin had done was stupid, I thought, but I did understand how galling it had been for him to be faced with Callan's wall of clan pride and clan justice.

"We have a long and bloody history, Dina," said the head of the Laclan clan. "Back in the Time of the Feuds, not many of our men lived long enough to reach middle age. This is why the head of the clan is nearly always a woman. But all the blood that was shed during the feuds did teach us something. We have the Ring of Iron now. We have clan justice. We no longer butcher one another by the hundreds just because one man steals another man's wife. But there are few who do not fear the return of such evil times."

Her gaze became distant, and I suddenly realized that she was old enough to have lived through the last of the great feuds.

"What did he look like, this false Ivain?" she asked.

"Dark-haired, with a tiny triangle of beard on his chin. Very . . . refined. He did not talk like a Highlander. But he wore a Laclan cloak, so we did not suspect him."

"How old was he?"

"I don't know. Perhaps thirty."

"Hmm. It does not sound like anyone we usually count among Laclan's enemies. But who else would benefit from sowing strife between Kensie and Laclan?"

I don't think she meant for me to say anything. She was posing the question to herself. But I answered anyway.

"Maybe Drakan. . . ."

She snorted delicately. "I nourish no gentle feelings for a man who would buy children from a peddler, the way the rest of us buy mules or frying pans. But other than that, Laclan has no charge to make against the Dragon Lord, and I doubt he wishes enmity with us. He would not dare."

Laclan was a great and powerful clan, far bigger than Kensie. But I thought that that would be all the more reason for Drakan to try to set the clans at each other's throats.

Having them kill one another, rather than risking anything himself—that sounded like a very Drakan-like scheme. But although she had called me "Medamina Tonerre" and entertained me at her own table, I did not think that Helena Laclan would ever act on advice from an eleven-year-old girl, and so I took another bite of my honey bread and kept my thoughts to myself.

Before I could go looking for plantain, I had to tell everything I could remember about the false Ivain to Helena Laclan's clerk, who carefully wrote down every word I said. I did as Callan said and asked for someone to come with me, and Helena Laclan laid that task on her youngest grandchild.

"Tavis, you go with Medamina Tonerre and show her the way. Behave, now, and do as she says!"

I thought Callan had had a guard in mind, rather than a guide, but I didn't like to say so. Besides, Tavis was a lively looking boy with a shock of red hair, a host of freckles, and a mischievous smile that made you uncertain whether to cuddle or to throttle him. I would rather have him along than a grown-up like Ivain, who would probably get impatient and grumble about having better things to do.

"How old are you?" I asked, once we were out of Helena Laclan's hearing.

"Nine," he said. "How old are you?"

"Eleven."

He took my measure. I was only about a hand's span taller than he. "Mmh," he said. "But ye're a girl."

"What is that supposed to mean?" I asked, even though it was pretty clear what he meant by it.

"Nothing," he said, and flashed his most innocent-looking urchin smile. "Where d'ye want to go, then, Medamina?"

"Find me an open field or a grassy verge. Do you know what plantain looks like?"

"Mmh. What d'ye need it for?"

"For my brother's hurts. But only the ones with the pointed leaves will do. *Plantago lanceolata*."

"What?"

"That's what they're called in Latin." Just to show him that I knew a thing or to—even if I was a girl.

We had to leave the town to find a bit of grassy ground that had not been trampled to mud, and the first place Tavis showed me was so riddled with buttercups that precious little else grew there.

"Let's just go down the road a bit," said Tavis hopefully. "We'll be sure to find something."

"As long as it doesn't take us halfway to the Lowlands," I said. It sounded a little surly, but that was mostly because I was worried about Davin.

"Oh, so ye're not so used to walkin'?"

"Of course I am." There he went again with his what-are-girls-good-for-anyway manners. It was starting to annoy me. Perhaps a real guard *would* have been better than a nine-year-old brat with freckles and a cheeky manner.

We walked along the road—a cart track cutting through the hills, sometimes sunk so deep that we couldn't even see over the sides. Above our heads hung a lark on flickering wings, and the sound of its song brightened my mood a little. The sun was near its noontime height now, and the day was getting warmer.

"Are ye thirsty?" asked Tavis, and I thought that *he* probably was.

"A bit."

He clambered up the side of the road and extended a polite hand to help me. I hesitated a bit before taking it, remembering a trick Davin had had of letting go halfway up a slope, but Tavis really was being the gentleman, for the moment at least. A small path led over the hill. It seemed to be trodden mainly by sheep; little round black pellets of sheep dung were everywhere, and I had to watch my footing, because I didn't want to ruin my nearly new boots. Tavis wore clogs and didn't care.

On the other side of the hill, the path crisscrossed down toward a hollow overgrown with birch and hazel. Water gleamed brightly among the leaves, and I could hear the gurgle of a stream. We slid and skidded down the last sharp dip of the path, and Tavis sat down on a rock, kicked off his clogs, and dangled his feet in the water. Crouching, I cupped my hand, dipped it, and drank my fill.

"What's that noise?" I asked, because there was a not-so-distant rushing that seemed to be more than a brook this size should make.

Tavis pointed downstream. "There's an old water mill down there. It doesn't work anymore, so no one lives there." He looked at me sideways. "We can go and look if ye like. But it's not really a place for girls. It's haunted."

"Haunted by what?" I asked. "You're only saying that to try to scare me."

He shook his head. "No, it's true. I've heard it. If ye stand at the top of the mill wall, ye can hear her weepin'. And in the night, ye can see her too, or so I've heard."

"Who?"

"Auld Anya. Anya Laclan. My great-great-grand-mother. She's searchin' for her drowned child."

I snatched a quick look at him, just enough to see whether he was telling the truth. He was. Or at least he believed what he said.

"They found Anya in the Mill Pond some weeks after her little girl drowned. No one knows if she did it on purpose or if she slipped while she was searchin'."

Tavis cautiously peeked at me to see whether he had frightened me. And I did suddenly feel a chill come over me, despite the heat of the noonday sun.

"We're looking for plantain," I said. "We don't have

time for water mills." And that was quite true, but I could tell by his smug smile that he thought he had succeeded in scaring me.

We sat there for a while, watching the dragonflies skim across the surface. Then I noticed that we weren't the only ones drawn to the coolness of the stream.

"Look," I said, "peddlers."

Tavis looked the way I pointed. Farther upstream, by the proper ford, some men were leading their horses down to the water. Two covered wagons stood on the bank, hung with copperware and other tinker's goods.

"Well met!" shouted Tavis at the top of his voice, waving at them. One of the peddlers looked up. He seemed to stare at Tavis and me longer than was really polite, but in the end he raised an arm in greeting.

"Let's go and see," said Tavis. "Let's have a look at what they're sellin'."

"Plantain," I reminded him. "*Plantago lanceolata.*"

"Oh, come on. Just a peek. It'll only take a moment. Then we can look for yer plantago what's-its-name afterward."

I agreed unwillingly. "But only for a moment!"

"That's what I said. . . ." Tavis had already pushed his wet feet into his clogs and was trotting upstream along the narrow path next to the brook. I followed him more slowly. Living deep in the Highlands the way we did, we did not get many visits from peddlers and traders, and despite my worry for Davin, a flutter of curiosity rose inside me. What did they have in those wagons? Bartol Tinker, who passed by Baur Kensie about once a month, always had some boiled sweets, white and red and yellow, and every child got one—if you wanted more, you would have to buy them, and I never had the money; there had been so many boring and necessary things we had to have, nails and rope and things like that. But that one piece of candy . . . if I sucked it carefully, I could make it last nearly an hour. My mouth watered at the thought, and I hoped the peddlers by the ford would be as generous as Bartol. They looked as if they could afford to be—I had never seen such fine horses in front of a peddler's wagon before. One of them, a leggy chestnut, positively shone in the sunlight.

"Well met, and welcome to Laclan," said Tavis as he produced a bow worthy of a chamberlain with lace on his sleeves. It looked a little out of place when done by a freckle-faced kid with bare wet feet in his clogs. "May I ask what such fine tradesmen as yerselves keep in yer wagons?"

"This and that," said one of them a bit curtly. He was a broad-shouldered, black-bearded man who actually looked more like an armsman than a peddler. There was something about him . . . hadn't I seen him before? A strange unease fluttered in my stomach.

"Tavis," I whispered, "come on. Let's go back."

"Now? But we haven't seen anything!" He walked up

to one wagon and patted the chestnut's neck in a familiar fashion. "A handsome animal," he said approvingly. "Master Tradesman has a good eye for horseflesh."

"Get away with you, boy!" barked the black-beard. "Hands off that wagon. Don't even think of pinching anything!"

What an ill-tempered man. And rude. Where had I seen him before?

"Come *on*, Tavis."

But Tavis had drawn himself up to his full height—roughly level with Blackbeard's belt buckle—and had gone rigid with offended pride.

"We are not thieves, Mesire. And ye would do well to speak us fair. My name is Tavis Laclan. Mesire may have heard of my grandmother—Helena Laclan, head of the clan? And this"—he flourished a hand in my direction, like a mountebank showing off a three-headed wonder—"this is Dina Tonerre, the Shamer's daughter."

Oh, do be quiet, Tavis! I thought furiously. No good ever came of mouthing off about Mama being a Shamer. And now that someone had tried to kill her, it seemed even less wise. Blackbeard stiffened for a moment, threw a quick glance my way, then looked away.

"I see," he said. "Tavis Laclan. And the Shamer's daughter. Fine company for a humble trader. Forgive my suspicion, but one meets all sorts of riffraff on the roads. Step inside and have a look at the merchandise." He waved a hand at one of the wagons. And suddenly I knew where I had seen him before. I had had only a brief glimpse of his face, just before I had nearly ridden right over him, letting the gray pony shove him into the lake. He was one of the ambushers—he might even be the one who had shot my mother.

"I'm afraid we don't have the time," I said, backing a step. My whole body felt icy cold and empty of blood. "Come on, Tavis, we have to go."

"What's the matter with ye?" asked Tavis in irritation. "Just the one peek."

But I shook my head.

"No, thank you. I want to get back to Baur Laclan. Now." I turned and began walking.

"But ye said— Hey! Let go of me!"

Blackbeard had hooked Tavis by the belt, holding him so that he wiggled in the air like a fish at the end of a fisherman's line. Yet another man had come out of the wagon. And although he too was dressed like a peddler, I recognized this one right away. The false Ivain Laclan.

I ran the only way I could, downstream, toward the old water mill.

The Mill Pond

"Gone? What do you mean, 'gone'?" I stared at Callan as best I could, with my right eye swollen almost shut.

"Her and the Laclan boy they sent with her. They went lookin' for plantain and did not come back."

I remembered very well the last thing I'd said to her. *Dina, go away.* And I had asked Callan to get her to leave. For a brief confused moment I thought she might have done exactly that. Maybe she had just left. Gone back to Baur Kensie, and to Mama. But no, she wouldn't have. Dina was much too stubborn for that.

I pushed the blankets aside and tried to sit up. Callan had to help me.

"What time is it?" I had dozed for most of the day, and now I only knew that daylight no longer fell though the thick leaded panes of the chamber's window.

"The sun went down about an hour ago," said Callan. "Lie down, lad. There's nothing ye can do. I only came to tell ye that I'm ridin' out with the Laclans to look for them."

It had been dark for an hour. Dina would never have stayed out so long of her own free will. The unheated air of the chamber chilled my bare chest and arms, but I felt colder still inside.

"I want to come."

"Do ye now? Try standin' on yer own first."

"Dina is my sister! If something has happened to her . . ."

"Likely they got lost, that's all." He handed me a pewter mug. "Here. Drink a bit, then lie down. What can ye do that the Laclans cannot do better? There's an unholy lot of them, they're all fit and healthy, and they know this place inside out. We'll find the children, never fear."

"And if you don't?"

Callan got up. "We will. If we have to look under every blade of grass, we will. Lie down, lad, and try to get some rest. I'll be back as soon as I can."

I waited until the sound of Callan's steps had faded in the passage outside. Then I grabbed hold of the windowsill and hauled myself to my feet. Where were my boots? At the foot of the bed, it seemed. Bending to pick them up, I nearly fell flat on my face. Callan was right, it was horribly difficult to stand without hanging on to something. At least it hurt less—the pain had faded into a strange kind of numbness the minute I realized what Callan meant by "gone." With thick, clumsy fingers I pulled on my boots and reached for the shirt. I could barely raise my arms, but somehow I managed to get it on.

I got up again and put a hand against the wall to steady myself while I waited for the room to stop spinning. But I *was* able to stand. I was fairly certain that if I could only get onto Falk's back, I'd be able to ride, or stay on at least. That would have to be enough. The Laclans might know the land inside out, like Callan said, but I knew Dina. And I couldn't just lie here and let them do the searching if there was the least little clue, the least little lead that I might understand because it was my sister we were looking for.

There was only one problem.

Callan had locked the door.

He returned shortly before dawn, spattered with rain and mud, and with an oddly helpless droop to his shoulders. I knew at once that they hadn't found Dina.

"I'm sorry, lad," he said, his voice hoarse from shouting. "We haven't found them yet."

"Are there any tracks?"

"The hounds lost the scent by the millrace. They'll . . . they'll drag the pond once it gets light."

They'll drag the pond. That was something you did

when you were looking for drowned bodies. My stomach turned to ice once more

"Dina would never go swimming in a mill pond. She's not that stupid. She wouldn't even come close. Didn't you say she was looking for plantain? They don't grow by water." My voice sounded oddly breathless, although I had done nothing except lie still, trying to sleep.

"Let's hope so," said Callan. "Are ye any better? Can ye walk today? There's breakfast downstairs in the common room, but I'll bring ye some if ye cannot make the stairs."

"I can walk," I said. "And I won't let you lock me up again."

He peered at me. "Another day in bed would do ye no harm, lad. How's yer head?"

"Fine. Let's just go." My head did hurt, but what did he expect? My sister was missing. Did he think I would stay in and nurse a bit of a headache?

He had to help me down the stairs. My back and my arms were the most badly battered parts of me, but it's amazing how hard it is to lift your feet when your back hurts. When I caught sight of Ivain among the men seated at the long table, I squared my shoulders and tried not to limp. His eyes followed me all the way from the stairs to the table, but he didn't say a word. At least no one laughed. They just moved aside, making room for Callan and me on the benches.

It was a silent and hasty meal. Most of the men had been out searching all night, and they ate hungrily. But there were no jokes, and no laughter, and very little talk. I remembered that it was not just Dina who had disappeared. A Laclan boy had been with her, and he was gone, too.

"We'll start by the mill," said Ivain, and rose without further comment. Benches scraped against the slate flagstones of the floor, as most of the men around the table got up to follow him.

"I want to come," I hissed at Callan. "You're not going to leave me stuck in that bloody chamber all day."

He looked at me. Then he slowly nodded. "If that's what ye want. But turn back if ye start feeling poorly. There's no shame in takin' it easy after a beating like the one you got."

Someone had fetched Falk from the White Doe, and Callan helped me get him ready. I couldn't raise my arms far enough to brush his back, and when I tried to pick his hooves I nearly fell flat on my face again. It was very annoying. Callan practically had to lift me onto the horse.

"Are ye sure ye shouldn't rest a bit more, lad?" he asked, eyeing me dubiously.

I shook my head and gathered the reins.

"Let's get moving," I said, nudging Falk forward.

It was a gray and windy day. The water mill had probably once been a busy, useful place, but now it was little more than a ruin. The old works squealed and creaked when the wind came whistling through the gaping holes where windows used to be. Half the roof had fallen in, and only owls and crows lived here now. And water rats. I caught a glimpse of a slick brown body diving into the water as we approached.

"What a gloomy place," I said, shuddering a bit. "Dina would never come here."

"The hounds think so," growled Callan. But even he looked dubious.

"The hounds are wrong," I said. "Dina would go out of her way to avoid a dismal place like this one."

There were two ponds, an upper and a lower. The upper pond was dammed by a wide stone wall and lay silent and dark like a mirror. The one below it was much more turbulent. Water tumbled into it not just from the millrace where the wheel had once gone round and round, but also through a big, jagged hole in the dam.

"Is the water supposed to do that?" I said, pointing.

Ivain heard me, and shook his head. "No," he said. "The water broke through one night, and no matter what they did to repair the dam, it didn't hold. Some say it's the ghost's doin'. In any case, it's why the mill was abandoned."

"The ghost?"

He nodded. "Auld Anya. If ye stand on the wall there, ye can hear her weep."

I didn't believe him, and it probably showed in my face.

"Come," he said. "Callan can hold yer horse. Or . . . likely ye're not so steady on yer legs yet. We wouldn't want ye to get a duckin'." There was a challenging glint in his gray eyes, and I felt my anger boil in response.

"I'm fine," I said, slipping off Falk's back with as much ease as I could muster.

The wall was wide, almost like a bridge. One could tell from the worn smoothness of the stones that people had been using it to cross the millstream for ages.

"Here," said Ivain, stopping nearly halfway across, "listen."

At first all I heard was the rushing of the waters. But then it came.

"Aaaaaahhhh . . . aaaaaahhhh." A drawn-out plaintive moan, a long wet sigh of sorrow.

"It's Anya weepin' for her drowned child," Ivain murmured very quietly, as if he didn't want to disturb her grief. "At night ye can see her too, they say." There was no gleam in his eye now, and I felt chilled all over, because it really did sound like a grieving woman. Below the wall,

Laclan men had begun the miserable task of dragging the bottom, and drowned children was the last thing I wanted to think about right then.

One of the dogs had begun to bark furiously, and there were sudden shouts, not from the men below us, but from the upper pond. Something had been found. I forgot all about ghosts and hurried back to the bank.

"What is it?" I asked Callan, even though he could hardly know better than I. He grunted noncommittally and got a lanky Laclan boy to hold both our horses.

"Let's go look," he said.

At first all you could see was something green and shapeless below the surface, caught between the roots of a large willow. Ivain tied a rope around his waist and clambered down the steep bank to fish it out.

"It's a cloak," he said, holding it out to us.

It hung there in his hand, moss green and sodden, looking strangely abandoned without the one who usually wore it. Like a body without a soul. I had to try twice before the words would come.

"It's Dina's," I finally managed to say.

The Ghost Country

My head was full of dark water.

It made no sense, but that was how it felt. Every time I moved, it sloshed and eddied, making me seasick. My thoughts drifted aimlessly like a dry leaf caught in a whirling current.

At some point someone tried to give me a drink of water, but it wouldn't stay in my mouth, it ran out the side and trickled down my cheek. I didn't do it on purpose—despite the watery feeling in my head, I felt thirsty and would have been grateful for the drink—but I seemed to have forgotten how to swallow.

"You haven't given her too much, have you?" someone said.

"If we are to hold this one, it's not enough just to tie her up, like we did with the boy."

"So you say. But if the brat dies on us, the Dragon won't be happy. Nor will Valdracu."

"I know what I'm doing. You mind your own business."

The voices went away, and for a while I drifted in lazy circles, round and round. If I could lie quite still, I thought, the seasick feeling might not be so bad. But it was hard to stay still. Whatever I was lying on was moving, tossing me from side to side. It was so unpleasant that I just wanted to be somewhere else. Anywhere else.

And then a strange thing happened.

One moment I was being rocked and shaken and tossed about, getting more and more seasick. The next, I really was somewhere else. I drifted upward and floated away, as if I weighed nothing at all, like I was a wisp of cloud and not a girl with a solid, warm body and "both feet on the ground," as my mother used to say.

I certainly didn't have both feet on the ground right now. Below me, so distant that they looked like dolls instead of people, some men were riding along beside two covered wagons. They were headed toward a narrow mountain pass, along a trail that cut like a streak of yellow ocher through the darkness of the heather and the gray rock of the slopes. Being so small, they looked funny, but I quickly tired of watching them. It was much more interesting that I had suddenly learned how to fly. Or float. Flying, I supposed, required more than just hanging there in the air.

Whusssh. Two ravens streaked by, close enough for one black wing to touch . . . no, it didn't touch. There was nothing *to* touch. The wing sliced right through my hand as if it wasn't even there. What had happened to me? I stared at my hand. It looked perfectly normal, five fingers, five nails, and so on . . . except that there was a strange bright edge to it, a weird kind of glowing.

I began to get scared. Down there on the ground, the men and the wagons were getting smaller and smaller. I was rising—slowly, perhaps, but steadily upward all the time, and this couldn't possibly be healthy. I wasn't meant to hover among the clouds like a falcon or an eagle. I tried to flap my arms as if they were wings, but that did no good whatsoever. Then I tried a few swimming strokes, although of course air and water weren't the same thing. Nothing helped. I just kept rising.

This was no longer interesting or exciting. I didn't want to be here. I wanted to be home. Home with Mama.

It was as if someone had hooked me on a string and was pulling it. The wagons and the mountain pass disappeared. The blue sky disappeared. For one long, endless moment everything, every color, every sound, disappeared into a shining gray mist. Then there was suddenly a window. A window, a bed, and a voice I knew.

"Thank you, Rose. That's just what I need."

Mama.

I was exactly where I had wanted to be, and I was so happy and relieved that I almost forgot how I came to be there. I stood between the bed and the window, watching Mama. She was still very pale, but she was sitting up, and she was able to hold the bowl of broth that Rose had brought her.

"Mama," I said quietly, so as not to startle her.

She didn't hear me. She sipped her soup and didn't even look my way.

"Mama!" I tried again, somewhat louder.

"Do you want me to open the window for a bit?" asked Rose. "It's such a lovely warm day."

"Please," said Mama, still not showing any signs of having heard me. And Rose walked toward the window, toward the window and me. *Through* me. Like I wasn't there. It was worse than the raven's wing. Much worse.

"Mama!" I screamed, and without thinking I used the Shamer's voice, because that was what you did when you wanted people to *listen*.

The bowl dropped from my mother's hand, and hot soup spilled across the bedclothes.

"Dina," she whispered, looking uncertainly toward the window, but not quite at me. With a startled exclamation, Rose fell to one knee by the bedside, dabbing at the soup stain with her apron and murmuring apologies and frightened questions.

"I shouldn't have . . . I'm sorry, I should have held the bowl for you. Do you have a fever?"

Mama paid her no attention. She was still staring at the window and me.

"Dina," she said sharply. "Turn around. Go back. What you are doing is dangerous. You can die from it."

"Mama."

"No! Turn back. Now!"

She used the Shamer's voice too, and she was much better at it than I was. Mama and Rose, the bedroom, and the soup-stained quilt all disappeared with a jerk, and I was once more whirled back into the shining gray mists. "Turn back," she had said, but I didn't know the way. The mist was everywhere, above me and below, and gradually inside me as well; dense and cold it went right through me and made it harder and harder to think. I couldn't see anything, but there were sounds, this time. I heard voices, faint like distant echoes, and I clung to the sound because there was nothing else. The voices were calling, searching. And one of them was searching for me.

"Dina . . ." It was so distant that I could barely hear it, but it tugged at me like the longing for home had done before Mama forced me to go back.

"Dina!"

It was Davin. And he wasn't whispering. He was shouting at the top of his lungs. He was crouched over Falk's neck although anybody could see that he belonged in bed, and his poor battered face was completely desperate and wet from tears. He forced Falk to trot along the millstream bank and paid no attention to our gelding's snorting attempts to shy away from the frothing, roaring water.

"Dina!" Again and again he called.

"Davin!" shouted Callan, close on his heels. "Halt. Stop it." Callan urged his robust bay gelding alongside Falk and seized the reins. "Stop it, lad!"

"Let go," Davin hissed, beside himself, and tried to jerk his reins from Callan's grasp. But Callan wouldn't yield.

"Lad . . . it's no good. She's gone. It's an evil thing, but there's no help for it. Chargin' along just askin' for a fall— what good will it do? Is it not bad enough that we must tell yer mother that . . . that Dina has drowned? Come home now, lad. At least she'll have you."

Drowned? Had I drowned? Was that why my head was full of dark water? Was that why people could walk right through me, as if I were a ghost?

"You go home," said Davin wildly and bitterly. "I'm not going back."

"Have ye lost yer wits, lad? D'ye think I can come home without ye?"

"Do you think *I* can go home and face my mother *now*? I can't, Callan."

Hesitantly, Callan let go of Falk's reins.

"What will ye do?" he asked.

"Search. Hope. As long as they haven't found . . . haven't found a body, Callan, I have to believe she's still alive." But although he was trying to sound hopeful, there was a toneless, dispirited ring to his voice. He looked so miserable that I felt like hugging him.

"Davin." I wasn't sure he'd be able to hear me. Maybe only Shamers could, and contrary to me, he had inherited no hint of my mother's gift. But he started and looked about him wildly.

"Dina?"

I wanted to tell him that I didn't think I had drowned. That he shouldn't despair so. But something seized me by the arm and I was jerked back into the shining gray mist. And this time, I wasn't alone.

"Riana! I found you. I found you!"

A gaunt woman was clutching my arm with cold fingers. "Where have ye been, sweetheart? Mama has looked so hard for you!" She drew me into an embrace that felt as cold as her fingers. "Wicked child, to scare me so!"

She was not just cold. She was wet too. Sodden with water, as if she had just risen from the Mill Pond. Suddenly, Tavis's story came back to me: *She's lookin' for her drowned child.* Auld Anya. Tavis's great-great-grandmother, who had drowned herself so many, many years ago.

"Let go," I pleaded, struggling to escape her wet embrace. "I'm not your little girl!"

"Wicked child," she said, clutching me still more firmly. "Wicked child, I told ye to stay in the garden. I told ye!"

"Let go of me. Let *go*."

"No. This time I'll not let ye go. This time ye'll stay right here with me!"

"If I have to stay here, I'll die!"

"No. Mama will take care of ye. Mama will take such good care of her little girl." She began kissing my cheek and throat, kisses cold and wet like toad's skin.

"Let me go. I'm not your child!"

She released me as abruptly as if I had chopped off her arms. Her hungry, searching eyes met mine. And, like the living, she too looked away.

"I did not mean to," she moaned. "I was only gone for a minute! How was I to know she could climb the fence on her own. I could not know that!"

Her hair was as soaking wet as the rest of her. It stuck to her face in dark streaks. She wrapped her wet gray shawl more closely around her shoulders, as if she herself could feel how cold she was. Around her, the mist was less dense. I could see the waterwheel behind her, and the slumping outline of the mill.

"Riana," she whispered. "I want my Riana back." And she moaned so plaintively that it cut me right to the soul.

"Riana is dead," I told her as gently as I could. "And so are you. You must stop searching."

She raised her head, and her eyes gleamed with rage.

"I want my Riana! What did ye do to her? *Where is she?*"

She snatched at me with skinny fingers and would have seized me again, but I threw myself backward and wished myself far away—far, far away. I whirled through the fogs of the gray ghost country and closed my ears to all the calling voices. For a moment, I hung once again in the blue air above the mountain pass, with the wagons and the men below me. This time I didn't try to flap my arms. I just closed my eyes and willed myself *down*, down to the wagons, back to my place in the normal, living world, with a body that weighed something, a living body that other living people could see.

"Come on, girl! Wake up. Sandor, get me that water, damn you!"

No more water, I thought, I never want to be wet again! But nobody paid any attention to what I wanted. A cold wet cloth was placed on my forehead, and somebody was patting my cheeks in the most irritating way, so hard that it felt like he was hitting me.

"'Trust me, Lord. I know what I'm doing!' Wasn't that what you said, Sandor? I remember it quite distinctly. If the brat dies, *you* may have the privilege of explaining it to the Dragon!"

"It's just witch weed, Lord. Nobody dies from witch weed! It was Herself as gave it to me."

"For the mother, fool. Not the girl."

"Pardon, Lord, but it was for the mother *and* the girl. We were told to be just as careful with the brat."

I didn't want to die. I didn't want to go back to the

ghost country to wander searching through the mists, cold and restless like Auld Anya.

"Stop hitting me," I mumbled. My head hurt quite badly enough. Like one huge toothache.

The slaps stopped, and I slowly opened my eyes. The face of the false Ivain hovered over me, and I gradually realized that he was crouched next to me, a wet rag in one hand. I was no longer lying in the wagon, but on some stiff yellow grass. I wrinkled my nose; there was a smell of vomit, and I was afraid that it came from me.

The false Ivain straightened and looked at somebody standing behind me.

"It's your lucky day, Sandor," he said. "It seems she has decided to live after all."

Shortly after that, we went on. I lay in one wagon, still feeling weak and unwell, but at least this time they'd given me something to cushion the jolts—two heavy cloaks bordered in black and blue. The colors of the Skaya clan, I thought. Where had they got those? For the first time I was able to pay some attention to my surroundings. The wagon was loaded with thick bundles of cloth, some Skaya-colored, others in the green-and-white of the Kensies. Next to the bundles was a long wooden box that I kept bumping into whenever the wagon wheel hit a rock or a bump in the road. I eased the lid open and looked inside. Straw. A boxful of straw? Not very likely. Fumbling in the straw, my fingers touched something cold and sharp. It wasn't something I was used to holding, but I recognized the shape. Swords. The box was full of swords.

I let the lid drop. Clan cloaks and swords. Where was the false Ivain going with such a load?

Fault

For three days we searched, from daybreak till it became too dark to see. Except for Dina's cloak we found no trace of either child, alive or dead.

"We have to go tell yer mother," Callan said on the fourth day. "She has to know."

I didn't want to; nor did Callan, judging from his expression.

"I heard her voice, Callan."

"Aye. So ye say."

"Don't you believe me?"

Callan moved his shoulders uneasily. "Aye. There's more than most folks ken of this world and the one beyond."

He was thinking of ghosts, I knew. "She wasn't dead," I said. "I don't think she was dead."

Callan looked down at his hands. "That's as may be. But lad . . . folks rarely hear the voices of the livin' in that fashion." He tightened the laces of his pack and swung it across his shoulder. "Well? Are ye comin'?"

"I suppose so." What else could I do? It was as Callan said: Mama had to be told.

Callan went down to get the horses ready. I called on Helena Laclan to bid her good-bye and to thank her for the Laclans' long searching. They had spared no effort. That they had also been looking for a Laclan child made no difference. I might not be a Highlander, and the Tonerre family was not a clan, but still I knew that Tonerre owed Laclan something now.

As I came down to the courtyard, I saw a woman in a black shawl, standing by the Ring of Iron. She was staring at me, rigid and unmoving as a pillar, so that I became uneasy and tried to hurry past her. But she stepped in front of me, forcing me to stop.

"Tonerre." Her voice was iron hard, and her eyes as gray and cold as Ivain's had ever been.

"Medama?" I said in my politest tone.

"Are ye happy now?"

"Happy? Medama, I don't—"

"Ye came to take a life," she said in a voice that raised chills down my back. "And when ye could not have Ivain's, you and yer witchy sister led my Tavis to his death."

I stood there, openmouthed, and could think of no way to answer her. How could she think I . . . that Dina . . .

"No," I finally whispered, "it wasn't like that."

"I want my Tavis back," she said. "And if I cannot have that, I'll curse you and yer family to blackest hell every day for the rest of my life." She raised her clenched hand and held it in front of my face. Her fist was blackish gray, smeared with something greasy and dark.

"Here," she said. "I'm givin' ye a gift. I give ye one night of my dreams. D'ye know what I dream? I dream that fish are eatin' Tavis's eyes." And then she hit me, right between the eyes with her black hand. The blow was not a hard one, and yet it shook me more than anything Ivain had done to me. I couldn't protect myself against this, much less strike back.

"I never hurt your son," I said dazedly, for this had to be the Laclan boy's mother. "And Dina didn't either, I'm sure of it!"

"I know what I know," she said, and walked away from me, her back still rigidly straight.

"What kept ye?" growled Callan. "The horses are frettin' to be off."

One of them certainly was. Falk was busy flinging his head about and pawing the ground to show how impatient he was. Callan's bay just stood there, much too well trained for that kind of silliness. Debbi Herbs's gray pony yawned, showing all its long yellow teeth.

"I . . . I met Tavis's mother."

"Mmmh. Can't have been easy for ye."

I shook my head but said nothing more about it.

"Ivain gave me this," said Callan, handing me a long bundle wrapped up in old sacking. I knew immediately what it was, but I unwrapped it anyway.

It was my sword, or what was left of it. Seeing that I lost, it rightfully belonged to Ivain now, but I don't suppose he had much use for a broken blade.

"What should I do with it?" I asked Callan.

He shrugged. "That's for you to know," he said.

At that moment I felt like flinging it on the middens. It had brought nothing but evil, and I suddenly understood Nico much better; right now I didn't care for swords either. Still, I wrapped up the broken pieces and found a place for them in my pack. It *was* iron. Perhaps it could be made into something useful—a pot or some such thing.

The marks Ivain's sword had left on me had faded now to yellow and green, but Callan still had to help me into the saddle. I gathered the reins and made ready to ride.

"Wait, lad," said Callan. "Ye have something on yer brow."

I felt my forehead. There was a greasy spot right between my eyes, where Tavis's mother had hit me. I tried to rub it with my sleeve, but it wouldn't come off.

"Did she hit you, the boy's mother?" said Callan, suddenly looking worried. "With the Black Hand?"

"She hit me all right," I said. "And her hand was smeared with something."

Callan stood quite still. He stood quite still for so long that even the well-bred bay got impatient and shoved him gently with its muzzle.

"What is it?" I said. "What about that hand?"

Callan pulled something out from under his shirt, a small bag he apparently wore around his neck. I had never seen it before. "Here," he said. "Best borrow this, at least until we can get ye home to yer mother. She is a wise woman, she understands such matters too, I think."

"What is it?" I asked, weighing the small bag in my hand. It was very light, and there was a faint rustle when I squeezed it. "What do I need it for?"

"Just some dried herbs. Clover, catnip, vervaine, and dill. My gran made it. I don't know if it works, but it's worth a try."

"Works? On what?"

"Against the Evil Eye and suchlike. The Black Hand is no jest."

"You mean that she . . . that she cursed me?" *I'm givin' ye a gift,* she had said. *One night of my dreams.* And she had talked about cursing me and my family to blackest hell. "What was that on her hand? What is this, Callan?"

"Grease. Ashes. Likely other stuff as well. I don't know much about witchy matters. Put that thing on, now, and let's get out of here."

· · ·

Even leading the gray pony we made better time than I had done alone, as Callan knew the way much better. If I hadn't been so sore and tired still, we might have made the trip in one day. But late in the afternoon I could barely stay on Falk's back anymore, and Callan found us a good campsite under some birches by a small brook. I used the cold, clear water to scrub at the greasy spot until the last remnants of the woman's black fist had gone. Her words stayed with me, though. And that night I had hideous sunken dreams of black water and slimy water weeds and cold, cold rocks. And fish. Fish eating Dina's eyes.

I woke in the middle of the long, cold hour when the first pale light is in the sky but the sun has not yet risen. I was so grateful to be awake and so frightened to go back to sleep that I felt like saddling Falk on the spot. But Callan was still asleep, and the horses too were dozing, heads low and haunches slumped. I leaned against the trunk of a birch tree and tried to forget about the fish and Dina's eyes. And Mama. Most of all I tried not to think of Mama and her eyes when she heard what we had to tell her.

We reached Baur Kensie in the late morning. It was strange to come across the crest of the hill and see the cottage there below, so small and ordinary. Naturally, it hadn't changed much in the time I'd been away. It was only me. I had a strange feeling of . . . of not really living there anymore. Of not belonging. And that made me suddenly fond of every silly chicken down there, every row of cabbage plants, every turf we had so laboriously put on the roof last autumn.

Mama sat on the chopping block by the woodshed, enjoying the morning sun. I hoped that meant she was stronger now. She would need her strength. She waved at us. And then she got up suddenly, propping herself against the wall of the shed with one hand. She had seen the gray, and the empty saddle.

She didn't say anything until we had reached the yard.

"Where is Dina?" she asked.

My mouth had gone dry, and my cheeks felt wooden. I couldn't seem to say the words. Callan couldn't either, at first. But then she put her hand on his knee and forced him to meet her eyes.

"*Where is Dina?*" she repeated, using her eyes and her voice as ruthlessly as only my mother can. And Callan had to tell, word by difficult word, what had happened.

"We . . . we found no body, Medama," he finally ended his tale. "But no trace either of . . . of any livin' child."

She let him go. He slumped on the horse as though she had snapped something inside him. Mama whirled without a word and strode into the cottage. I heard Rose's voice in there, and Mama's answering her. Then Rose came running out. She flew straight at me, like an arrow toward a target.

"You . . . You . . ." She hit me on the thigh so hard that Falk started at the sound.

"You fool! You numbskull! How could you *do* it!" Her pale braids danced, and there were red spots on her cheeks from sheer rage.

"It's not the lad's fault," said Callan, sliding off the bay's back. "Ye think this is easy for him?"

"Why did he have to run off like that?" spat Rose. "He could've stayed at home, and looked after his mother and Melli and Dina, like he was supposed to! This . . . this *never* would've happened!"

A burning feeling spread through my body, a mixture of fury and shame.

"Mind your own business," I hissed. "Or mind your own family. Where are *they*?"

It was a cruel thing to say, for Rose had more or less run away from home. To get away from Drakan, yes, but also to escape her grown-up half brother, who beat her. Rose's mother still lived in Dunark and had made no answer to any of the letters we had helped Rose write to her.

"At least I didn't drown anyone!" Rose cried, tears in her eyes.

"Neither did I," I said, feeling suddenly more tired than angry. I got off Falk and led him into the stable, not looking at anyone.

•   •   •

I stayed in the stable for a long time. Much longer than it took me to unsaddle Falk and rub him down and see to his water and feed. I suddenly remembered how Dina used to hang about the animals when she was feeling low. That made me so miserable and guilty that I didn't see how I could ever face another human being. What was Melli thinking about all this? She was only five. Did she even understand what it meant that someone was dead?

Finally the door opened. I half-expected it to be Mama, but it wasn't. It was Rose.

"Davin?" she said tentatively. "Aren't you coming in?"

"Why?" I said, my anger flaring up again. "It's all my fault, isn't it?"

"I didn't mean it like that," she said. "It's just . . . I got so scared and furious and miserable, all at once." She put her hand on my arm, very cautiously, as if she expected me to hit her or something. "Won't you come in? Your mother is asking about you."

I nodded. "I'll come. In a minute."

It was a long, horrid day. An evil day. Worse, even, than the days we had spent searching and searching and not finding anything. Worse, because there wasn't anything left to do. That night, Rose lit the fire even though it wasn't really cold. Mama sat with Melli on her lap, looking completely exhausted. No one said much. It was almost a relief when it finally became time to go to bed, except that I was scared of the dreams that might be waiting.

In the new cottage, I had a place of my own. One couldn't really call it a room; it was really just a curtained-off section of the kitchen. But there was a narrow bedstead, a wooden chest, and a row of pegs, and I no longer had to share an alcove with Dina and Melli. Melli. It was a good thing we had Rose now, so that poor Melli didn't have to sleep alone. Her eyes had looked so huge and scared all night. She hadn't said a thing, not even to ask about Dina. It was hard to tell what she was thinking.

I must have slept a bit, though I don't remember any dreams. I woke because I heard something. It was very faint, and not a sound I had ever heard before. Yet I knew right away what it was.

My mother was crying.

I sat up. There was a light on in the kitchen. I pushed aside the blankets and pulled on my breeches.

She was sitting in the chair by the fire. The faint glow from the fire flickered across her gray linen skirt. And something else. Something green. She was sitting there with Dina's dark green cloak in her arms.

"Mama . . ."

She raised her head to look at me, making no attempt to hide her tears. I looked away.

"Davin. Come and sit down."

When I was younger, I used to sit at her feet and lean against her legs. I was too old for that now, I thought. I sat on the bench instead.

"It's so strange," Mama said quietly. "I heard her voice some days ago. And I . . . I sent her away. What she was doing was dangerous to a living person, so I sent her away. I didn't stop to listen to her. If I had, we might at least have known where she was."

"Do you mean that she . . . was alive?"

"I thought so then. Now I'm not so sure. Maybe it was because . . . because she was dying that she was able to come to me."

"I heard her too," I said. "The day after she went missing."

I could feel her eyes on me, but I just kept staring into the fire.

"What did she say?"

"Nothing. She just called my name."

"How long?"

"Just once. I nearly fell off my horse. We turned over every bush and rock in that place because we thought she might be nearby. But we found nothing."

For a while, we were both silent. A log in the fireplace sighed and broke in the middle. New flame leaped up, lapping hungrily at the wood.

"Mama? What does it mean?"

"I don't know, my love. But I'm not about to give up hope yet."

We sat there quietly for most of the night, I with my thoughts, and she with hers. We didn't say much to each other. But it was better than being awake alone.

"Davin?" she said at last, close to dawn. "Will you . . . will you please look at me?"

I tried. I really tried. But every time I raised my head, shame burned in me. Rose was right. It *was* my fault. In a way. And yet, it wasn't. Was it? I hadn't meant to . . . It was only because . . . I never intended . . . Excuses poured into my mind, but excuses were no use with my mother.

"I can't," I whispered. "I'm sorry, Mama. But I really can't."

She got up a little stiffly. "It doesn't matter, Davin. Let's go to bed now, and catch some rest while we can."

But it mattered. Of course it mattered.

"I—I'm really sorry," I stammered.

"Forget it, love. It doesn't matter. I shouldn't have asked."

And then, of course, my shame stung worse than ever.

The Whipping Boy

"Catch him!" yelled Blackbeard, tumbling out of the other wagon. "Catch the little bastard!"

He was holding his nose with one hand, and blood welled between his fingers. Among the pines on the other side of the track I caught a glimpse of Tavis's small and agile form, running as if the devil himself were at his heels. And that might not be too far off the mark; three of the false traders set off after him, two on foot and one on horseback.

Run, Tavis! I thought. Run for your life! I looked around quickly. Perhaps, while they were all busy chasing Tavis, I could . . .

"You stay here." A hand closed around my wrist in an iron grip, dragging me back to the ground. I was still queasy and weak after the business with the witch weed, and my knees buckled limply.

"That hurts!" I protested; it felt like he was twisting my hand off my arm.

"What a pity," he said drily, not loosening his grip.

I glared at him, but he was careful not to let me catch his eyes. The false Ivain. The others called him "Lord" or "Mesire Valdracu," and I gathered he came from Sagis and was some sort of relative to Drakan's mother. Drakan's cousin, more or less. Somehow, that didn't surprise me—they probably got along famously.

I tried to see what was happening in there among the trees, but both Tavis and his pursuers had disappeared from sight. All day we had been traveling through a dense forest of pines, and it had taken the woods only moments to swallow up Tavis, three grown men, and a horse. I could hear shouting but no hoofbeats or footsteps; the ground was covered with a thick carpet of old yellowed pine needles.

Valdracu stirred impatiently.

"Sandor," he said to Blackbeard, "take the gray mare and go and see where they went. It shouldn't take this long to catch one small contrary boy."

"He is clever," growled Sandor, dabbing at his bleeding nose with his kerchief. "I untied him because he said he needed to piss, and when I was undoing his feet the brat kicked me in the face and got past me out the back of the wagon."

"One doesn't *need* to be clever to fool you," said Valdracu acidly. "See that you catch him. We don't want him running all the way back to his clan to tell them he hasn't drowned after all, now, do we?"

Oh, yes. Please. If only he would. My family must think I'm dead, I thought. No one would come looking for me here, days away from Baur Laclan.

Sandor swung himself onto the dappled gray mare that usually pulled one of the wagons and headed for the shouting. Time passed. More time passed. Valdracu let go of my wrist, but kept a watchful eye on me. He was not about to let me run off too, that much was obvious. But Tavis? I rubbed my tender wrist and began cautiously to hope.

But when the men finally returned, Sandor had Tavis slung across the saddle in front of him, like a roll of blankets. Tavis had a large bump over one eye, and his face was very pale under the freckles. But he wasn't the only one who had come to grief. The other horse, the chestnut, was limping badly, and the man who had been riding it was walking all hunched up, clutching his elbow.

"The little rat isn't worth the trouble," raged Sandor. "The chestnut is lame, and Anton has a broken shoulder." He grabbed Tavis by the scruff of his neck and jerked him more or less upright. Tavis's head dangled, as if it had become too heavy for him. "Can't we just get rid of him?"

Get rid of . . . It took me a moment to understand. They did not, of course, intend to let Tavis go. Sandor was asking permission to kill him.

"No!" I cried, terrified, and the Shamer's voice came quite naturally to me. *"You can't kill a—"*

Valdracu hit me so hard that I tumbled to the ground and crouched there, while pines, horses, and wagons spun around me. Then he hauled me to my feet and clapped one hand over my eyes and the other over my mouth, clutching me to his chest.

"Shut up," he hissed. "Shut up and listen." His voice was low and cold, but he had no need to shout. He held me so close to him that I could feel the rasp of his beard against my cheek.

"We still have plenty of witch weed—" he began.

"No . . . ," I pleaded, or tried to, but it came out as a muffled moan because of the way he held me. I didn't want to go back to the Ghost Country. Mama had said that I could die from it, and I believed her. Die, or become insane. It was not a place meant for living people.

"Shut up, I said!" He shook me. "We can drug you. It's easy, and there is no danger in it except to you. Or we can do something else. Do you know what a whipping boy is?" This time he loosened his grip to let me answer.

"No," I whispered.

"Every child needs a beating now and then," he said, as if that was a fact of life. "But in some lands laying hands upon a prince is a capital crime. How, then, does one raise a royal child? I'll tell you. One gives him a whipping boy. If the little prince misbehaves, the whipping boy gets his beating."

It sounded crazy to me, and I didn't see why he was telling me this. But I soon found out.

"The Laclan brat is your whipping boy. If I am not happy with you, he gets the punishment. And if you *ever* raise your witch eyes or your witch voice to me or my men, we'll kill him. Do you understand?"

I swallowed, not knowing what to do.

"Do you understand?"

"Yes."

"Good. You must learn to behave yourself. We shall start with two simple rules. Keep your eyes to yourself—if anyone looks at you, you stare at the ground. Is that clear?"

"Yes."

"And you must learn to keep your mouth shut. Do not speak unless you are told to do so."

He released me and told Sandor to get Tavis back into the wagon.

"And this time, make sure he stays there!"

He turned his attention back to me. I stared rigidly at the ground, as I had been told to do.

"You," he said, "get into the other wagon."

"There's no way the chestnut can pull it, not with that leg," said Sandor.

"No. We shall have to use Mefisto."

He was speaking of his own mount, a big mean bay that would lay back his ears and snap at anyone who came near. At first I had thought it was only me he didn't like—after all, I had pricked his rump with a knife once. But he was just as ill-tempered with everyone else, and in the end Valdracu had to harness Mefisto himself. Sandor claimed the horse would have taken his hand off if he had tried.

Valdracu mounted the box and grabbed the reins. He clicked his tongue. Mefisto's only reaction was an irritated kick at the traces. He obviously wasn't used to playing the cart horse and didn't like the job. But when Valdracu raised his whip in warning, the bay stallion decided to move forward after all. Anyway, the wagon was nowhere near as heavy as it had been. Its load was gone now, both the clan cloaks and the box of swords picked up by a group of men we had met at the edge of the Highlands. They hadn't paid for it, as far as I could see. On the contrary—Valdracu had actually given one of the men a leather purse, which the man had received without a word. A strange trade, I thought.

Mefisto kicked at the traces again, and Valdracu had to slap his dark brown quarters with the reins. I understood how the horse felt. I wanted to fight my harness too—I just didn't dare. Not when my rebellion could cost Tavis his life.

"Come up here where I can see you," Valdracu said, patting the box, and I obediently went to sit next to him.

"It's not that I mind hitting you," he explained, as if it

were important for me to understand all the finer points. "It's just that killing you doesn't suit me at the moment. The boy, however—I have no real need of him. You are the only reason he is still alive. Remember that."

I didn't say anything. I hadn't been asked.

The Shamer's Signet

Daylight was fading when Valdracu finally ordered a halt. He was annoyed—the lame horse had delayed us, and we had not traveled as far as he had meant to.

"Get some firewood," he ordered as he jumped down from the box. "But stay in sight. Remember what happens to your freckled friend if you misbehave."

I clambered stiffly down from the box myself and began on the task I had been set. Tavis apparently was not going to be allowed out of the wagon this time. After his last stunt, they probably didn't feel like untying him.

The pines still crowded densely around us, and there were plenty of twigs and branches I could gather. Pine might not be the best fuel in the world, tending to spit and hiss and explode into sparks, but there wasn't much else.

"What's that?" asked Anton, the one with the broken shoulder. He had caught a glimpse of my Shamer's signet that my mother gave me when she made me her apprentice.

I normally wore it under my shirt, but it had slipped free as I bent to pick up a branch.

"It's just a kind of pendant." I quickly pushed it back out of sight.

"Let me see." He held out his good hand. The other arm was couched in a sling since his accident.

"It's only pewter," I said, hoping he'd lose interest. "It's not worth much."

"Give it here," he said, annoyed. "Do as you're told, girl."

But I couldn't. I stood there, staring at the ground and clutching the round pewter plate as if it had been made from the purest gold. It was strange, really, because when my mother first gave it to me, I didn't like it at all. But somehow it had ended up becoming something I would be heartbroken to lose.

"It's mine," I whispered. "You have no right to take it."

I didn't look at him. And I didn't use the Shamer's voice. But Valdracu struck like a buzzard swooping on a mouse. A hard and bony hand closed around the back of my neck and squeezed until tears clouded my eyes.

"Misbehaving already, Dina? Perhaps you didn't quite understand me."

"I didn't mean to misbehave," I protested. "My mother gave me this, and he has no right . . . no right to—" I stopped. Valdracu's hand on my neck felt nearly as cold as Auld Anya's.

"Apparently you really don't understand it yet," he said. "Sandor, get the boy."

My skin felt clammy with fear. "No," I said. "That's not—I'm not—"

"Shut up," said Valdracu. "Who asked you?"

Sandor came out of the other wagon, hauling Tavis along by the arm. Tavis was still pale, and the bump on his forehead had darkened to something close to black, but he kicked and fought as best he could, despite his bound hands.

Valdracu let go of me and approached Tavis.

"Stand still, boy," he said. And Tavis stopped fighting, just like that. A new expression had come into his freckled face, and it was not one I liked to see. Tavis was scared. He would fight Sandor, biting and kicking and scratching— Sandor and probably all the other men. But not Valdracu. Valdracu scared him.

"Pull off his shirt," commanded Valdracu.

Sandor pulled the shirt over Tavis's head. Because of his bound hands it wouldn't come all the way off but dangled from his wrists like a white flag. Or nearly white; it wasn't very clean anymore.

Valdracu cast a searching glance at his surroundings.

"Across the horse," he told Sandor, and although I had no idea what he meant, Sandor obviously understood completely. A white grin glistened in his black beard.

"Yes, Lord," he said. He threaded the end of a rope

between Tavis's wrists and drew it across Mefisto's back. The big bay was still harnessed to the wagon. He twitched his ears sullenly, but apart from that he didn't move, not even when Sandor hauled on the rope until Tavis's bound wrists were drawn halfway across the horse's back and he had to stand a-tiptoe, if he wanted to stand at all.

Valdracu put his hand on the stallion's dark brown neck.

"Stand, my friend," he told him almost lovingly. "You will not be hurt."

He loosened his belt. It was no ordinary belt, but a metal chain with a leather loop at either end. The chain was not an overly heavy one—perhaps as thick as my little finger.

"I've made an agreement with Dina," he said to Tavis, who was standing with his cheek pressed against Mefisto's flank, staring at the chain. "It's not nice to hit a girl, you know. So when she misbehaves . . . well, I'm sorry, lad, but that means you get the beating."

I wanted to object, I wanted to shout out that there was no "agreement," that it was all something Valdracu had made up. But I was afraid I'd make things even worse if I said anything, so I bit my lip and kept my mouth shut. Silently, I stared into the ground, hoping, *hoping*, that Valdracu would see that I had learned my lesson and that it wasn't necessary to hit anybody.

He did it anyway. There was a whistling sound as he

swung the chain, and a sickening sort of *thwap* when it hit Tavis's back. Tavis screamed. And I could no longer look at the ground. On Tavis's pale, freckled back a dark welt had appeared, about as thick as my little finger. And as I stood there, watching helplessly, blood welled from the broken skin and started to trickle down his side.

I was so furious that everything inside me had gone black. If I had looked at Valdracu then, my eyes would have seared holes in him. How could a grown man hit a small boy that way? How could he stand there with his disgusting chain and *hit*? It was all I could do to hold back the words.

"He is still alive," said Valdracu icily, and I knew it was a warning. *If you ever raise your witch eyes or your witch voice to me or my men, we'll kill him.* That's what he had said. And I was in no doubt that he meant it.

Valdracu held out his hand. "Give me that pendant."

Tavis stood with his face pressed against the horse's side, but although he was trying to hide it, I could see that he was crying. I loosened the narrow leather thong and put my signet into Valdracu's palm.

"That's better," he said. "Very well, Sandor. Get the boy back into the wagon." He held the signet so that it caught the day's last light. "Pewter," he said. "A bit of enamel. Hardly worth the effort." He threw it to Anton, who caught it with his good hand. "Take it, if you want it so badly."

Anton rubbed at the enamel with his thumb and did not look overly excited, but he still stuck the signet into the leather purse he carried in his belt. I felt lost. It was just a bit of pewter on a leather thong, and still it felt as if I had lost a part of myself.

"I hope you learned something," Valdracu told me in a low voice. He patted Mefisto's neck. The big animal shook his head and snorted, and in the middle of everything I suddenly wondered why he hadn't shied at the blow, the way most horses would have done. How could he know that only Tavis would feel the lash?

Then I remembered Sandor's expectant grin. He had known straightaway what Valdracu intended. And there was a very simple explanation why Mefisto had stood there, steady as a rock despite whistling chains and Tavis's scream.

They had done it all before.

In the late afternoon the next day, the cart track widened, and the woods around us became less dense. There were clearings here and there where the pines had been felled and taken away to be used for timber, and in their absence grass and lupines and tiny birch saplings had found enough light to thrive. And slowly a new sound grew: the constant rush and roar of falling water.

Valdracu peered at the setting sun. "Get that horse to move its feet," he told the man leading the lamed chestnut. "We want to be in Dracana before dark."

Dracana? Where was that? What was it? I would have liked to know, but I didn't dare ask. Not after what Valdracu had done to Tavis. That night I had been wakened by the sound of someone crying. It wasn't very loud, not much more than a half-choked sniffling. Even so, it was enough to annoy Sandor, who was standing guard.

"Stop that blubbering, boy!" he hissed. The quiet sniffs stopped abruptly. But I lay awake for a long time after that, thinking about Tavis and his sore back, and how he was lying tied up in the other wagon, frightened and alone. If only I had given up the signet right away. It was Valdracu who had hit him with his beastly chain, but it felt as if it were my fault too, somehow. If only I hadn't been so stubborn. I *knew* that Valdracu would stop at nothing to get what he wanted.

The wagon in front of us labored up a sharp rise and then disappeared from sight. Then it was our turn. Mefisto had to strain with all his strength to get us up the last steep incline. Then the road dipped, and we were suddenly in a narrow valley. At the bottom of the valley was a river, and by the river a town. Some of the buildings were very tall, almost four times as high as most ordinary houses. Across the river's rushing waters a kind of bridge had been built, and below it I could see not just one but . . . but a number of waterwheels, so many that I couldn't count them at first.

The horses pricked up their ears and began to move with a will, even the lame chestnut. They had been here before, it seemed, and knew that shelter, food, and water awaited them. They needn't move so quickly, I thought. Not for my sake. I was in no hurry to find out what was in store for *me*.

Like a Disease

The wind whipped across the heather, and Falk was acting skittish, trying to turn around all the time so that he wouldn't have to face into it. I was freezing cold; that morning the weather had been sunny and mild, and I was only in my shirtsleeves. If Callan had seen me, he would have scolded: "Never trust the weather in the mountains, lad; it can change quicker than a woman's temper." But the only thing on my mind then had been to get out of the house.

Mama was out of bed now, but she grew tired very quickly, and she was as pale as a ghost. It stung to look at her. I had managed to swallow only a few mouthfuls of porridge at the breakfast table before rising.

"I'm taking Falk out," I said.

At first she didn't say anything. Then she nodded. "Take care, my love." She was always careful not to look straight at me now, the same care she took with strangers.

"Perhaps . . . ," I began, and then couldn't make myself say it out loud after all: Perhaps today I'll find a lead, some rumor, someone who has seen her. I no longer believed it myself, but sitting around at home was unbearable.

"Yes," she said, "perhaps."

So here I was, trotting along in the borderland between Laclan and Kensie, and I had almost given up even the pretense of looking. When I met someone, which didn't happen often, I asked them whether they had seen two children, but I was no longer disappointed when they said no, because I no longer expected any other answer.

Falk trudged along a narrow sheep trail skirting a hollow. The wind now carried little icy raindrops in it, and it was time to turn back. Time and more than time; and still I kept postponing it, going on just a bit farther, just another half mile.

Suddenly I caught sight of two travelers below, on the more traveled trail at the bottom of the hollow.

"Hello, down there!" I called.

They looked up. One was a woman, the other a man leading a donkey. They were both sensibly dressed, he in a woolen cap and a sleeveless sheepskin coat, she with a scarf over her head and a large shawl wrapped warmly around her shoulders. Common folk, it seemed, of the kind who could not afford to feed a horse but had to make do with the hardy little donkey. Two large wicker baskets hung on either side of its woolly gray back. Trading goods, it might be, or perhaps simply whatever they had brought for the journey.

The man briefly raised his hand. "Hello! Can you tell us—" and then he broke off, peering more intently at me. "Davin? Davin, is that you?"

Now it was my turn to stare. I couldn't seem to—oh, of course. The clothes were different, and I had not expected to see him here, but it was the Weapons Master from Dunark, the one who had helped Dina and Mama and Nico to get away from Drakan last year. And the woman by his side was Master Maunus's niece, whom everybody called the Widow. For years, she had been running her dead husband's apothecary business in Dunark.

"Welcome to the Highlands," I called, and made Falk clamber down the slope to the bottom of the hollow. "What brings you here?" For although the Widow was related to the Kensies just like Master Maunus—she was in fact Maudi Kensie's granddaughter—they had chosen to settle in the Lowlands, in a fortress city called Solark.

"War," said the Weapons Master curtly, and I saw now that his left hand was wrapped in a stained and dirty bandage.

The Widow smiled at me, but it was a tired and joyless smile.

"We were lucky to meet you, Davin. We didn't dare travel by the road, and I'm afraid I don't know the trails up here as well as I did when I was a girl. Are we going the right way?"

I nodded. "I'll take you. I was about to turn back

anyway." Curious, Falk sniffed at the donkey. The donkey tipped back its long ears and looked bored.

"Won't you ride, Mistress Petri?" I asked, getting down from Falk's back.

"Thank you, Davin," answered the Widow and cast a sideways look at the Weapons Master, "but it might be better if Martin—"

"You ride," he grunted. "Nothing wrong with my feet." She still looked at him.

"Ride," he repeated. He obviously didn't want to be treated like a wounded weakling.

"As you please," she said, and I held Falk for her while she mounted. Her long brown skirts flapped in the wind, and Falk was fresh enough to pretend to be startled.

"Stop that," she said, and did something with the reins that made Falk stand stock-still with a sheepish cast to his ears. "We have no time for such silliness!"

She rode on a little ahead of us, and Falk behaved much better for her than he ever did for me. The Master and I trudged along in the trail left by Falk's hooves. I offered to lead the donkey, and he wordlessly handed me the rope.

We walked silently for a while, the donkey between us. Down here in the hollow I couldn't see for miles the way I had been able to up on the ridge, but the wind was less fierce, and walking warmed me up much better than riding Falk.

"What happened?" I asked, nodding at his hand.

"Drakan has taken Solark," he said with an edge to his voice like rusted iron.

"Solark?" I was so surprised that I stopped in my tracks. "But I thought—"

"That Solark was impregnable? Yes, we all thought so."

"But . . . how?"

"Treason." He spat the word as if the taste of it was bitter. "He paid a man to poison the water supply. From one day to the next, everyone, city and castle, got sick. Many died, and those of us who lived were hardly able to stand upright. After that it was easy." He looked at me, and there was such rage in his eyes that I took an involuntary step backward. But his anger was not for me. "People were dying in the houses and in the streets, and no one had the strength to help them. The bluebottles had a grand feast in Solark."

I wished he hadn't said that. Often enough, I had seen the flies cover some small dead animal like a swarming blue-black blanket. The thought of that happening to a human being . . . I lowered my eyes and swallowed.

"How did you get away?" I finally asked. Drakan was unlikely to have forgotten the role those two had played in Dunark last year. If he had had them within his reach, I don't think he would just have let them leave.

"Luck," said the Master. "And an old friend."

He clearly didn't want to say any more about it. And I don't like to ask. But the Widow had halted to wait for us, and she looked even more furious than the Master.

"As soon as they realized who Martin was, they took him to Drakan," she said. "And then they began to break his fingers. One finger a day."

Ouch, I thought, instinctively clenching my hands to protect my own fingers.

"Did they want the Master to . . . reveal something?"

He shook his head. "Wasn't much I could tell them that they didn't already know. It was meant to be revenge, I think, and perhaps a warning to anyone from the old Dunark Guard who might be thinking about joining the Young Lord." The Young Lord was Nico, I knew. Many people from Dunark called him that.

A finger a day. I eyed his bandaged hand. How many . . . ?

"Three days," said the Widow in a voice that could pierce steel. "Three fingers. Before we got him out, and got out of the city."

"Most of Drakan's trained men are still from the old Dunark Guard," explained the Weapons Master. "His so-called Dragon Force is a bunch of runaway apprentices, beggars and bandits, and ignorant peasants who are more dangerous with a hoe than with a sword. He cannot command without the Dunark Guard, even though some of them are not as blindly loyal to the Order of the Dragon as he might wish."

In the old days, when Nico's father was still the Castellan at Dunark Castle, the Weapons Master had had the training of the castle guards, and most of them had served under him at some time or another. That was probably what he meant when he mentioned an old friend. The Dunark Guard would have had little stomach for Drakan's bone-by-bone revenge.

The raindrops were much fatter now. The Widow eyed the heavy-bellied thunder-gray clouds.

"Is it far?" she asked.

I shook my head. "If we hurry, we can be home inside an hour."

"Then let's hurry," she said. "I think it would be a good idea to find a roof very soon."

We picked up speed.

"Will you be staying up here?" I asked after a while.

"Perhaps," said the Widow.

"No," said the Master. "There *are* people who do not want Drakan for an Overlord. Quite a few people. There must be something we can do."

"Eidin surrendered," objected the Widow. "Not a hand raised against him. If Arkmeira falls too, Drakan holds all of the coastlands in the palm of his hand."

"I'm not saying it will be easy," he muttered. "But shame on the man who seeks only easy victories."

The rain was a heavy gray blanket around us when we finally reached Baur Kensie. The donkey's coat was nearly black with moisture, and Falk was snorting and shaking his head, trying to rid his eyes, ears, and nostrils of the wet. My shirt was sticking to me like a second skin, and despite their more sensible travel clothes, the Master and the Widow both looked chilled and tired. Luckily Mama and Rose already had a fire going, and hot black-currant wine was steaming away in our new copper kettle. Mama found blankets and dry clothes for her unexpected visitors, and Rose put on her clogs and went to tend Falk and the donkey.

"We can go to Maudi's," said the Widow, protesting. "There will be room for us there—"

"There is room for you right here," Mama said firmly, "And you are not walking another step in this weather."

"Thank you, then, for your warm welcome, Melussina," answered the Widow, sipping her black-currant drink. She was one of the few people in the world who called Mama by her first name. "But where is Dina? I had been looking forward to—"

There was a strained movement in Mama's face, and the Widow broke off.

"Melussina . . . what has happened?" She could tell by my mother's face that something was horribly wrong.

I could have kicked myself. Why hadn't I told them on the way?

Mama stood there with the black-currant jug in her hand, staring at the floorboards.

"Dina isn't here," she finally said. "She is . . . missing. We don't even know if she is still alive, or . . ." And then she had to put the jug down. She hid her face in her hands, and I could tell by the way her shoulders trembled that she was crying.

The Widow got to her feet abruptly, and the blanket that had warmed her fell to the floor in soft green folds. In two paces she was at my mother's side, putting her arms around her.

"Oh, Melussina" was all she said, and then she held her and let her cry until she was finished. And I could see that Mama had needed that, had needed a grown-up person to hold her so while she wept. I was only sorry that she hadn't thought I was old enough for that.

The Weapons Master cleared his throat and looked as if he would rather be anywhere else.

"I'm sorry," he said a little stiffly, but one could see that he meant it. "But remember that Dina is a strong little lass. I don't think you should give up hope too soon."

Mama nodded, dabbing at her eyes with the corner of her apron.

"No," she said. "I still have hope."

Mama looked at the Master's broken fingers, but the Widow was herself wise in the ways of the human body and the injuries it could suffer. There wasn't much for Mama to do that hadn't been done already.

"The bones have been properly set," she said. "Two of the breaks are healing nicely, I think. The third, the compound one . . ." She hesitated briefly and gave the Widow a rapid glance. "We must be careful, and watch out for gangrene."

The Weapons Master grunted. "It's a good thing that they started with my left," he said. "At least I can still hold a sword."

Mama carefully splinted his battered fingers and wound a clean bandage around his hand. Although her movements were gentle, one could see the anger in her.

"That anyone could do this to another human being," she said.

"Yes," said the Widow. "There is a need for Shamers in this world. But . . ." She hesitated, asking the Master a wordless question with her eyes. He nodded faintly.

"Medama Tonerre needs to know," he said. "Ignorance makes a poor shield."

Still, the Widow hesitated. Mama had to prod her along.

"Know what?"

The Widow cleared her throat. "They . . . there was a Shamer in Solark, and one in Eidin. Drakan . . . had them both burned. Called them witches, held a summary court, and burned them at the stake. He claims that the Shamer's Gift is witchery."

Mama stood quite still, clutching a bit of unused bandage.

"This is nothing," said the Master, raising his damaged hand. "Nothing compared to what else happened in Solark."

"He is spreading shamelessness around him," my mother whispered, and none of us was in any doubt who "he" was. "Like a disease. So that the people he corrupts will do things they would never have countenanced before. No wonder that he needs to kill the Shamers. But if we lose all common decency, if we lose all sense of right and wrong, how are we to live with one another?"

"Like beasts," answered the Weapons Master bitterly. "Like a pack of his damned dragons, who devour one another when they are given the chance."

A Rare Weapon

It was the strangest town I had ever seen. Not that I was any kind of expert on towns—Dunark was the biggest I had ever been to—but I knew one thing: towns were supposed to be full of people.

In Dracana there was no one.

There were houses enough, set in neat lines like soldiers on parade. The streets were the straightest I had ever seen. And the houses all looked new, with fresh timber still unpainted. Outside the town itself there was a giant ring of tents, more than a hundred, I think; a hundred dark gray tents all exactly the same. There was *room* for plenty of people. But although the sun still hung huge and orange just above the mountains behind Dracana, there wasn't so much as a peddler, beggar, or pickpocket in sight. There was a pretty little square with a well, but no one had gathered there to get water or do laundry or catch up on the latest gossip. No snotty-nosed kids were playing in the streets, no grandfathers perched on the benches by the walls, warming their bones in the evening sun. No dogs barked at us. No chickens squawked. It was all as still and silent as if an evil fairy had swung her wand and magicked away every living creature in the town.

"Where are—" Where are all the people, I wanted to say, and I barely caught myself in time. Valdracu half turned his head toward me, but let it go. I breathed a sigh of relief. I was determined that Tavis would get no more beatings because of me, but although Valdracu's two rules were simple enough, they were terribly hard to obey. *Look at no one. Talk to no one unless you are asked.* I was not used to being the quiet little mouse, but I would just have to learn. For Tavis's sake. So I kept my mouth shut and my thoughts to myself. Where had they all gone? Someone had to live in these straight new streets.

The wagons rattled across the square and onward, toward the big mill houses I had seen from the ridge. The tall walls cast long shadows in the evening sun. There were a lot of strange rasping, thumping sounds from inside, not at all the creak and rattle I was used to from the mill in Birches. But then, who would need this many waterwheels—thirty-six, I had now counted them—just to grind flour?

Suddenly, a bell pealed loudly. The thumping sounds stopped, and a moment later the gates to the nearest mill house opened, and a closely packed crowd of women and children swarmed through. For a moment it was like being in the middle of a flock of sparrows. The women and the girls were all dressed the same way—coarse tan aprons over gray skirts and blouses, and black head scarves. The boys were not quite so alike. They all wore black pants, but some had gray shirts, some tan, and others were bare-chested. I saw no grown men at all.

Some of the women were laughing and talking, tugging off their head scarves and running their fingers through sweat-dampened hair. Others simply looked bent and tired. A girl with short brown hair stuck out her tongue at one of the bare-chested boys, but he pretended not to notice. Other than that, the children did not look very lively, and when they caught sight of Valdracu, all talk and laughter stopped. Some of the women who had taken off their scarves were suddenly in a hurry to get them back on. The nearest ones curtsied, just a quick little duck, and stepped aside to let the wagons through.

Who were they? What were they doing in the big mill houses? Where were all the men? I was choking on questions I couldn't ask.

The wagons rolled past the mill houses and turned into a large courtyard surrounded by buildings that had clearly been here longer than anything else. The barns and stable wings were black-tarred timber with turfed roofs, not so very different from those you saw in the Highlands. But the main building was a grand white stone house with broad granite steps in front of it. Valdracu halted in front of the steps and tossed the reins to a groom who had come running at the first sound of hooves.

"Put the boy in the cellar," Valdracu told Sandor. "If we let him in among the others, he will only make trouble. And you"—he meant me—"you're coming with me."

I had been perched for many hours on the not very comfortable box seat of the wagon. Stiffly, I clambered down and followed him up the steps. Before we were even halfway to the blue door at the top, it flew open, and a girl of about my age came out. This was certainly no sparrow: shiny turquoise silk skirts gleamed at every move, and the bodice of her dress was richly embroidered in black and green and gold. Her black hair, held back by a pearl-studded headband, fell shinily to her waist and beyond. Everything about her was shiny in some way, but her eyes shone more brightly than anything else. She looked at Valdracu like he was some kind of a fairy-tale prince or hero. No, more than that. She looked at him as though he were a god.

"Welcome home, Lord," she said breathlessly. She must have been running in order to reach the door before him. And then she curtsied, a sweeping, graceful movement far different from the quick duck of the sparrow girls.

"Thank you, Sascha," said Valdracu, resting his hand for a moment on the shiny black hair. "Have you been well?"

"No," she said, flashing a brief and strangely shy smile. "But I am now."

Despite myself, I stared. Around Valdracu's waist I could see the chain he had used on Tavis. How could that little goose gaze at him like he was the adored center of her universe? As if everything was wonderful just because he was around?

"Sascha, this is Dina," he continued. "She will be staying with us for a while. Put her in the Green Room. And see to it that she is given something slightly less displeasing than what she is wearing at the moment."

I finally remembered to lower my eyes. But even though I wasn't looking at her, I could feel her glare.

"Yes, Lord," she said with another curtsy. "The Green Room. This way, please."

I followed her into the white house and up a curving staircase. She turned right at the top, past several closed doors. At the fifth, she stopped.

"This is yours," she said, and opened the door for me.

I stared. I wasn't sure what I had expected. Anything but this, certainly. I thought of Tavis and the cellar Valdracu had mentioned, and found it very strange that I was to be given a room like this, a room almost as big as our entire cottage. The walls were shiny with green silk tapestries, green carpets covered the floor, and moss-green velvet curtains dimmed the light and made me think of marshlands and bogs. Hesitantly, I stepped across the threshold.

A hard, unexpected shove sent me sprawling. Angrily, I leaped to my feet and turned on the girl, Sascha, or whatever her name was.

"Why did you do that?" I snapped, entirely forgetting Valdracu and his rules.

"There's just one thing you need to know," she said, her voice dark with fury. "I don't know what he wants you for. But you'd better not think you can take *my* place!"

Her place? What on earth was she going on about? I didn't ask. I thought of Tavis and forced myself to shut up and lower my eyes. But even though I had caught only a brief glimpse, her feelings were unmistakable. Her dark eyes shone with a hard glare, and her pretty heart-shaped face was pale with hatred.

"Mesire Valdracu said for you to come to the Marble Parlor as soon as you were presentable," said Marte, the cook. She was clearly uncertain what "presentable" meant in my case. Bathed and combed, of course, but how was she to dress me? Silken skirts like Sascha's, or something slightly less fine? Marte herself looked severe and newly ironed in black skirts, white blouse, and a laced-up black bodice. A starched white cap hid most of her auburn hair. I stood there with a thin towel wrapped around me, wishing that she would make up her mind. It was nice to be clean again, but the flagstones of the kitchen floor were icy beneath my damp bare feet.

"First these," she said, pointing to a pile of linens. I looked at the pile uncertainly. All of them? Did she want me to put on all that, just for underwear?

Apparently. First a pair of long white stockings held up by a complicated system of buttons and suspenders. Then a pair of short knickers. Then some long white linen underpants ending at midcalf in a flare of frills. Then three underskirts, each more frilly than the next. To say nothing of the underbodice that laced up at the back— Marte had to do that for me.

"You're not exactly tall," she muttered, tightening the laces. "And there really isn't that much we can do with the hair."

My hair is black and coarse and would look better on a horse. Instead of falling tidily to my shoulders, it stuck out in all directions. I couldn't even braid it anymore, not since Master Maunus had done what he could to make me look like a boy last year in Dunark. A pearly headband like Sascha's would suit me about as well as a tiara would fit a toad.

"Wait here," she said. So I stood there for another long while, feeling the chilly air against the skin of my bare shoulders and the cold of the flagstones beneath my stockinged feet.

When she finally came back, she was carrying a striped linen dress and a white blouse like her own.

"Try this," she said, passing me the dress. "It was once . . . it once fitted a girl about your size." She smoothed the striped skirts with a sad, gentle motion. Who was the girl who had once worn that dress? Marte's daughter? Or her little sister? It was difficult to guess her age. Her hands and her face looked worn, but I had a feeling they were marked more by the kind of life Marte had had than by the length of it. There was no gray in the hair left visible by the cap.

I put on the blouse and the dress on top of all the frilly underskirts. The dress was fine linen, with narrow stripes in green, pink, and gray. The bodice had silver hooks up the front, shaped like flowers. It was a very nice dress, I thought.

"Thank you," I said quietly. No one had told me to say anything, but surely I was allowed to thank somebody without permission?

"It suits you," she said, delicately straightening the shoulder seam. "You look very nice."

And I suddenly began to like Marte quite a bit.

Marte took me down to the Marble Parlor, and I was glad to have her there. I had no particular wish to face Valdracu again. *I don't know what he wants you for,* Sascha had said, and I didn't know either, but my stomach turned itself into a small hard ball just wondering about it.

There was a fire in the huge marble fireplace, and in front of it sat Valdracu, comfortably ensconced in a stuffed armchair. He too had bathed, I could see. The trader's clothes had been exchanged for a fur-lined black velvet coat, black breeches, and embroidered gray felt boots with pointed toes. He looked completely different— highborn and foreign. No one would take him for a common peddler now. One thing hadn't changed, though—he still wore the thin metal chain around his waist.

Behind the armchair stood Sascha in her turquoise silk dress, combing out the damp tangles of her master's hair with a silver comb. She gave me a single furious glare and then carried on as if I didn't exist.

"Come here," said Valdracu.

I didn't hang back on purpose. It just took a while before my legs obeyed me, and Marte had to give me a gentle shove.

Valdracu rose and circled me, like someone judging the worth of a horse.

"Very good, Marte," he then said. "She will do."

Marte curtsied and turned to leave. On the threshold, she paused for a moment.

"Dina hasn't had her meal yet, Lord," she said. "There wasn't time."

Valdracu raised an eyebrow. "Has she made you her

caring friend already? You need not worry. I shall allow you to feed her as soon as she has worked for her keep."

Work? What did he want me to do?

Valdracu turned to me again.

"You see, Dina, in Dracana we all work. Most of us work very hard indeed, and there is no room for shiftless idlers. I could make use of you at the looms or in the forges, but it has occurred to me that you may serve me better in another way. Sascha, will you fetch the mill-house girl?"

"Yes, Lord." Sascha put the comb down on a small lacquered table next to the armchair. It already held the remains of a fine meal, judging from the chicken bones and the ruby dregs of wine at the bottom of the glass. My stomach turned over. But perhaps some of the pangs were really just from hunger.

"I've sent a messenger to my cousin, the Dragon Lord," Valdracu continued. "I'm sure he has plans for you, but he is a busy man, and we may not hear from him right away. Meanwhile, you belong to me. Your time here need not be unpleasant, as you can see from the room you've been given. I punish sloth and incompetence severely, but I can be equally generous to those who serve me well, and I may even be able to shield you somewhat from my cousin's intemperate ways. You would do well to serve me, Dina. Your small Highland friend might benefit as well."

What did he mean by all this persuasion? What did he

want me to do? He was normally so good with threats, it was almost more frightening to hear him fly the lure at me in this way. I stirred uneasily.

"Did you want to say something, Dina?"

I shook my head.

"Speak up. You have my permission."

I cleared my throat. "What is it Mesire Valdracu wants me to do?" No way would I call him "Lord," he was no lord of mine!

"You possess something rare. Your eyes and your voice are a weapon, and only a foolish man casts away such a weapon unused."

A weapon? Was that how he saw it? My mother called it a gift, and although I had once considered it more of a curse, she was closer to the truth than he was, I felt. I did not ask him what plans Drakan had for me. I didn't think he'd tell me, and in any case I wasn't sure I really wanted to know.

Sandor came in with one of the sparrow girls—still in her tan and gray work clothes, but without the black scarf. It was the girl with the short brown hair, the one who had stuck out her tongue at the bare-chested boy. She looked both frightened and defiant. Sandor nudged her, and she curtsied to Valdracu, but no deeper than she had to.

"Come here, girl," said Valdracu impatiently. "What is your name?"

"Laisa." Sandor nudged her again, harder this time, and she mumbled a belated "Lord."

"I hear ill reports of you, Laisa. You are late, you giggle and sing and make foolish jokes during the workday, and on several occasions you have been rude to the Master Weaver."

Laisa pulled herself up straight. "I do my work—Lord." Again this "Lord" came late, as if she grudged him his title.

"Yes, well, that is the question. Are you an obedient and industrious girl, or are you really a troublemaker? We shall let Dina decide."

"Me?" The word escaped me unintentionally.

"Dina. Look at Laisa."

Oh, so that was what he meant by a weapon. He meant for me to make a lively and somewhat impertinent girl ashamed of singing while she worked!

Laisa just looked confused. She had no idea what she was in for if I did what he wanted me to do.

"That's not—" That's not a proper use of the Gift, I meant to say. But he brought me up short with a slicing motion of his hand.

"Remember what I said about the good servant and the bad, Dina." He rested his hand on the chain around his waist. "Do your duty. I would much rather reward than punish."

In my mind, I saw the bloody welt on Tavis's back, and I remembered how he had cried that night.

"Look at me, Laisa," I said halfheartedly, with not a trace of the Gift in my voice. She looked at me anyway. She didn't know any better.

Our eyes met. She made a startled movement and looked away. But Valdracu gave Sandor a small nod, and Sandor wrapped his great paw around the back of her neck so that she could no longer turn away from me. Her gaze flickered this way and that. Then she closed her eyes and screwed them up tight.

"Do your duty, Dina," said Valdracu quietly, and once more let his fingers play with the slim chain.

I'm sorry, Laisa, I thought. So sorry. But if I don't do this, he will hit Tavis again.

"Look at me, Laisa."

It was an effort to get the voice right. Normally I did it almost without thinking, but not this time. There was a strained tremor to it that made it sound nearly false, like a singer ever so slightly off-key, but it still worked. Laisa's eyes opened and looked helplessly into mine. And images started to flicker between us, memories that leaped from Laisa's mind to mine.

"Run along now, Laisa, girl, and don't dawdle. Come straight home with the rest of the money!" Laisa's mother was pacing the floor with a howling baby on her arm, Laisa's

new kid brother, ooh, ain't he a cute one, the aunties said, but Laisa didn't think so, he was puking and screaming with one end and spurting stinking yellow stuff out the other, what was so cute about that? And Ma was always tired now and couldn't work much, so Laisa was hungry all the time, and all because of that stinky little brat. "Come straight home . . ." But at the market there was a woman making pancakes, pancakes with thick golden syrup on them, and Laisa was so hungry, the smell of the pancakes nearly drove her wild. Just one, she thought, just a taste. And suddenly the money was gone, and she hadn't even got the flour and the lard. And so there was nothing for it but to throw the purse away and scrape her knees. "They just pushed me right over, Ma, and took all the money," but she got her ear clipped all the same, 'cause Ma was tired, and the brat howled, and her little sister was whining with hunger, and in Laisa's belly, the pancakes lay like lead.

I closed my eyes, stopping the stream of pictures in my head. My head throbbed, and I felt sick to my stomach. But Laisa was worse—on her knees, weeping and clutching at my skirt, promising never to do it again, never; and Valdracu, who had no idea that she was talking about stolen pancakes and starving sisters, only smiled and said that that was fine, she could go now.

Still crying, she backed out of the room, as if she were afraid to turn her back on us. Her hands had disappeared beneath her apron, and I knew very well what they were doing there. Hidden beneath the cloth she had her forefingers crossed in the witch sign that was supposed to ward off evil. It did no good whatsoever against someone like me, but I guess she didn't know that. I could tell that she was now more afraid of me than of Valdracu, and this made the sick feeling worse, but what else could I do? It was her or Tavis, and at least she was now crying because of something she had once done. If Valdracu hit Tavis again, it would be because of something *I* had done.

Valdracu put his hand on my head in a loving way, smoothing my impossible hair. I would rather let a spider crawl all over me, but I didn't dare shake him off.

"Excellent, Dina. You will be of great use to me, I can see. Go to Marte now, and get your supper."

He would do it again. He would use me as a weapon over and over again. And if I refused, Tavis would pay the price. I stumbled from the room, no longer hungry. Sickness was clawing at my belly, and I had no idea what to do.

The Boy from the Forge

"Mesire requires you in the Marble Parlor."

I had come to hate those words. Every time I heard them my hands froze and my stomach became a sick little knot of fear and loathing.

Nineteen days had passed since Valdracu had made me use my eyes on Laisa. Nineteen. I had counted them carefully. And on every one of those days, sometimes more than once, there had been somebody, some poor wretch who had aroused Valdracu's anger. It was then that I was "required" in the Marble Parlor, or sometimes in the Gold Room where Valdracu kept his desk, and while he watched us hungrily, I had to shame his poor "miscreants" until they wept and begged for forgiveness. They might not be ashamed of whatever it was he thought they had done, but that was all one to him. For him, the important thing was to see them grovel and sob and beg to be released. Then he would smile and stroke my hair and brag about me to Sandor: "What powers! Isn't it amazing,

Sandor? A mere slip of a girl, and she can bring grown men to their knees with a single glance! We have caught us a rare bird indeed."

There were few enough grown men among the wretches, though. Mostly they had been children from the mill houses, children like Laisa who wasted the workday with "giggles and foolery" or simply weren't fast enough or strong enough to please Valdracu. Once it was two women who had come to complain about one of the big looms that was broken and had become dangerous to work with. And one night there had been a battered tramp that Sandor had found by the forges where the poor beggar had been trying to hide in one of the woodsheds. Him they accused of spying and treason, and Valdracu had hit him many times with that damn chain of his, so that his back had become a mass of bloody welts. But although the tears were streaming down his poor bruised face when he looked at me, he spoke nothing except a garbled string of nonsense rhymes and children's chants, and then he passed out on the floor, and Sandor had to carry him back to wherever they kept him.

Who was it this time? The tramp again? I was in no hurry to find out.

"Hurry, girl! You know how he hates waiting." Marte gave me a nervous little push.

I nodded, but I kept on walking as slowly as I dared. It did no good, of course. Even if it took me all day, the

Marble Parlor would still be there, with Valdracu in his favorite chair by the fireplace, expectantly eyeing some wretch who would be shivering already at the thought of having to meet Valdracu's tame witch. Oh, yes, I knew what they were calling me. Even the guards looked at me sideways now, with a mixture of revulsion for me and admiration for Valdracu, who had so ably mastered such a monster. "The Lord's little witch."

This time it was a boy, a year or two older than I. He was dressed in black work pants and a stiff brown apron and nothing else. I could smell the forge on him as I got closer, a fierce smell of sweat and soot and hot metal. On his bare back there were marks and scars where sparks from the furnace had singed him. His dark hair was oily with sweat, but he kept himself straighter than most of the people who had been where he now stood.

"It's dangerous," he said, glaring rebelliously straight at Valdracu. "If it wasn't, how come it's only us no-man's-brats doing it? Four accidents in three weeks. Four! One death, and three of us badly hurt. Imrik"—his voice broke, the first sign of weakness he had shown—"Imrik will never walk properly again."

He was holding out his hand, palm up, but it did not make him look like a beggar. More like a man expecting to shake hands on a deal fairly made.

"It's not that I mind working," he said. "I want to learn the craft. I'm good at it. Ask the Master Smith if you don't believe me. But using us like that, as if we were nothing, as if it didn't *matter* that you lose a few every month . . . that's . . . that's wrong, and it's also . . . it's also wasteful. We are worth more than that!"

But if he thought he could make a deal with Valdracu, he was much mistaken. Valdracu got up slowly. With careful movements he brushed a few crumbs from his velvet sleeve. He looked at the boy's outstretched hand. And with the speed of a snake, so quickly that the eye could hardly follow it, he drew his chain and slashed it across the boy's naked palm.

"I don't make deals with thralls," he said.

The boy yelled with pain. He stared at his hand, at the blood welling from the thin, swollen cut. Then he raised his head again and glared at Valdracu, and for a moment I was afraid that he would actually hit him. Afraid not for Valdracu's sake, but for the boy's. If he laid a hand on Valdracu's lordly body, I didn't think he would leave the room alive.

But the boy held on to his temper. His eyes blazed with fury and hatred, but he made no move to hit back.

"I am no thrall," he hissed. He turned on his heel and began to leave.

But he was not allowed even that much freedom.

Sandor blocked his way to the door.

"Not so fast, thrall," said Valdracu. "There are still a couple of things we have to teach you. Humility. Respect. Shame."

The boy seemed to see me for the first time. His dark eyes flickered, taking in the silver hooks on the neat bodice of the dress, and I suddenly wished I had been less finely dressed.

"I've heard of you," he said. "I've heard of your witchy eyes. But I'm not afraid of you. I have nothing to be ashamed of!"

Valdracu smiled, slowly and maliciously.

"We shall see," he said. "We shall see."

He was strong, that boy. There was already an uncommon width to his shoulders, and one could see that he would become a big man in a few years. And he was strong inside as well, in heart and in spirit.

It did him no good. Against me, he didn't stand a chance.

I caught his eye, forced him to meet my gaze. And the images began to flow.

A peddler's cart was rattling down the road, drawn by two mules. Behind the cart two barefooted boys trotted along, somewhat breathlessly; one of them was the boy from the forge, strong and road-hardened, the other a much slighter boy, small-boned and soft-featured. The smaller boy was sniffing, and every few steps a tear slid down his cheek.

"Oh, stop it, Imrik," said the larger boy. "It's not that bad."

The small one sniffed even harder. "No, but . . . my foot hurts so. Tano, can't you . . . can't you say you're sorry?"

"No." Tano was both angry and adamant.

"But, Tano, if only you said you were sorry, I'm sure he'd let us back in the cart."

"No. I'm not groveling to that bastard."

They trotted on yet a while.

"Tano."

"What is it now?"

"Tano, my foot is bleeding."

The larger boy stopped. "Let me see."

Imrik showed Tano his left foot. There was a bloody cut on the heel, perhaps from a sharp rock.

Tano swore. Although he was still only twelve, he knew a lot of juicy curses.

"All right," he said furiously. "I'll tell him I'm sorry." He let go of Imrik's foot and straightened. "But one of these days we're out of here. One day soon."

"Tano, that's dangerous—running off. I'm . . . I'm not as brave as you are."

"Of course you are." Tano put his arm around Imrik's slight shoulders. "And anyway, I'll take care of you. Haven't I told you so, at least a hundred times?"

"Yes."

"Well, then, don't I keep my promises?"

"Yes."

"There you are, then. You'll be safe with me."

The fireplace and the room around us slowly returned. I was still standing in front of the boy from the forge—Tano, as I now knew. His dark eyes met mine. But there were no guilty tears. He did not lie crouched on the floor, begging forgiveness.

"Get on with it." I heard Valdracu's voice somewhere in the background, sharp and impatient. "Do your duty, Dina. You don't want to anger me, do you?"

No, that was the last thing I wanted. I had seen what happened to Tavis when Valdracu was displeased with me.

"Look at me," I told Tano. And dug a little deeper.

The air in the forge was hot enough to scorch the lungs. The fire, too, flared so hotly that the iron at its heart grew white in moments. The great bellows that kept it so worked tirelessly, driven by an inhuman power. Nor did human hands and arms make the great hammers rise and fall, rise and fall, blow after blow, the same unvarying beat all the time, until the pounding entered your blood and you heard it in your sleep, thump bang, thump bang, *over and over again. No mere man could have worked so tirelessly. But the river flowed incessantly, and it was the river's current that powered the bellows and the hammers of Dracana's weapon forges.*

A smith's hands were needed for the finer work that gave the swords their final form. And the smiths were treated with the respect due their craft, and were well paid for their efforts. Even their apprentices were decently treated, as a rule. But the no-man's-brats—children like Imrik and Tano who had no father or mother or master at the forge—now, that was a different matter.

It took no special skill to carry the iron from the furnace to the hammer mill. Nor did you have to be very clever to hold the iron in place while the great hammerheads pounded it into flat bars. All that was needful was that you were just strong enough and not too big, because there wasn't much space, and the tall ones had to keep ducking their heads to avoid the gears and driveshafts overhead, and the ones that were too fat . . . if you were too fat, or too clumsy, the machinery might catch you, the way it had happened to Malik. And a hammer designed to flatten iron took no particular notice of human skin and bones and blood. Malik only had time to scream once.

Imrik wasn't really strong enough. But Tano and Imrik were a pair, and Tano watched out for Imrik. Until one day . . .

"Stop it!"

One day Tano had gone to get a drink from the water barrel, and Imrik had to carry the iron from the furnace to the hammer mill on his own. He had done it many times before—Tano couldn't always be there to help him. He couldn't. He really couldn't.

"Leave me alone. Let me go!"

Imrik seized the iron with the big pincers and held it as tightly as he could. He raised the white-hot iron bar out of the flames and turned to—

"It wasn't my fault!"

—turned to edge past the driveshaft. But just then—

"I tried to get to him. I tried! I was just too far away."

Just then the pincers slipped, and the white-hot iron dropped, and Imrik had to leap aside to avoid it, stumbling, catching his foot—

I broke off. I had no desire to see exactly what had happened to Imrik's foot as it got caught in the gears.

Tano was no longer standing defiantly upright in front of me. He was kneeling. Tears glistened on his soot-stained cheeks.

"I promised to take care of him," he whispered. "I promised. A hundred times, at least."

He lowered his head and hid his face in his hands as if to prevent me from looking at him again. But I just stood there, knowing suddenly which peddler the cart belonged to, and how Imrik and Tano had come to work as no-man's-brats in the weapon forges of Dracana. The little peddler. The one who sold children. He had been paid fifteen silver marks for the runt, he had said, and twenty-three for the lout, who was big and strong for his age.

As if he could read my mind, Valdracu began to talk to Tano.

"I bought you, thrall," he whispered. "Bought you and paid for you. You are my property. My dog. And you know what? You weren't even very expensive. I paid more for my horse than I did for you. I paid more for my *boots*." He set the toe of one embroidered boot against the boy's shoulder and sent him sprawling. "Well? Are you a good boy now? Have you learned some respect? Are you a good thrall, *thrall*?"

At first Tano didn't answer. Valdracu had to prod him again with his booted foot.

"Well?"

"Yes," whispered Tano. "I'm sorry. I'm sorry. May we get back into the cart now?"

Valdracu and Sandor exchanged glances.

"Raving," muttered Sandor. "The boy has taken leave of his senses."

"It hardly matters," said Valdracu. "It doesn't take much wit to work at the hammer mill. Send him back to the forge, we've already lost hours because of his rebelliousness."

He put his hand on my shoulder and tugged gently at my hair.

"Well done, Dina. For a moment there I thought you were going to disappoint me, but of course you didn't. You are my rare bird still."

I hardly heard him. My headache was so bad that I thought I might pass out, and all of a sudden vomit surged in my throat, and I threw up, over and over, until nothing was left but the bitter green gall. There was only one tiny glimmer of light in all my misery. I had managed to vomit all over Valdracu's expensively embroidered boots.

The Stone Girl

Lying between smooth white sheets and a quilt of green silk, I felt miserable. I had never before slept in such a fancy bed. I had never before worn night robes such as these, so white and soft and frilly that I felt like a cross between a cloud and a snowflake. Cilla, the miller's daughter in Birches, would have been sick with envy. Except for my hair, I might be mistaken for what Rose called "one of them rich girls," someone who lacked for nothing and had every reason to feel spoiled and happy. But inside me, something had curled up and was starting to rot.

There was a light tapping at the door.

"Dina? Are you awake?"

I felt like pulling the silken quilt over my head and saying no. But it was Marte, and there was no fooling her.

"Yes," I said, and realized a little belatedly that I would have to say "Come in." I wasn't used to giving orders and permissions.

Marte pushed the door open with her hip. She was carrying a breakfast tray.

"Are you feeling any better?" she asked.

I felt like a worm—a worm with ugly stiff bristles on the outside and something slimy and disgusting on the inside.

"I'm fine."

Marte looked at me gaugingly. She was the one who had put me to bed the day before, when I had vomited all over Valdracu's boots. I had been so dizzy then that I couldn't stand up.

"Do you think you might be able to eat a little?" she asked, setting the tray on the small bedside table. "It would do you good."

I shook my head dumbly. I didn't feel like eating. I didn't feel like anything.

"I made the bread fresh this morning," she coaxed. "It's still warm. And there's honey."

It was not the bread that I couldn't refuse. It was Marte. She looked so worried, and in some ways she reminded me of my mother, although the only real similarity was the auburn hair. I forced myself to bite into the bread, chewing slowly.

Marte put a cool hand on my forehead. "I think you have a touch of fever," she said. "Drink the tea. I've put in a bit of allheal. And stay in bed for as long as you like. Mesire said that you should be allowed to rest."

"Can't I go out for a little while?" I pleaded. "It's so stifling in here."

Marte hesitated. "Mesire doesn't want you to leave the house. You know that."

I lowered my head. I could feel tears on my cheek, hot and heavy, and I wiped them away with the back of my hand. It might be very grand, this Green Room, but I felt like I was being smothered in fat gleaming green carpets and curtains and pillows and pom-poms. It had been twenty days since I had had a breath of outside air, and it was hard for me to be shut in like this, even if the prison walls had silken tapestries on them.

"Oh, sweetheart, don't take it so." Marte stroked my cheek and looked terribly upset. "Look, I have an idea. You can sit for a while in the Rose Court. You'll have sunshine and fresh air, and it's still part of the house, sort of. If Mesire asks."

I asked Marte if there was something I could do—slicing cabbage or peeling celery or something. But she wouldn't hear of it. I was to rest, those were Mesire's orders. So I sat on a white bench in the Rose Court, kicking my heels and doing nothing at all. Still, it was so much better than kicking my heels in the Green Room. Summer had come now, and the earliest roses were blooming, with small pink blossoms and a sweet scent that teased the nostrils.

It was a strange kind of garden, this Rose Court. Everything there had been planted for looks. Not at all like Mama's gardens where even the smallest plant had its purpose, either because she used it in her cooking or because it was useful against some ailment or other. In this place, there was just a bit of lavender and box, and then roses, roses, and more roses. Rose hedges, rose arches, roses big and small, roses climbing and creeping. Gravel paths wandered among the roses in rough circles, creating a kind of maze. I suppose it had been made this way so that the ladies of the house could go for "walks" without ever having to step outside the high walls that surrounded the courtyard.

Where were the ladies of the house? I had seen no one, unless you counted Sascha, and despite her silken skirts I didn't think she was a real lady. Valdracu was the only lord in the house now. Maybe he had taken it away from the people who used to own it. It had been a good long while since anyone, lady or not, had walked the circling paths, for the roses now grew fiercely and so untamed that in many places it must be impossible to pass without having skirts or sleeves torn by the dark red thorns.

I looked back at the house. No one seemed to be watching me. And Valdracu may have ordered "rest," but surely there was no harm in walking a bit among the roses?

I got up and smoothed my striped skirts. Then I slowly

began to wander into the maze of roses, and no angry voices called me back.

It was strange. I knew there were walls all around me, and that the garden was not that large. But a little bit into the maze it seemed as if the house and the walls disappeared entirely, leaving me to walk in a magic briar wood. Roses curled and tangled overhead, and all around me. Shiny dark green leaves, paler green vines, and red thorns were everywhere, and through the thicket led only a narrow white ribbon of pearly gravel. I followed the white paths, back and forth in soft curves, ever inward to the heart of the maze. This proved to be a small clearing in the rose forest, a small circle of gravel with two benches and—what was it? A statue of some kind? Vines clung to it like thick green tentacles, and at first I could see only what I thought was a human form. Clearing away some of the vines, I realized that I was mistaken even in that. It was the statue of a girl, slender and delicate, but when I pushed the leaves aside, I saw that she had horns. Not big ones like on a goat or a cow, but two soft little points like those of a very young deer.

The white stone face was frozen in an expression of despair. And as I stood there, staring at her, a shiny beetle ran down one cheek, so that for a moment it looked as if she were crying.

It terrified me. I don't know why. Suddenly it seemed that the green vines belonged to a tentacled monster that had caught her and was slowly smothering her, and I couldn't bear to watch. I spun and ran, back into the maze.

Briars caught at me like claws. I jerked free, ripping a long tear in Marte's white blouse; I knew this was not a good place to run, but I couldn't help myself.

Then I suddenly caught a glimpse of green that was not leaves, and this made me stop.

It was a door. A door in the wall. It was nearly hidden by tangled roses, and I don't think I would have found it at all if I hadn't been tearing so frantically through the thicket, unmindful of paths, without caring how badly I was scratched. There was something secretive about this door, something forbidden. It was not meant to be found and used by just anybody. Maybe it had been made so that some lord could get in unseen to visit with the ladies walking the maze. But to me, it was a door leading *out*.

I tore at the tangle of roses. My hands had already been full of scratches, and I now acquired deep new ones, but I barely noticed. A door. A way out! The handle was a huge iron ring, rusty and difficult to turn, but I was stubborn. And finally there was a muffled click from the old mechanism, and I was able to open the door.

Behind it, there was a small meadow of stiff yellow winter grasses, so tall that they nearly reached my waist. Behind the meadow, there was forest. Dark and silent pines. And rising behind the forest were the mountains. The Highlands.

My feet took off without waiting for further orders. I didn't even close the door behind me. I waded through the tall grass, wet from the dew of the night. My skirts were soaked in moments and clung clammily to my legs, and little yellow seeds stuck to the striped material. But it took me no time at all to reach the forest's edge.

Among the pines, it was a dim and silent world. My feet passed soundlessly over the thick carpet of brown needles, and only a few frail sunbeams reached the forest floor. It felt more like evening than midmorning in there. Distantly I heard the rushing falls of the river and the clangor from the mills, but they no longer concerned me. I was not in Dracana anymore; I was on my way to the Highlands. I was going home.

How long would it be before Valdracu discovered that his rare bird had flown the coop? Marte would be the first one to worry. She would look for me in the Rose Court, call my name, perhaps. Sooner or later they would find the door, and I supposed they would figure out the rest. And Valdracu would gather some men and—

I stopped abruptly. I knew exactly what Valdracu would do. He would send Sandor down into the cellar to get Tavis. And then he would kill him.

I dropped to my knees on the forest floor. For a brief moment, I had forgotten all about Tavis. For a brief moment, I had been free. Now the trap closed its jaws about me once more. I could squirm and fight it, but it wouldn't change the facts: if I ran without Tavis, Tavis would die.

My legs still wanted to run, on and on, through the pines, as far away from Dracana as I could get. It was terribly hard to turn back, and harder still to hurry. But I had to get back, and preferably before anyone discovered that I had been gone.

I had barely reached the green door when I heard Marte call my name. I hurried through the maze as quickly as I could.

"Sweet Saint Magda, girl, will you look at yourself!" she said when she caught sight of me. No wonder. My scratched hands, the torn sleeve, the wet skirts—no wonder she looked crestfallen.

"Come on in," she said. "Hurry. We have to get you into some decent clothes. Mesire wants you, and this won't do at all!"

"Why did it take you so long?" Valdracu glanced up, coolly and disapprovingly, from a letter he had been reading. "When I ask for you, I expect you to present yourself immediately."

"I had to change my clothes," I mumbled, which after all was just the truth. No need to tell him *why* I had needed the change.

"I see," he said. "Go with Sandor. I'll join you shortly."

Where? I thought, but I didn't ask. Although Valdracu was mostly happy with his rare bird, he still upheld his rules, and in his presence I didn't speak unless I was told to.

Sandor opened the door for me. "This way, Medamina," he said with false courtesy. Sometimes it amused him to treat me as if I was some grand lady.

I followed him out of the Marble Parlor, down the hall, and into the cobbled courtyard in front of the house. A groom was wiping down an exhausted-looking horse with the Dragon Crest on its saddle blanket. It probably belonged to the messenger who had brought Valdracu his letter. The groom aimed a silent bow in our direction as we passed.

Apparently, we were headed for the stables, or at any rate for the tack room. Harness and saddles hung in neat rows, and there was a smell of leather and linseed oil, with just a hint of dust. In the floor, there was a bolted trapdoor with a big ring in it. Sandor shot back the bolt and hauled on the ring until the hatch came open, no easy job by the looks of it. He waved at it with an extravagant flourish.

"Ladies first."

No great prize, that—not when the door in question was a hole in the floor with some narrow steps that were really just a ladder. A sour, fusty smell flowed up at me, making me think of rotting turnips.

"Why do we have to go down there?" I asked, even though it was against the rules.

"You'll find out," he said. "Down you go."

Whenever I had thought of Tavis and his cellar, I had always imagined it to be below the big house. It had never occurred to me that it might be below the stables instead. The darkness down there was almost total. I sincerely hoped that this was not where he had been stuck for twenty days, but what other reason could there be for us to go down there?

Sandor was getting impatient. "Down!" he snapped, and I didn't dare to hang back any longer.

At first I was almost completely blind, but slowly my eyes got used to the darkness, and there were a few weak glimmers of light. Mostly from the open hatch, but also from cracks between the rough floorboards over our heads. Along one wall there was a row of large cagelike crates of the kind winter stores are kept in. In the nearest one were some cabbages, packed in straw to prevent them from rotting. It soothed me a bit to see them. This was no longer a dark mysterious cave, but a root cellar not unlike the one we had had in Birches. This one just happened to be a bit bigger and darker.

There was a rasp of steel and tinder, and a small flame grew between Sandor's cupped hands.

"Get that," he said, nodding toward a square lantern hanging on a nail by the hatch.

I took it and carefully lifted one of the soot-stained glass panels, so that he could light the candle inside. With a hissing sound, the wick caught fire and began to burn with a small but steady flame.

"Down that end," Sandor said, this time jerking his head in the direction of the back wall of the cellar.

The ceiling was low, and Sandor had to duck his head to avoid the beams. I eyed the storage crates as we passed. Most were empty or nearly empty, and the beets in the third one looked distinctly unappetizing. Most of the rotting smell came from them.

And then I stopped in my tracks. In the second to last crate, on a layer of straw that was thinner than the one the cabbages rested on, lay Tavis. He had curled himself into a ball and didn't even look up when the light of the lantern touched him.

"Tavis. . . ." My voice was nearly soundless, a stunned whisper. He heard it anyway. He turned to look at me, shielding his eyes with one hand. Even the weak glare of the lantern was too much for someone who had spent weeks in the dimness of the cellar.

"Go away," he said, but his voice was more scared than angry. "Stupid cow. This is all your fault." His voice was cracked and hoarse, as if he had been doing a lot of shouting.

"Move," said Sandor, shoving me in the back. "Mesire has no interest in him today."

What did interest Mesire, it appeared, was still the crazy tramp. He was crouched inside the last crate, and I realized immediately why they hadn't dragged him along to the Marble Parlor this time. There was no way he'd be able to stand or walk, the way they had beaten him.

"He's just a poor beggar who's not right in the head," I whispered. "Can't you let him go?"

"Mind your own business," snarled Sandor. "You just do as you're told, girl."

At that moment we heard someone making his way down the ladder. It was Valdracu, and he was angry. Whatever had been in the letter, it hadn't pleased him. When his boot heels hit the floor it sounded as if someone was cracking a whip. Sandor straightened like a soldier coming to attention and was suddenly in a great hurry to open the front of the tramp's crate and drag him out onto the cellar floor.

"Right," said Valdracu, not too loudly but with a chill that I could practically feel on my skin. "Get me the truth from this beggar."

He was not a big man, the tramp. He had been hunched and skinny and dirty even before they started hitting him, and now he looked a wreck. His face was swollen and streaked with blood, and his breathing sounded all wrong, sort of wet and uneven. Yet he raised a hoarse chant when he saw Valdracu.

"The Devil came to the honest man and said: / You must learn how to tell a lie / Then you shall rise in the world like a sun / And have all the friends that money can buy."

"Stop that nonsense," said Valdracu. "This madness is nothing but playacting, and I am not fooled by it in the least. It seems the last lot of swords we sent to Dunark was short by two dozen, and my cousin the Dragon Lord wants to know why—and so do I. Dina, look at him."

I swallowed. The headache had come back the minute I heard Valdracu's steps on the ladder. Now, sickness lay like lead in my stomach, and I had a hideous, rotten taste in my mouth. I wanted to say that I couldn't do it, that I was too sick, but he wouldn't have believed me.

"Look at me," I told the tramp. His gaze met mine for a brief moment. He could barely see out of one eye, and I stood there hating Sandor and Valdracu with a will. How could they beat a poor simpleton like that? He was no kind of spy, I thought. What did he know about missing swords?

"Evil eyes are bought and sold / Witches answer rich men's call / Naked beggars feel the cold / But Death's cold hand touches all."

I wasn't sure whether he had learned his rhymes somewhere or just made them up as he went along. But when his brown eyes met mine, it was suddenly as if he were the Shamer, not me.

"I'm not a witch," I muttered, looking down. "I can't help this!"

"What's wrong with you, girl?" hissed Valdracu, seizing my arm. It felt as if his fingers went right to the bone.

"I don't have time for this! Get the truth from this piece of filth—or someone gets hurt."

I knew he meant Tavis. My temples throbbed, and the sickness was like a living thing twisting inside me. What would he do if I vomited on his velvet coat this time?

"Look at me," I said once more, the voice more nearly right. My head hurt so badly I could barely see, but I heard the tramp's snuffling breath catch and stumble, and I knew that my eyes and voice held him now.

"Ask him what he is doing here," said Valdracu, calmer now that his rare bird was once more an obedient weapon in his hand. "Why was he lurking around by the forges?"

"Sharp new steel, shiny blade / How many orphans has it made? / Feel the edge, cold as ice / Ask a dead man for the price." The tramp's breath whistled as he rattled off yet another nonsense rhyme. But when he said the word *blade,* something happened between us. I saw his hand on the hilt of a sword, I saw an opponent. The two blades met with a chiming sound.

"Cruel hard is a beggar's lot / Grant him mercy, grant him bread / Or if you won't, then keep what you've got / And this starving poor beggar will soon be dead."

There was no longer a sword in his hand. It was stretched out, palm upward, open, empty. But the sword *had* been there. This beggar had once held a sword, and he had known how to use it. He was trying to keep his true

189

story hidden behind a screen of rhyme and madness, but Valdracu was right—this was much more than a poor half-crazed simpleton.

"Tell me—" I began, but he interrupted.

"No," he said very quietly, very calmly. "Don't. What you do is wrong, and you don't have to do it."

His words struck me as forcefully as if my mother had said them. *What you do is wrong.* But if I didn't . . . Tavis . . . if I didn't do it . . .

My thoughts whirled, and then ceased to move at all. Something inside me snapped, like a string on a lute tuned beyond its breaking point. Suddenly I was down on all fours on the damp cellar floor, and no matter how much Sandor hauled at me, I couldn't stay on my feet.

"I'm sick," I finally managed. "I can't do it." Something was broken, I could feel it as clearly as if it had been a broken bone. I really *couldn't* do what he asked; it would be like telling a man to walk on his broken leg. The mere thought of it made my head spin sickeningly, and I brought up all the breakfast Marte had so carefully managed to feed me.

Valdracu leaped away from me and cursed in disgust.

"Children!" he said in the sort of voice most people use when they say "Roaches!"

"I reckon she really is ill," Sandor said cautiously. "I mean, not even girls throw up over nothing."

"No," said Valdracu icily. "I don't suppose they do. Get her to bed. We'll try again tomorrow. And get me Anton. I need the pendant he took from her."

"Errh . . . that might be a bit difficult," mumbled Sandor nervously.

"What is that supposed to mean?"

"I can get Anton. But he sold the pendant."

"He sold it?" Valdracu's voice was so cold that it practically left frost in one's ears, and Sandor was obviously wishing he had kept his mouth shut. "To whom?"

"Some woman from Solark who thought it looked pretty. She paid him two copper marks, I heard."

"Tell Anton to go find that woman. If he is not back with the pendant in three days, he would do well to stay away entirely. Otherwise *he* can have the privilege of explaining to my cousin the Dragon Lord just why we are not able to send him what he wants."

I would probably never see my Shamer's signet again, I thought, and felt still more miserable. But there was some comfort in knowing that Valdracu wouldn't have it either.

Who Steals Dead Sheep?

It was the middle of the night, and Black-Arse was pounding on our door. Or at least it felt like the middle of the night, and it was still mostly dark outside.

"Where is Callan?" he asked the moment I opened the door.

"At Maudi's, I think," I mumbled sleepily. "Why? And why did you think you would find him here?"

"Killian saw him with yer mother last night," said Black-Arse breathlessly. "Late. So when he was not at the croft, we thought he might be here."

Mama had been out on a sick call, to someone who had tried to chop off most of his foot with an ax. It was the first time she had been out since the ambush, and even though it was only a short ride, Callan had been adamant: She was going nowhere without him!

"We don't have that much space," I said. "Maudi has. But why did you want him?"

"Someone raided Evin's place and stole all his sheep,"

Black-Arse called, already back in the saddle and heading his sturdy little Highland horse toward Maudi's. "If we hurry, we might still catch them!"

"Wait," I yelled. "I'm coming with you."

Black-Arse halted his horse briefly and gave me his can-ye-really-trust-a-Lowlander look. Then he nodded.

"Good," he said. "But hurry. We're meetin' at the Dance. I'll go get Callan."

Rose had appeared in the doorway behind me, with her fair hair in wild disorder and an old brown shawl of Maudi's wrapped around her shoulders.

"Where're you going?" she muttered, not really awake yet.

"With Black-Arse and Callan. Some sheep have been stolen."

"Aren't you going to tell your mother?" Rose suddenly looked much more alert—alert and reproachful.

"No time," I said. It sounded a bit wooly and muffled because I was pulling on my thickest sweater at the time. Luckily, I had put on my breeches before answering the door. "You tell her."

I trotted across the yard to the stables without looking at Rose again. I knew how she would be glaring daggers in my direction, almost as if she had the Shamer's Gift. But luckily neither Melli nor Rose had any such powers. Two Shamers in one house were quite enough. And then it hit me again—bang in the belly—that right now, there was only one. Now, and perhaps always. I slapped my hand against the stable wall, hard, as if that could chase away the thought.

Falk was in a lousy mood and used every trick he knew to avoid being saddled. Such an early start on top of his late night made him feel sulky and put upon, but we had had him for nearly six months now, and he rarely got anything past me anymore. Whether he wanted to or not, we were soon headed for the Dance.

I was the first one there, but only just. Black-Arse and Callan were already on their way up the hill. Callan scowled like a thunderstorm when he saw me.

"What are you doin' here?"

"I want to come."

"Come? It's not a bloody party, boy. And ye don't even have a sword anymore."

"I've got my bow."

"My bow, ye mean," Callan said, as I was still using the one he had lent me. "And besides, we're dealin' with outlaws and peaceless men here, not deer. Green pups like yerself can get killed."

"You're letting Black-Arse come!" I said without thinking, and Black-Arse gave me a sour look. He didn't much care for being called a pup.

Callan eyed me. "Do ye not think yer mother has lost enough children?"

I looked down at Falk's black neck. "I can't sit at home forever, Callan. You know I can't."

Actually I wasn't home all that much—ever since Dina went missing I had used any excuse to get out of the house. I knew that, and so did Callan. But he didn't say it. He just sighed.

"Right, then. Come if ye want. But stay in the back and do as ye're told!"

I nodded. "I will."

Evin Kensie was a bit odd—a silent old man who preferred the company of his dogs to that of most humans. Perhaps that was why he had chosen to live about as far from Baur Kensie as one could get without leaving Kensie lands. He had a small croft that clung to a rocky slope about halfway up Maedin Mountain, and he came down to Baur Kensie only twice a year—in the spring when he had wool to sell, and in the autumn when he had to buy supplies for the winter.

"I tell ye, I got me one hell of a surprise when I saw him," said Killian Kensie, Evin's nearest neighbor, whom the old man had called from his sleep in the middle of the night. "What a sight he was! Blood pourin' down his face and him staggerin' like a drunken man. My Annie got him to sit down and gave him a hot drink, though I think he'd rather've had whiskey. But he was like a wild man. Ravin', he was. Wanted me and him to go after those devils by ourselves, just the two of us. Paid no mind to the cut on his face, and it wasn't the sheep so much, either, but they shot one of his dogs. I'm tellin' ye, he was ravin' mad."

Killian had gathered about a score of men now, me and Black-Arse included. Enough, as he said, to "teach those devils a lesson." In the early dawn we reached Maedin and the slope where the raid had taken place. At first it was easy to see which way the devils had gone. They had driven the sheep right through a thicket of blackthorns, trampling it and leaving tufts of wool stuck on every other bush. They must have been in a tearing hurry to get away, it seemed, and the trail led straight toward the lands of the Skaya clan.

"Evin said those devils wore Skaya cloaks," said Killian. "I didn't rightly believe him. Skaya would not break the clan peace, I told myself. And black and blue, who can tell such colors in the dark? But it looks like he was right. Damn Skaya devils!"

"Calm yerself. We'll see," said Callan in his broadest Highland drawl. But he looked angry and worried, and I remembered how he had refused to interfere in the matters of another clan even when we thought a Laclan had led my mother into ambush.

"What if it *is* Skaya?" I whispered to Black-Arse. "Do we just go home?"

"I do not know," Black-Arse answered in the same low whisper, careful not to let Callan hear him.

We followed the trail as fast as the horses would go

over the difficult ground. Around midmorning we reached the cairn that marked the end of Kensie lands. Callan brought his gelding to a halt.

"If we go on from here," he said, "I want a word from each of ye."

"What word is that?" asked Killian.

"I want yer word that ye'll use no blade, knife, or bow against anyone—unless I tell ye."

"Who made you the leader?" grumbled one of the men.

"Oh, shut up, Val," said one of the others.

That was all that was said about that. Nobody had made Callan the leader. He just was—and even Val the Grouch knew it.

Sometimes I get a bit envious of Callan. Sometimes I wish I was more like him.

"Well, Killian," said Callan. "Do I have yer word?"

Killian nodded, a resigned look on his face. "Aye," he said, "ye have."

Callan asked every one of us—even Black-Arse and me. We all agreed. And only then did we enter Skaya lands.

It was as if somebody had suddenly waved a wand over the trail, magicking it away. One moment it had been as wide and obvious as a caravan road; the next, it dwindled away to nothing. Suddenly the sheep raiders made every effort to hide it—splitting up, riding through water, riding over rock.

"A fox gets careful near his own lair," said Killian. "We're gettin' close now."

We had to split up too, of course.

"You two are comin' with me," said Callan to me and Black-Arse.

We spent the rest of the morning searching, without seeing hide nor hair of any raiders or sheep. The sun had reached its midday height before something happened.

Black-Arse found them. Not the raiders, just the sheep. In a narrow cleft, almost completely hidden by blackthorn.

"Here!" he yelled, but something was wrong with his voice. There was no trace of triumph or pleasure in it, not the least little bit. And when we got closer, we could see why.

All the sheep were dead.

Some had been shot, but most had had their throats cut. The cleft was clogged with dead sheep, and the flies were already buzzing about them in a black cloud. I suddenly thought of the Weapons Master and his story about the fall of Solark.

"I saw the flies," said Black-Arse, pale-faced. "And then I found them. They're all dead." He looked at Callan and me with puzzlement in his eyes. "Who on earth would steal dead sheep?"

The sheep had not been dead when they were stolen, of course, but I could see his point. Why go to all this trouble to get hold of the beasts and then just kill them? It wasn't even for the meat. Dumped like that in the cleft, it would take less than a day before they were meat fit only for scavengers.

"Skaya must answer for this," said Killian savagely when he saw the dead sheep. "Attackin' an old man, shootin' his dog, stealin' his livin'—how will Evin survive this winter?"

"Maudi'll not let him starve," said Callan. "But ye're right. Skaya must answer. Some of us will have to go to Skayark."

Any chance of catching the raiders had fled, now that we knew they no longer had the sheep. After a bit of discussion we all rode on to Skayark except Val, who went back to tell Evin and the rest of the Kensies what had happened. It took us most of the day to get there, and although we met several Skayas on the way and passed more than one village, Callan forbade us to do anything more than give polite greeting.

"We bring our complaint to Astor Skaya," he said. "As is right and decent. Let no one say *we* break clan peace."

Skayark was a fortress city, the only one in the Highlands, and Astor Skaya was the only male clan leader in the mountains—the closest thing the Highlanders had to a castellan. Skayark lay at the mouth of the Skayler Pass, an important site, because there was nowhere else that you could cross the Skayler range with wagons and caravans of some size. It was said of Astor Skaya that his ancestors had been robber chiefs more than castellans, but these days Skaya made enough on ordinary trade and the pass toll that Astor demanded in return for keeping the pass free from rock slides and bandits.

Skayark looked awe-inspiring in the afternoon sun. The city walls spanned the whole of the narrow valley, gray and massive like the mountains themselves, and from the three tall towers the Skaya banner fluttered in the wind, blue at the top and black at the bottom, with a golden eagle in the middle. I eyed our little troop anxiously: sixteen dusty, sweat-soaked Highlanders, who had been torn untimely from their nighttime rest and had been riding ever since—and looked accordingly. Sixteen dusty Highlanders, and me. Not an impressive force, I thought, looking up at the massive walls. Once we entered, Skaya could crush us the way a nutcracker cracks a nut. If Skaya really intended to break clan peace and cause bad blood and warfare among the clans.

"Who comes?" called the guard at the gate.

"Men of Kensie," Callan called back, and if he felt like a nut in a nutcracker, he showed no signs of it. "We have a matter to bring before Astor Skaya."

"And what matter is that, Kensie?"

"Clan justice" was all Callan said, but his voice was iron.

The gate opened.

"Enter, then, Kensie," said the guard. "In the name of clan justice."

Astor Skaya received us in the Falconer's Court. He had been about to go hunting; he was dressed in leathers and wore a heavy falconer's gauntlet, and a shiny black horse stood saddled and ready. On a smaller horse next to the black was a rather unusual rider: an eagle, tied to its perch by jesses and wearing a plumed and jeweled hood.

"What is yer business, Kensie?" Astor Skaya asked impatiently, eyeing the sun. "I haven't much time."

Flying an eagle at the hunt could only be done in daylight, which might be why he was so eager to be gone.

"Evin Kensie was raided last night," said Callan. "His dog was shot and his sheep stolen. The raiders wore Skaya cloaks, and the trail led straight to Skaya lands. We found the sheep on Skaya land, all dead. Astor Skaya, this is an ill deed that must be answered."

Astor Skaya raised his chin and looked at Callan as if he had just detected a foul smell. "Are ye accusin' us of stealin' sheep?"

"I just want an answer."

"Ye want an answer? Here it is: Skaya are not sheep stealers nor ever have been. Good day." He turned his back on Callan and went to mount his waiting horse.

"Not so fast, Skaya."

At first I thought Callan had spoken, but this was a different voice, hoarser and more hate-filled. A rider had entered the Falconer's Court, an old man who could only be Evin. His long white hair stuck out all over the place, and there was still a bit of blood encrusted in his beard and an angry dark cut on his forehead. His horse was soaked in sweat both before and behind and looked to be only moments away from collapsing. But it still obeyed him and walked a few staggering steps so that Evin could look down on Astor Skaya.

"Evin." Callan put out a hand to stop him, but Evin had eyes only for Astor. From the blanket roll at the back of his saddle he drew a sword—a sword so ancient that it was black with age.

"Look yer fill, Astor," said the old man. "This sword was my father's, and his father's before him. It has tasted Skaya blood before. And it will again when I catch the bastard who shot my Mollie." And then he spat Astor Skaya in the face.

For a moment, we all sat completely stunned, except for Evin, who turned his tired horse around and left, without another word spoken.

Astor Skaya put a hand to his face as if he didn't quite believe what had happened.

"Mollie?" he asked, sounding momentarily more astonished than angry. "Who is Mollie?"

Callan cleared his throat. "The dog. The one that was shot."

Astor Skaya stared at Callan, and now the fury rose in him in a visible wave.

"A dog?" he said in a voice trembling with rage. "He insults me, he threatens me, he *spits* on me—because of a *dog*?"

"He was very fond of it," Callan said, for once looking uncertain. It had not gone quite as he had planned, this visit to Skayark.

An embarrassed groom handed Astor Skaya a rag, and he wiped his face carefully.

"I see. Ye have run yer errand, Callan Kensie. Now go home. And go swiftly. From tomorrow at sunrise no Kensie is welcome in Skaya lands."

We caught up with Evin not far from Skayark. His poor horse was walking so slowly that he would have been better off on foot.

"Evin," said Callan, "that was not a wise thing to do."

Evin's face remained closed and stubborn.

"It was my right."

Callan sighed. "Only if a Skaya did this. And even then . . . Evin, do ye really want Skaya and Kensie at war? Do ye really want men to fight and kill—over a dog?"

"Aye," said Evin, and rode on.

. . .

The ride back was a long one. Horses and men had already had to endure more than was good for them, but no one doubted that Astor Skaya was deadly earnest: come sunrise, no Kensie would be safe in Skaya lands. We had had to leave Evin's horse behind, or we would never have made it out of Skaya before dawn. He now rode double with Black-Arse, who was the lightest of us.

By the time we reached the cairn, night had fallen, cold and bright with stars, and more than one rider had been on the point of toppling from his horse from sheer tiredness. But it was easier to go on to Killian's than to make camp in the dark, and so it was in the hay of Killian Kensie's barn that I could finally let myself drop, so weary that I could barely hold my head up.

And yet, once there, I found I couldn't sleep. I kept seeing Astor Skaya's furious face, and Evin's, blood-encrusted and pale with hatred.

"Black-Arse?" I whispered. "Are you asleep?"

"Not quite," he answered in a sleep-slurred voice. "Why?"

"Do you really think there will be war between Kensie and Skaya?"

"I do not know." The hay rustled as Black-Arse turned to face me. "I hope so. Skaya deserves it."

I was suddenly angry at Black-Arse. He had no idea

what he was talking about. War—that meant people dying. War meant coming home to a blackened ruin and a lot of butchered animals, like at Cherry Tree Cottage. We had done it once. I could not bear to think of having to start over again. And this time without Dina.

"You don't know what you're talking about," I said, but I don't think he heard me. At any rate, he didn't answer, and a few moments later he began to snore.

I had expected Mama to be angry, or at least upset. I knew that I should have told her myself that I was going with Black-Arse and Callan, instead of leaving Rose to do my dirty work. But as soon as she heard Falk's hoofbeats, she flung open the door, and I barely had time to dismount before she threw her arms around me, hugging me tightly.

"Davin," she said, laughing and crying at the same time. "Look. Look what the Widow has sent me!"

She dangled something in front of my face—a pewter pendant on a leather thong.

It was Dina's signet.

Hopes, Fears, and Oatmeal

Every thought of war and dead sheep flew right out of my head.

"Where did she get this?" I asked.

"A man sold it to someone who—no, you'd better read the letter yourself." Mama gave me a small sheet of thin parchment. Tiny letters filled very inch of it, and there were creases where it had been wrapped around Dina's signet.

"Dear Melussina," it began. "I have news for you which is mostly good. We think Dina is alive, and we think we know where she is. . . ."

I suddenly felt as if I needed to sit down. The tiny letters wouldn't stay still, and after those first few lines, nothing else made sense. I was never very good at reading, but right then I seemed to have forgotten the trick entirely.

"Won't you read it?" I asked Mama. "It'll take me forever."

"Perhaps you should practice your letters more," said Mama with something of her old sharpness. "Weapon skills are all very well, but being able to read and write would do you no harm either."

"I can read!" Just not right now.

Mama put her hand on my arm. "I know," she said. "I'm sorry. I don't know why I'm snapping at you like this. It's just . . . suddenly everything is upside down, and one minute I'm crazy with joy, and the next I'm scared out of my wits. Here. Give it to me. I'll read it to you."

And so it was on the day after the sheep raid that I learned that my sister was probably alive after all. The Widow told us how she and the Master had begun to gather people who "feel like we do," as she cautiously put it. People who were tired of having Drakan for a lord and wanted to put an end to the Order of the Dragon.

"There isn't much we can do at the moment," she wrote, "except get together, gather a few weapons, and keep our eyes and ears open. We count men. We count swords. We find the strengths and weaknesses of the Dragon."

One of the strengths was apparently Dracana, a completely new town where Drakan's people were somehow using the power of the Eidin River to weave cloth and forge swords faster and in greater numbers than anybody had been able to before. The Widow and the Master were keenly interested in Dracana, for Dracana's secret was the reason Drakan had been able to raise such a large force so quickly.

Unfortunately, it was not a town just anybody could walk into. Only men of the Order of the Dragon and their families lived there, and it was the wives and the children who worked the looms and did much of the work in the forges, while the men served in Drakan's Dragon Force.

"We talk to people from Dracana whenever it is possible, which is not often. The town is governed by a certain Valdracu, a relative of Drakan on his mother's side, and he rules his people with a ruthless hand. A woman we know bought this Shamer's signet from one of Valdracu's men. I think it might be Dina's. And there are rumors that Valdracu has a girl with the Evil Eye in his service. We are trying to find out more, but it is not easy—I fear that one of our people, a friend of Martin's, may have been caught, as we have not heard from him for many days now. So, Melussina dearest, a hope has been kindled. But a hope surrounded by fear and danger. If it is she, she is alive— but captured by the Dragon."

Persuading my mother to let me go took some doing. At first she wanted to go herself, but I came down hard on that idea.

"They *burn* Shamers down there. Didn't you hear what the Master said?"

"She's my child, Davin. And so are you. How am I to sit here idly waiting, while you are both in terrible danger?"

"You will just have to," I said harshly, "because we would be up to our necks in it the first time you looked at anybody."

She knew I was right. I knew that she knew.

"But Davin, do *you* have to go?" Her voice was completely different from how it used to be. Smaller. More afraid. It hurt me to hear it. "Let Callan do it," she begged. "He would if I asked him to, I know he would."

Now that war with Skaya threatened, Maudi needed Callan. Yet I still think my mother was right. Callan was no longer completely a Kensie man. The day he had come home without Dina, a part of him had become the Shamer's. If my mother asked him to do this, he would. Whatever Maudi said. I wondered if Maudi knew that.

"You can't do that to him," I said. "You shouldn't force him to go against Maudi's word. And there are other reasons I'm a better choice. For one thing, I don't sound like a Highlander every time I open my mouth."

"There are others who don't."

"Mama. There is another reason. The most important one."

"And what is that?"

"If I don't do this, I'll never be able to look you in the eye again."

She looked utterly dismayed. "Davin . . . Of course you will. Always. You're my son!"

I shook my head. "It's not something you decide. It's not even something I decide. It's just the way it is."

She was quiet for a very long while. Her hands rested in her lap, open and empty, looking strangely helpless. One rarely saw them so still. They were always working, or dancing in the air as she spoke. They would smooth Melli's hair, or scratch Beastie's ears until he sighed with delight.

"All right," she finally said in a very low voice, looking at her empty hands. "Go if you must. But Davin . . ."

"Yes?"

"Promise to come home again. No matter what."

I nodded. "I'll do all I can."

"No," she said. *"No matter what."*

If I die, I thought, my ghost will have to come home. It was not a voice one could refuse.

I borrowed a horse from Maudi, a stolid brown mare of no particular beauty. Hella, she was called. I would rather have had Falk, but I dared not risk anybody recognizing the Shamer's horse the way they had at the White Doe in Baur Laclan. The good thing about Hella, except for four sound legs and an easy temper, was the fact that she had not yet been branded with Kensie's clan mark. Maudi had only just got her in exchange for some young rams.

"I'm sorry I cannot let Callan come with ye," she said. "But I cannot spare him, the way things are with Skaya."

"I know," I said. "It doesn't matter." Although to be perfectly truthful I would have liked to have Callan at my back, Callan with his unflustered strength and calm good sense. "Well, then." She patted my shoulder a couple of times. "Good luck to ye, lad. Ye be careful, now."

"I will."

I checked the straps of my pack one last time and swung myself onto Hella's comfortable back.

Mathias, the Lowlander who had brought the letter and the Signet, sat up a little straighter on his dun gelding.

"Ready?"

"Yes," I said. "I'm ready."

And off we rode, headed for the Lowlands, and Dracana.

There was a sharp crack from the bonfire, and a burst of sparks took flight, riding the smoke as birds ride the wind. I just lay there, rolled up in every blanket I had brought, and felt the heaviness of sleep creep over me. On the other side of the fire, Mathias was still awake—I could see the glitter of his eyes in the glow from the flames. Next to me, snoring comfortably, was Black-Arse. I was still a bit surprised at that. Shortly after we had set out, he had come chasing after us at a gallop, hollering like a madman.

"Wait!" he yelled. "Wait for me!"

He had decided to see me on my way, he said, "at least as long as ye're still in the Highlands." He made it sound as if a single breath of Lowland air would poison him on the spot. But I was very glad to see him. Maybe we were closer to being real friends than I thought, despite my being a Lowlander and all. And in any case, riding next to Mathias, whom I didn't know at all, had been an odd and silent experience. He didn't say much, the good Mathias—if he had suddenly been struck dumb, I think it would have been weeks before anyone realized. When he wanted you to do something, like gather the firewood, he just pointed. If he thought you had fallen too far behind, he turned and looked at you with those weird yellow eyes of his, and you knew that you had better make your horse catch up.

He was tall and skinny and so long-legged that his feet hung quite a bit below the belly of the dun. But there was nothing clumsy about him despite his lankiness. Every move he made was precise, as if he had decided to be as sparing with his strength as he was with his words. He looked a bit like a large bird of prey, I thought, with those yellow eyes and the wary way he cocked his head. If I wasn't careful, I could easily have become just a little bit scared of Mathias.

Black-Arse, on the other hand, talked constantly, which was nice, as it saved me from thinking too much. Hella followed Mathias's dun with the steadiness of a rock; riding her made no great demands on my attention. So if Black-Arse hadn't joined us, I would probably have spent the entire afternoon throwing wary looks at Mathias and worrying about Dina. What did it mean that Valdracu had her in his service? I couldn't imagine my stubborn little sister serving anybody, least of all a relative of Drakan's.

No, it was a good thing that Black-Arse was there. Even if he did snore and talk in his sleep. And even if his foot was digging into my back right now.

Suddenly Mathias was standing over me. I could have sworn that he was still lying rolled up in his blankets on the other side of the fire, but either he was quicker than any magician, or else I must have dozed for a moment. He put his hand on my shoulder and jerked his head in a fashion that clearly meant "Get up!"

"What is it?" I asked, or rather, I meant to ask him, but as soon as I opened my mouth he put a finger to his lips to stop me.

My heart beat a little faster. What was going on? I freed myself from the blankets and got up. Mathias pointed at his own spot by the fire. No wonder I had thought he was still there: His blankets were wrapped around something, so that it looked like a sleeping figure. I took my pack and a log from the pile by the fire and tried to copy his handiwork. He waited for me, just outside the circle of light cast by the fire, and was already almost invisible. I pointed silently to Black-Arse, but Mathias shook his head. Apparently, it was to be just the two of us. He disappeared into the thicket, and I followed him.

We had camped by a small stream not too far from the road, in a hollow overgrown with brambles and lanky birches. The pale trunks shimmered whitely in all the darkness. Mathias had made himself invisible simply by squatting in the brambles, and I got down next to him and looked at him questioningly. He held a hand to his ear. Listen, he meant. I listened. And now that I was a bit more awake, I heard it clearly: a great rustling and snapping of twigs, quite loud, in fact. Something was coming our way, drawn by the light of the fire. Something big. A bear, perhaps?

A bear . . . and my bow was still by my pack near the fire, next to the shrouded shape that was supposed to be me. Callan would have made my ears burn. Mathias, of course, said nothing.

Crash. Snap. The sounds were coming closer. The bushes moved. Then the crashing stopped, and the night grew quiet. So quiet that I was able to hear a sort of hoarse snuffling. Did bears sound like that?

We waited. I could *see* my bow from where I crouched. It might as well have been on the moon for all the good it did me. How could I have been so stupid?

Black-Arse moved in his sleep and called out something slurred and incomprehensible—the only thing that stood out clearly was "blueberry pie." He must be dreaming. Suddenly it felt very wrong that he should be lying there, defenseless and ignorant of his danger. If the bear suddenly decided to rush our camp, would we be able to stop it before it mauled Black-Arse?

The bushes moved again.

So did Mathias.

There was a sharp cry and a lot of rattling and crashing and moving about. A little late off the mark, I stumbled through the thicket trying to come to Mathias's aid. He had flung himself on something and was now thrashing about on the ground. In the dark, I could hear him better than I could see him, and I ended up tripping over him and whatever it was he was fighting. It wasn't a bear, at any rate. Bears don't have braids. Braids . . .

"Rose?" I hazarded. "Rose, is that you?"

"Let go of me!" yelled Rose. "Let go of me, you bastard!" And when Mathias didn't: "Let go! I'm warning you, I have a knife!"

Oh, it was Rose, all right.

"Let her go, Mathias," I said. "It's my . . . it's my foster sister." I didn't know what else to call her so that he would understand.

Mathias let Rose get to her feet and pulled her out of the thicket and into our camp. When I turned to follow him, I bumped my shin on a huge basket of the kind some people use to carry firewood. A basket? It had to be Rose's, but what was she doing with a firewood basket so big that she could barely carry it? I dragged it with me to our small camp, clanking and clattering as if she had an entire tinker's stall in there.

Rose looked terrible. Bits of leaves and little twigs were caught in her fair hair, and her hands and knees and one side of her face were covered in filth. Tears made pale runnels in the dirt, and the hoarse snuffling I had heard was the sound of Rose crying.

"I thought you were a bear," I said without thinking. She gave me an acid glare but said nothing. She rubbed at her face with one hand, trying to wipe away the tears, but her hand was so grubby that it only made it worse.

"What are you doing here?" I asked.

"What do you think?" She spat a few times. I couldn't tell whether it was to show her opinion of me, or to rinse the dirt from her mouth. She managed to cry and look completely furious at the same time, but I didn't quite understand why she was so angry.

"Rose, you can't just—"

"I'll tell you what I can't!" she cut me off. "I can't just sit at home and let you blunder around in the Lowlands. Dina is *my* friend. Only nobody seems to remember that!"

That stung, because there was more than a little truth to it. We hadn't thought a lot about Rose and how she was feeling lately. I certainly hadn't. She was just there—helping Mama, feeding the animals, cooking and doing the dishes, and so on. But still . . .

"You can't just come barging in on us like this," I said. "In the middle of the night. What about Mama? She must be beside herself with worry."

"Look who's talking," sneered Rose. "At least *I* left a note."

I wasn't touching that one. It might not be too clever of me to get into an argument on who scared Mama the most.

"You can stay the night," I said, in my best and-that's-final voice. "But tomorrow at daybreak you're going home. Black-Arse can take you."

Rose glared at me in defiance. "That's not up to you," she said, tossing her head so that her braids danced on her back.

"Rose, you don't even have a horse!"

"I'll just have to walk then, won't I?" she said. "Shank's mare is good enough for most people."

I threw Mathias an entreating look. Couldn't he explain to the girl that it was no good? But he just stared at us with his yellow falcon's eyes and showed no signs of wanting to interfere. Rose crouched next to the fire, dug into her basket, and brought out a blanket. If I wanted her to go back, I would probably have to tie her to Black-Arse's horse, and the thought of having to fight a girl was not very appealing. Particularly not when the girl was Rose. After all, I knew that she really did have a knife.

"Until daybreak," I said as firmly as I could, "and not a minute longer!"

Rose snorted. "Shouldn't you get some sleep?" she said. "We all have a long day ahead of us." She lay down and wrapped the blanket closely around her. I tried to glare at her, but I don't have Shamer's eyes, and I had the feeling that nothing less would do the trick with Rose.

"You have to use niter," said Black-Arse suddenly, loudly and clearly. I turned and stared at him. But his eyes were closed, and he was far away in his own dreamland. He had managed to sleep through both the bear hunt and my fight with Rose without twitching an eyelid.

I woke up with a wonderful smell of roast sausages in my nostrils. It made me smile even before opening my eyes, particularly since lunch *and* supper the day before had consisted of dry bread and a lumpy, unsweetened oatmeal porridge Mathias made. Perhaps it wasn't so odd that Black-Arse should dream of blueberry pies.

I sat up. Sunlight fell in slanted streaks through the dark thicket, and at our small fire Rose was sitting on her haunches, turning sausages and—yes, she even had sliced potatoes in her frying pan. My mouth watered.

"Oh, you're awake?" she said, smiling a little too sweetly at me. "There's fresh tea in the kettle. You have a cup of your own, don't you?" She nodded at a small tin kettle sitting on a flat rock near the fire. Steam curled from the spout.

Yes, I did have a cup, even if I hadn't thought of bringing frying pans and kettles and sausages and potatoes. No wonder Rose had sounded like a bear, crashing through the thicket with that load. I couldn't think how she had made it all the way here from Baur Kensie.

"Where did you get all this stuff?" I asked. I could tell it wasn't my mother's frying pan she had pinched.

"Nico helped me," she said.

"Nico? *Nico* helped you?" I stared at her in disbelief. Why on earth would Nico help Rose run away from home—which in effect was what she had done? Mama certainly hadn't given her permission.

"He said that if we were to rescue Dina, there had to be at least one person along with a bit of practical common sense."

"You aren't rescuing anybody," I said. "You're going home."

"Before or after breakfast?" she said, smiling again—even more sweetly than before. And my stomach was no help at all, choosing to growl loudly just then.

"Breakfast?" muttered Black-Arse, sitting up sleepily. "Is breakfast ready?" And then he caught sight of Rose, and his face lit in a brilliant smile.

"Rose! And ye have cooked sausages! I thought we were in for the oatmeal again." He made it sound as if she had saved him from a fate worse than death.

We drank the tea and ate the sausages and the fried potatoes. At first I was determined not to eat any. Then I had just a bite. And then the rest of my share, seeing that she had already made it. It tasted wonderful.

"But don't think you and your frying pan can make me change my mind," I said around a mouthful of sausage. "Once we've eaten, you're going home!"

Rose made a skeptical little sound. "You know what Nico said? He said that a frying pan might be more use to us than a sword."

"I'm sure he did," I said sourly. Nico didn't think much of swords. "But you're still going home!"

We packed our stuff. Mathias finished his in seconds. It took me and Black-Arse a bit longer, and Rose, of course, finished last, what with all the gear she had to clean and put away.

"Black-Arse, will you see that Rose gets home?" I asked.

"Aye," said Black-Arse. "If that's what ye want. But I had reckoned on riding with ye yet a while."

"Don't trouble yourself for my sake," Rose told him. "I'll be fine on my own." She threaded her arms though the carrying straps of the basket and levered herself upright. It was so large that when you saw her from behind, she was really just a basket with legs.

"Can you find your own way back?" I asked.

"Don't trouble yourself," she repeated, and I quite realized that she had not agreed to go home. But if nothing else, at least we could outride her. With that load, she had not the slightest hope of keeping up with three riders, and sooner or later she would have to give up and go back. And it was better, anyway, than manhandling her onto Black-Arse's horse by main force.

"Let's get going," I said, mounting Hella. And so we rode on. And of course Rose followed.

"She's followin' us," said Black-Arse after a bit.

"I know," I said through clenched teeth. "She'll soon get tired of that."

I could hear her behind us. The basket clanked at every step she took, making me think of frying pans and teakettles. And sausages and fried potatoes. But I refused to look back.

Time marched on, and so did Rose. Mile by mile she followed us, farther and farther behind, until we could see her only on the longest straight bits of the road, a tiny toiling ant on the horizon. A tiny ant with a very large basket.

"Are ye not goin' to wait for her?" asked Black-Arse.

"No," I said, my teeth now clenched so hard it made my jaw hurt. "She said she could manage on her own, and she will have to do just that. If we help her, we'll never get rid of her."

"Aye, but . . . after all, she is . . . well, she is a *girl*."

"So?"

"So nothing," muttered Black-Arse. But he kept turning his head even though Rose was now completely out of sight. I knew how he felt—just knowing she was there gave you an odd sort of prickling at the back of your neck.

It was hot, and we were all sweaty, men and horses both. The road wasn't much—barely a cart track—but the ground was so dry that yellow dust rose in little bursts at every step, layering itself on the horses' legs and bellies and on my own damp skin. Irritating little black flies kept buzzing around us, and Hella was constantly shaking her head and swishing her tail to be rid of them. I tried not to think of Rose toiling along with her heavy basket, but it wasn't easy.

"There's a stream up ahead," said Black-Arse. "Can we not halt there? I'm all over dust."

Mathias nodded silently. And soon after that, a stream did appear. The horses stopped without any signals from us and buried their dust-streaked muzzles in the cool water. Gratefully, I got down and splashed water on my face and at the back of my neck. Black-Arse simply dipped his entire head and then shook himself like a dog, spraying water everywhere from his thick mane of red hair.

Mathias dug out his dented pot and filled it with water. Then he poured oatmeal into it, stirred, and left it to steep in the sun.

"Aren't you going to heat that?" I asked, eyeing the watery gray mush.

"No need," said Mathias, and lay down in the shade of a birch. "Just wait." He tipped his old greasy leather hat so that it covered his eyes and appeared to fall asleep instantly. No wonder, I thought, he had just said four whole words in succession. That must be downright tiring for a man like him.

Black-Arse peered into the pot.

"Oatmeal again?" he said sadly.

I nodded.

Black-Arse heaved a sigh and looked even sadder. "Is there not a bit of sausage left?"

"No," I said. "But you have no reason to complain. Oatmeal is excellent and nourishing food for travelers. And practical too. Look, you don't even have to heat it." I gave the contents of the pot a stir. The oatmeal flakes had already begun to soak and swell. In an hour's time the porridge would be quite edible. More or less.

Mathias obviously was not going anywhere anytime soon, so I pulled off my boots and dangled my feet in the stream. Black-Arse wandered about a bit and returned with a few blueberries. They were very tart and not quite ripe yet, but at least they cleared the taste of travel dust from my mouth.

About an hour later we were getting stuck into the oatmeal. It had not been particularly exciting the day before, and now, served cold, it was even less of a thrill. The oatmeal had gone mushy and water-soaked without really turning into porridge, and we had neither honey nor apples, nor anything else, to sweeten it. Mathias strewed a little salt on his and passed the bag silently to me. It improved matters slightly. Very slightly. I wolfed down my share anyway, both because I was hungry and because I wanted to get us back on the road. Unless we got moving soon, Rose would—

"Hello."

I turned. I wouldn't have thought she could catch up with us this quickly, but there she was, absolutely plastered with sweat and dust. She had to lean forward to balance the weight of the basket, and her braids swung from side to side at every step. But her smile was triumphant.

Black-Arse positively lit up when he saw her.

"Hello," he called. "D'ye have any more of that sausage?"

"No," said Rose. "But there's a bit of cheese if you want."

Black-Arse leaped to his feet. "Oh, aye," he said. "Thank ye. Let me give ye a hand with that." He practically ran to get the basket from her and carry it the last bit of the way. And soon he and Mathias and Rose were filling their bellies with cheese and bread.

"Are you sure you don't want any, Davin?" asked Rose sweetly, holding out a slice of fat yellow cheese.

"No, thanks," I muttered darkly. "I've just had my oatmeal. And anyway, shouldn't we get moving? I do actually have things to do."

"No need to rush so," said Black-Arse, biting into his bread and cheese and gazing at Rose all the while as if she was an angel descended from heaven just for him. The way to Black-Arse's heart definitely went through his stomach. And when we finally did ride on, Black-Arse went last, and it wasn't long before Rose's basket had somehow ended up on Black-Arse's horse.

At first I pretended not to see. But when I looked back a bit later to see that she was now riding double with him, it was too much.

"Let her down," I said angrily. "This is not a picnic, and we're not bringing any girls!"

"She can ride with me until I turn back, can't she?" said Black-Arse and gave me a glare almost as defiant as Rose's. "And anyway, who said you could decide who gets to ride on my horse?"

It was hopeless, that much I could see. I could yell at them and kick up a fuss, but it wouldn't do any good. Rose did exactly as she pleased, and, apparently, so did Black-Arse. I might as well face it—Callan might be a born leader, but I clearly was not.

"All right," I said. "But only until you turn back. And that's final!"

"Oh, aye," said Black-Arse. But Rose said nothing at

all, and I thought darkly that she would no doubt stay with me like a persistent tick all the way down to the Lowlands, with or without Black-Arse, with or without a horse.

That night Rose made rabbit stew, from a small brown rabbit Black-Arse killed with his slingshot. He skinned it and cleaned it for her, and she brought out onions and dried mushrooms from the depths of the basket. Nobody mentioned oatmeal.

Serving the Dragon

Getting into Dracana was not easy.

"Move your elbow," I hissed at Black-Arse once the Dragon patrol had gone by. "That's my rib!"

Black-Arse moved his elbow, and a bit later the rest of his bony body. It was a relief to sit up. Strange that someone so thin could be that heavy.

"That was close," said Rose. She too got up slowly and began picking pine needles out of her shawl. "Do you realize we nearly got caught this time?"

She glared at me as though it was my fault.

"If you can't stand the heat, feel free to leave," I snapped. "I'm not keeping you!" As a matter of fact I had done everything I could to be rid of her, but it was like picking burrs out of sheep wool.

"Boys!" she said, rolling her eyes. "Why do they always turn everything into a pissing contest?"

There was a funny sound from Black-Arse, halfway between a giggle and a gasp. He probably didn't know a lot of girls who talked like that. Rose put a hand on his arm. "Not you, Allin," she said. "I didn't mean you. You're different, and that's the good thing about you."

Black-Arse managed to smile nervously and look embarrassed at the same time. It was enough to make you puke. Couldn't he see that she was twisting him around her little finger? Calling him Allin, for instance, when everybody else said Black-Arse. And the food. She kept serving him little tidbits and generally carried on like he was a prince of the blood royal. And it worked. He helped her all the time, letting her ride his horse, carrying that ridiculous basket for her, finding pine boughs and soft grasses for her to sleep on. Without him I would have been rid of her long since. And now she had even managed to lure him into the Lowlands.

It was all very irritating, but right now I had troubles far more important. Ever since we parted company with Mathias two days ago, we had been trying to sneak up on Dracana without being seen, and the closest we had ever come was the ridge we were hiding behind right now, well over a mile from the waterwheels and the houses down there. Dragon soldiers positively swarmed around Dracana, and I didn't see how we would ever manage to cross that last bit of open land, to say nothing of sneaking through the camp around the town and finding a way to get over the wall or through the gate. The patrol that had just missed us had come so close that I could have reached out and touched the leg of one horse—assuming I had wanted to, that is, and if Black-Arse hadn't ended up lying on top of me in the patch of ferns we had flung ourselves into to avoid being seen.

"What if they find the horses?" asked Rose, watching worriedly as the patrol made its way across that last irritating bit of open field.

"We lose two good horses. *And* they'll know that someone is sneaking about out here."

"We can't go on like this! We have to come up with a plan."

"Certainly, Madam Mastermind. Any ideas?"

"If we can't get in without them seeing us, why don't we *let* them see us?"

"Oh, brilliant. Let me see, we march up to the gate in full daylight and make a few polite inquiries—'Pardon me, Sir Dragon Knight, but do you happen to keep my sister Dina captive?' Yes, that would do the trick."

"Numbskull. That's not what I meant. But there are people down there, right? People who work in those mill houses. Ordinary people. Perhaps we can get them to hire us. And once we're in, it becomes a lot easier to ask around, doesn't it? And we might not even have to ask. Someone like Dina is . . . rather noticeable. People would talk."

It pained me to admit it, but it actually wasn't a bad plan. At any rate, I couldn't come up with anything better.

"All right," I finally said. "Let's give it a try."

We left Black-Arse and the horses in the woods a fair distance from the town. It would be better to arrive on foot, we thought. Most of the people we had seen on the road did. At least the ones not wearing Dragon tunics.

Black-Arse had not wanted to be left behind.

"Why do I have to stay here? Why can the three of us not go together?"

"Someone has to take care of the horses," I said. "And if things go wrong, someone needs to ride back to the Highlands and tell Kensie and . . . and the others." If things really did go wrong, I pitied whoever had to tell my mother. I hoped it wouldn't be Black-Arse.

"But how will I know if ye're all right? How will I know anything at all?"

"Every evening you go to that ridge where we were yesterday," said Rose. "If one of us can get to you, we will. But if not—" she rummaged in her basket—"look. My red scarf. You should be able to see that for some distance. Just before sunrise I'll be in the square down there where you can see me. If I'm wearing the scarf, everything's fine. If I'm not—well, you get on that horse of yours and go tell everyone where we are."

So here we were, trudging along in the noonday heat, while Black-Arse was hiding somewhere in the dense pine forest. I was carrying Rose's enormous basket.

"Why did you have to bring all that rubbish?" I complained.

"You never know when you'll need a good frying pan," she said. "But if it's too heavy for you, I'll take it."

Over my dead body. "No, I'm fine." No way would I admit how heavy the thing felt, or how the straps were chafing my shoulders. I was still wondering how she had managed to get it as far as she had before Black-Arse started being her Parfit Helpful Knight.

There was a drumming of hooves behind us, and I turned to look. A troop of Dragon riders were approaching, galloping at full stretch. Rose and I had to leap aside, into the ditch. Not to hide, this time, but simply to avoid being trampled. The riders barely glanced at us and certainly didn't slow down any. We were pelted with dirt and pine needles as they went past.

"Damn. Now my feet are wet," said Rose.

So were mine. It had rained last night, and the ditch was still full of rainwater. And I now had a big brown stain on my shirt where a clod of earth had struck me, right in the middle of my chest.

We climbed back onto the road.

"That was rude," said Rose, giving the already distant riders the kind of glare she usually reserved for me.

"What did you expect?" I said. "They're Dragon soldiers."

"That doesn't mean they can just trample people."

I shrugged. "Come on. Let's get it over with."

Close up, Dracana didn't look that awe-inspiring. It had walls, but they were nowhere near as tall and massive as those of Skayark. There were towers—one on either side of the river—but they were just wooden, hardly more than crow's nests meant for lookouts. Yet my heart was definitely beating at more than its regular rate.

"Name?" barked the guard at the gate.

"Martin Kerk," I lied. It would have been a bad idea to call ourselves Rose and Davin Tonerre. "And this is my sister, May."

Rose had teased me when she heard what I wanted to call myself. "Martin?" she had said. "Do you reckon that makes you just as tough as the Weapons Master?"

Heat had rushed into my cheeks.

"That's just a coincidence," I had said. "Martin is a perfectly ordinary name. It has nothing to do with him." But it had.

"What's your business?" asked the guard.

"Work, good sir. We heard there might be work for us here."

"There *might* be," he said, mustering us coolly. "But not for every drifter that comes calling."

"But we—"

"Save it, lad. It's not me you have to convince." He put his head through the door to the guard room and yelled. "Arno! Take these two to the Hire-Master."

The Hire-Master sat at a desk, writing long lists.

"Name?" he said, not looking up.

"Martin Kerk. But I already told—"

"And the girl?"

"Ro—erh, May. May Kerk. My sister. But—"

"Can she weave?"

"Yes. That is, I—" I nearly said, *I think so,* but caught myself in time. If Rose was my sister, I would know, wouldn't I? But we hadn't had a loom during the year Rose had stayed with us.

"I'm an excellent weaver, sir," said Rose, very polite, very subservient. I hardly recognized her.

"Hmm. And you, boy. Any weapon skills?"

"A bit, but—"

"But you don't have a sword?"

"It . . . got broken. But—"

"I see. You had better be more careful with the gear you

are issued here." The Hire-Master scratched our names on one of his lists and held out the pen to me. "Here. Put down your mark. If you can't write, a cross will do."

I made a cross. Most commoners were unable to write, and it was better not to draw attention.

"You report to the Blue Banner just outside the gate. The girl goes to the mill house over there, the door with the green letters on it."

"But . . ."

"Yes?"

"I thought . . . we want to work in the mill house. Both of us."

"No. They only take women and children there. What is it with you, boy? Too good for the Dragon Force? Or too cowardly?"

A bitter taste was in my mouth, but what could I do?

"No," I said, trying to look eager. "I'd like to be a Dragon soldier. Sir."

"Good, then. Dismissed."

"Damn," I cursed under my breath, once we had left the Hire-Master's office. "Damn and blast. I'll end up on the wrong side of the wall! *And* in Drakan's filthy uniform!"

"Yes," said Rose, giving me a quick farewell peck on the cheek—mostly for the benefit of the gate guard, I think. "So it's a good thing that you brought me along—isn't it?"

• • •

I didn't see Rose until two days later, a little after sunset.

"Hello, brother dear." Her voice sounded worn and strange, and at first I nearly didn't recognize her. Her fair hair was mostly hidden by a black scarf, and she was wearing a gray skirt and blouse I had never seen before. Around her neck was the red scarf that told Black-Arse that everything was all right, but that was the only bit of color on her. Her shoulders drooped tiredly, and she stood holding her elbows as if she were afraid that her arms would drop off.

"Hello, sweet sister," I said, lowering my own sore arms. In front of me hung what seemed to me an endless row of saddles and bridles, waiting to be cleaned and oiled and polished. Since noon, the Tack-Master had had me under his wing, or, more accurately, under his boot. My shoulders hurt so badly I wanted to scream, and my fingertips were shriveled like prunes and nearly as black. It was not what I had imagined the life of a Dragon soldier to be. But it could be worse. It *had* been worse. The day before I had had to clean the latrines. Those were the sort of heroic tasks newcomers were given.

"Can we walk for a bit?" she asked, with a tired jerk of her head—away from the camp, away from listening ears.

Gloomily I eyed the mountain of tack still waiting for me. The Tack-Master had said I wouldn't be allowed to turn in until I had finished, but at the rate I was going, that wouldn't be much before sunrise. A short walk with Rose wouldn't make much difference one way or the other.

"Yes," I said. "Yes, let's get out of here for a bit."

"Dina is here," Rose said as soon as we were outside the camp. "They talk about her in the mill houses. They are terrified of her, especially the children. He uses her to punish them when they don't do their work as quickly as he wants them to."

"Who? Valdracu?"

Rose nodded. "They talk about her like she's some kind of monster." She looked at me with anxious eyes. "Why does she do it?" she asked. "How does he make her?"

I shook my head silently. I could not imagine how anybody could make Dina do something like that. She would never abuse her gift like that. Only it seemed she had.

"Where is she?" I asked. "Do they talk about that, too?"

"She is up at the big house, the fancy house Valdracu lives in. I thought . . . maybe we could get in there one night? Soon? If I have to work much longer at the mill house, my arms will fall off."

I knew how she felt. I had no desire to spend many more days cleaning tack *or* latrines. "Tonight," I said. "We might as well do it tonight."

Getting past Dracana's walls was my first problem. New recruits were not allowed in town, I had been told. But if nothing else, my cleaning duties had given me an intimate knowledge of the riverbank—I had had to fetch water many, *many* times. The walls went all the way down to the river; but if a man was willing to brave the wild waters of the Eidin, there might be a way around them. Always assuming the river didn't sweep you away and batter you to a pulp against its rocky banks, which was a possibility I tried hard not to think about. And I had brought a precaution: a long rope I had pinched from the Tack-Master's stores. I tied one end of it around my waist and the other around the root of a young pine. With the aid of the rope, I then climbed down the steep cliff and lowered myself into the cold water.

I lost my footing immediately. It was as if a great hand of ice caught me and flung me downstream, in the wrong direction. I had thought I would be able to swim—I was a strong swimmer and I had swum rivers before. But this was nothing like the slow silted waters of the Dun back home in Birches. This was a maelstrom, a wild icy current that sucked me down and tossed me about as if I were a dry leaf in a meltwater brook.

Smack! The river threw me against a boulder, and my shoulder grew instantly numb and dead. If I didn't do something very soon, the rest of me would end up in the same condition. I grabbed the rope and hauled myself back upstream, tug by tug. My fingers were so cold I could barely feel the rough hemp of the rope, and my arms grew weaker and less obedient by the second. I was gasping and puffing like a steer with too heavy a load to pull, but I did finally manage to drag myself out of the water, up the cliff, and back to the pine tree. For a while I just lay there, panting and shivering with cold.

It couldn't be done. Swimming that river was not humanly possible. At least not here, where the current was forceful enough to drive the many waterwheels of Dracana.

I didn't know what else to do. I was soaked to the skin, and if I had ever had a chance of talking my way through the gate with some story, that was certainly gone now. Even the slowest of guards would become suspicious at the sight of a half-drowned water rat like me. And Rose was waiting for me. If I didn't show, she would be anxious. Perhaps scared enough to give the panic signal to Black-Arse tomorrow night.

Could I get past the wall without actually getting into the water? The cliff was very steep, vertical in most places. But perhaps, with the rope . . . it was only a distance of about twenty paces. It *might* be feasible.

For the second time I slipped over the edge, this time more carefully. I scrambled for a foothold—yes, there was a small crack in the rock, just big enough for me to dig my toes into. I let go of the rope with one hand and leaned sideways to grab at a tuft of grass growing from another small crack. Carefully, like a crippled spider, I crabbed my way along the bank, upstream, past the walls. I glanced upward. The wall was a massive shadow above me, a jagged black shape against the deep dark blue of the night sky. And at the moment, at least, it was a shape without men on it. So far, no one had seen me.

Suddenly, my right foot slipped, and for a moment I dangled helplessly, clinging to the rock face with rigid fingers. A shower of pebbles clattered into the deep, but luckily the rush of the water was loud enough to cover such small noises. I scrabbled about, found another foothold. If only I had thought to take off my boots before starting the climb. Bare feet would have been better. A mixture of sweat and river water trickled down my face, and I had to blink it out of my eyes. A small shelf to stand on . . . a sapling willow to clutch. I looked up again. Yes, I was past the walls. Now all I had to do was get back up onto properly dry land.

It sounded easy, didn't it? But suddenly I was stuck. I couldn't find purchase in any direction. I raked the rock face with my hands, and got nothing for my trouble except some scratches and a cracked nail. The rope was no good to me now, fastened as it was on the wrong side of the wall, and try as I might I couldn't find a way to move upward. My fingers hurt, and my shoulders shook from the strain. If I couldn't find a way to move on, I could only cling here until my strength gave out and I fell. And then I would have to start over—always assuming I didn't break a bone or two in the fall.

"Davin?"

It was just a whisper, so low I could barely hear it above the noise of the river. I looked up. A face was peering over the edge of the cliff, pale and round in the moonlight. It was Rose.

"Can't you get up?"

How amazingly observant of her.

"No," I spat. "If I could, I'd be doing it, wouldn't I?"

Rose held out her hand, but we were too far apart. And come to think of it, that was probably a good thing. I was a great deal heavier than Rose, and pulling her over the edge too would not have been the smartest of moves.

"Wait," she said. "My apron . . . perhaps you can reach that."

"Tie it to something," I said, trying to ignore the burning sensation in my fingers. They had become hooked and rigid claws, and I was beginning to think I'd never be able to straighten them again.

Something soft brushed my hand—one of the strings from Rose's apron. Would it hold my weight? There was nothing for it but to try. I couldn't cling here much longer. Cautiously I let go of my left handhold and clutched at the apron string. I tugged at it; there was some give to it, but it seemed to be holding. And it was not that far to the edge. I let go of my other handhold as well and clung to the apron for dear life.

"Come *on*, Davin," hissed Rose from the edge, and there was such a panic in her voice that I felt sure some guard was approaching. I wiggled and squirmed, clawing my way up the apron, hand over hand. Then Rose seized me by the collar and hauled me onto level ground, like a fisherman landing a flounder.

"Quick," she whispered, "someone's coming!"

She didn't even take the time to undo the knot, she just sliced through the apron string with a quick slash of her knife. Then she took off at a hunched run, nearly soundless in her stockinged feet. Breathing hard, I got up and tried to follow her, but an almighty jerk made me lose my balance and nearly sent me right over the edge again. In my haste, I had forgotten about the rope still tied to my waist.

"Come on!" Rose hissed furiously from the shadows, and now I too could hear the tread of booted feet. I cut myself free, tossed the rope over the edge, and ran after her as silently as I could.

A Family Outing

Among all the dark wooden buildings, the white walls of the big house glowed like pearl in the moonlight. The windows were dark, though, and I devoutly hoped everyone there was tucked up in bed and sleeping very soundly.

"Do you think there are guards?" Rose whispered.

"Can't see any. They guard the mill houses and the forges, and of course the storehouses, but maybe they don't think anyone is stupid enough to try to rob Valdracu's personal residence."

We were crouching behind a woodpile by the end of the stable. Above us an elder tree spread its branches, and the smell from its white flowers tickled my nose, sweet and bitter at the same time. It made me feel like sneezing.

"Well?" said Rose. "Do we go in?"

I hesitated. "We don't know where they keep her. We might end up opening every door in the place just to find her."

"Do you have a better plan?"

"No," I admitted.

"Well, come on then."

"Wait a moment," I said. "I want my boots off, at least."

I pulled off my slopping wet boots and hid them behind a few logs. The earth felt cold and damp beneath my feet, but barefoot I would be able to move more silently. Bad enough that I left a dripping trail like some forest slug; I didn't have to be a noisy slug. Should I take off the wet tunic of my Dragon uniform? No, at least it was black. With my pale chest I would light up the dark like a ghost.

There were some wide stone steps in front of the house, but sauntering up to the main entrance seemed a bit too foolhardy.

"There," I said. "The door at the end."

It was Rose's turn to hesitate.

"What do you think they'll do to us if they catch us?" she asked, a slight tremor in her voice.

"How would I know?" I said a bit more sharply than I meant to. "These are Drakan's people. We had better *not* get caught."

Rose muttered something about being able to figure that one out for herself. I didn't catch all of it, but the word *numbskull* stood out quite clearly. Strange—somehow it was almost comforting to bicker with Rose in the middle of all the danger and tension; it was almost like home.

"Wait here," I told her. "I'll see if it's locked."

I poked my head out from behind the woodpile, looking left and right. Not a soul. Taking a deep breath, I dashed across the cobblestones on my bare feet and ducked into the shadow cast by the gable wall of the big house. I lifted the latch and gave the door a very gentle push. It opened. No locks, no bars. I suppose if you have half the Dragon Force guarding your doorstep, locking the doors seems unnecessary.

I slowly pushed the door all the way open. At first I could see nothing whatsoever, but once my eyes got used to the darkness, vague shapes began to appear. None of them looked like people, and the only sound I heard was a slow, wet dripping. Tentatively, I moved forward—and took a nosedive. I slammed facedown onto a very hard floor with enough force to rattle my teeth. I didn't even have enough breath to curse with. Who the hell put stairs *inside* the door instead of outside? Whoever built this house, apparently. I had fallen down three worn steps onto the smooth, cool flagstoned floor of . . . of what? There was a soapy, wet, and slightly mildewed smell. A bathhouse? No, a laundry cellar. I could see the huge coppers now, big basins that one could light a fire under so that all the sheets and linens could actually be laundered in hot water. A bit more fancy than taking the washing down to the stream the way we did at home. But then, the whole house was a far cry from our cottage. Had I ever been in a house this big before? Only Helena Laclan's came anywhere near it.

Suddenly I remembered the chamber at Baur Laclan so vividly that I might still be in it. The chamber, and Callan staring down at his feet and telling me that they would drag the pond at first light. I could feel tears prickling at the corners of my eyes and blinked furiously. How stupid to sit here nearly bawling when I knew Dina was alive and not drowned, that she was *here,* in this house, and that I would soon find her. I wiped my eyes on my wet sleeve, climbed to my feet, and went out to get Rose.

"Mind the steps," I warned her.

She cautiously took the steps one by one.

"What is this?" she whispered.

"A laundry," I said.

"Hmm," she snorted. "Fancy place."

We sneaked through the laundry, up a few steps, and through a door into a large kitchen. There was a fire still glowing in the iron stove, and a rich and yeasty smell filled the air. Someone had left a pan of bread dough to rise, ready for the morning's baking.

In the darkness I bumped into a table, and there was a clatter of pans and pottery.

"Ssshh!" Rose hushed me.

I stood frozen for a moment, listening. The house was quiet; no steps or voices anywhere, no sounds at all except—was that someone snoring? Yes. A gentle fluttering snore, someplace near.

Rose grasped my arm and pulled me along, through the

kitchen and out through a door at the end. Immediately, I could feel that this was a different kind of room, big and empty and with a ceiling so high it vanished in the darkness far above our heads. Through big bay windows, moonlight fell on a floor tiled in black and white, and a tall curving staircase wound its way upward into the darkness.

"The cook often sleeps next to the kitchen," Rose whispered. "That was probably her. I think we need to go up. Servants usually live in the attic rooms in houses like this, and I don't suppose they'll have given her one of the master bedrooms."

"How do you know all that?" I asked.

"The people Ma does laundry for live in houses like this," she said. "Well? Do we go on? Or are there any more pots you'd like to break?"

"They didn't break," I muttered. That girl could be such a pain. And yet, although I was not about to admit it to her, I was glad she was with me right now.

We climbed the stairs slowly, hoping the steps wouldn't creak. When we reached the first landing I hesitated, but Rose pointed upward.

"All the way up," she said, "to the attic."

We climbed two more flights of stairs, the last one cruder and narrower than the ones farther down. Up here the darkness was nearly total; there weren't any windows with fancy glass panes in them, just shuttered slits that let in only the faintest traces of moonlight around the edges.

I halted because I couldn't see where I was going. Rose bumped into me and had to clutch at my arm to keep from falling. But for once there were no sharp remarks, and even after she had regained her balance she kept holding on to me.

There was a drawn-out eerie squeak, like the ones bats make when they fly.

"What was that?" breathed Rose.

"Someone sleeping?" I suggested. "People make the weirdest noises when they sleep."

"It sounded more like a bat," she said. It seemed to frighten her more than the fact that we might be about to trip over a sleeping Dragon soldier. Girls are strange.

It was hard to decide exactly where the sound was coming from. I stuck out a cautious foot, took a step, and then another . . . I still couldn't see a thing. I held one hand out in front of me and fumbled along the wall with the other. My fingers brushed some rough boards, and then something softer, like sacking. A curtain of some kind. The bat sound came from the space behind the curtain, I was pretty sure. It didn't sound like Dina, but then there might be more than one person sleeping in there. I gently pushed the curtain aside and peered into the alcove. There was slightly more light here because one of the shutters hung ajar, and I could just make out a body, much too large and coarse to be Dina's.

At that moment, the bat squeak stopped. I froze in the

middle of a movement. Sleep on, I prayed, sleep, there's nobody here. Just sleep.

The man stirred, making the bedboards creak. My heart skipped a beat. But he didn't sit up. I lowered the curtain again with infinite slowness. Just as slowly, Rose and I crept back the way we had come. We stood on the stairs for a while, listening. Still nothing. He really must be sleeping still, I thought.

"I don't think Dina is up there," I told Rose as quietly as possible, putting my mouth right next to her ear.

"We only looked behind one curtain," she whispered back to me. "There might be more."

"That was no servant girl," I said. "That was a Dragon soldier."

"So? Maybe he's guarding her."

"A bit inattentive for a guard, isn't he?"

For a moment it seemed that Rose would keep arguing. Then she heaved a discouraged sigh.

"Where else can we look?" she asked. "There's got to be dozens of rooms in a house this size."

"I just thought of something," I said. "Maybe we don't have to open every door to every room. Maybe we just have to find the one that's locked."

We found a locked door on the first floor—clearly locked from outside, too, as the key was still in the lock.

"This must be it," I said, my mouth suddenly gone dry. "Who else would they be locking up?"

"Open it," snapped Rose, sharp with impatience. "Don't just stand there, open it!"

I unlocked the door. Opened it.

It was nearly as dark in there as it had been in the attic. There were windows, large ones with plenty of glass panes, but they were mostly covered by heavy, dark curtains. When I took a step into the room, my bare foot all but disappeared into thick furry carpeting; it was like stepping on something live.

I stood there uncertainly, trying to get my bearings. It didn't seem like the kind of room you would give a prisoner. On the other hand, the door *had* been locked. And like I said, who else would they lock up?

I could make out a very large bed hung with velvet curtains.

"Dina?" I whispered tentatively. No one answered. I drew back the curtain, but the bed was clearly empty.

And then I saw her. Curled up on the window seat, half hidden by the heavy drapes. I knew at once it was she, even though all I could see was a slight figure in a long white nightgown.

I crossed the room in three steps. And then I stopped, suddenly afraid to touch her, as if she might vanish between my fingers like a ghost.

"Dina . . ."

She opened her eyes and blinked sleepily.

"Davin," she said in a totally ordinary voice, as if there were nothing strange about my being there. "Is it time to"— and then she stiffened and came fully awake—"*Davin!*"

She leaped to her feet and wrapped her arms around my neck, clinging so hard I could barely breathe. She was thinner than she used to be, but apart from that she seemed all right.

I can't begin to tell how it felt. As if I had finally fought my way out of a nightmare. As if I had been broken inside, and now wasn't. And at the same time, I was absolutely furious with her. Don't ask me why. For a moment it was as if everything, every awful moment we had had, Mama and Melli and Rose and me, as if that was all Dina's fault.

"Where have you *been*?" I whispered, hanging on to her as if I were afraid she'd run away. "Do you *realize* how frightened we've been?"

She pulled in a shuddering breath, like a sob.

"Don't be mad," she said, and her voice was hoarse with tears. "Davin, please don't be mad at me."

And of course then I felt like the world's biggest ass and the worst big brother anyone had ever had. After everything she had been through . . . and then, when I finally found her, I made her cry.

"Ssshh," I said, resting my cheek against her hair. "Shush. Stop it. I found you, didn't I?" I offered her my sleeve. "Here. Dry your eyes."

She put her hand on my arm. And then choked on a kind of weepy giggle.

"Davin," she said. "It's soaking wet. How do you expect me to dry anything with that?"

She was right, of course. The sleeve was as wet as the rest of me.

"You can have my handkerchief," said Rose.

"Rose!" Dina let go of me and hugged Rose instead. "What are you doing here? Both of you. How did you ever find me?"

"Oh, it was . . . teamwork, really," said Rose. Even in the dark I caught her teasing smile—a quick white flash of teeth. Then she became serious again. "But Dina, we've got to hurry now. We've got to get out of here before someone sees us."

Dina let go of Rose. Suddenly she looked utterly miserable.

"I can't," she said in a curiously dead voice.

"*What?*" Rose and I were almost a chorus.

"I can't come with you."

I was stunned. "What do you mean, 'can't'? Of course you can!"

She shook her head. "No. If I . . . if I don't . . . if I run away, he'll kill Tavis."

"Tavis?" For the moment, I had completely forgotten who that was.

"Tavis Laclan. The boy who was with me."

Of course. Helena Laclan's grandchild. His mother had hit me on the forehead with the Black Hand. *Ye came to take a life,* she had said.

"Where is he?" I asked.

"In the cellar," she said, "beneath the stable."

"I suppose we had better go get him, then."

Little Tavis Laclan was not exactly happy to see us. You would have thought we had come to cut his throat, not rescue him.

At first we could neither see him nor hear him in the dark cellar. There was a lantern hanging on a nail by the trapdoor, but we were afraid to light it. If anyone saw the glow of it and came to investigate, we would be caught like rats in a trap. There was only one way out of this place; all anybody had to do was bolt the hatch, and we would be finished. "Tavis," Dina called quietly, "are you awake?"

There was a rustle from somewhere, like an animal stirring up its bedding.

"What do ye want?" came a voice from the darkness, sulky and scared. "Stay away from me, ye filthy traitor. Ye'll not get any secrets out of me!"

Filthy traitor? Who did he think he was, talking to my sister like that? I waited for Dina to say something, but she just stood there, and I could hear from her breathing that she was about to cry again. That made me really angry.

"Listen, you little brat," I snapped, "don't you ever talk—"

But Dina put her hand on my arm and brought me up short. "Be quiet, Davin," she whispered. "There are . . . things you don't know."

What did she mean? Something had happened to her, I could feel it. She didn't seem . . . she didn't seem like herself, somehow. What had those bastards done to her?

"We've come to get you out, Tavis," she said. There was a scraping of wood on wood as Dina unbolted the front end of the crate they kept him in. "Come on," she said, "we're going home."

Right then somebody started singing. I nearly leaped a foot; and I did manage to crack my head on a roof beam.

"Long is the road and narrow the path / Heavy the heart that is forced to roam / Always we yearn for the warming hearth / To know we are safe, to know we are home."

A grating, snuffling voice. Certainly not Tavis. The voice of a madman, I thought. Normal people didn't sound like that.

"Oh," Dina sighed, "I forgot about him."

"Who? *Who,* Dina? Who is he?"

"A tramp. That is . . . not really. It's a long story. But, Davin, we have to take him with us."

"Dina . . . we can't—I mean, anybody can hear that he's

not right in the head. We'll never get him past the guards at the gate. Or through the camp, for that matter. He'll give us away." It would be hard enough with Dina and Tavis.

"If we leave him here, Valdracu will kill him." There was a stubborn note in Dina's voice that I knew only too well. "Besides, I don't think he is . . . completely mad. I think he knows enough to be quiet when he has to be."

"Gentle Lady," whispered the eerie, snuffling voice. "In this life, choices are few / A beggar does what a beggar must do."

I fumbled in the dark for the beggar's crate, and my fingers brushed against cold metal. A heavy chain secured the front of the crate.

"Dina, we can't even open the crate! This chain is as thick as my wrist."

Dina came to my side to investigate.

"Forget the chain," she said. "The slats are only wooden. Can't you smash a few of those?"

Who did she think I was? Sir Iron-Fist who could knock a dragon to the ground with his bare hands? Although, on the other hand, she said it as if she thought a big brother ought to be able to do that kind of thing. And the slats *were* only wooden.

"I'll need some light," I said. "I know it's dangerous, but if I can't see what I'm doing I haven't a hope."

"There's a lantern by the hatch," said Dina. "But I don't have a tinderbox."

Neither did I, and if I had, the thing would be soaked.

"I've got one," said Rose.

"Of course you do," I muttered.

We fetched the lamp, and Rose struck a fire and lit the wick. A gentle yellow glow spread through the cellar.

"Rose, will you be lookout? If anyone shows, we have to put out that lantern at once."

Rose nodded. "I'll whistle if anybody comes," she said. "Like this." She pursed her lips, and suddenly it sounded exactly as if there was a blackbird in the cellar. A blackbird who had just caught sight of a cat.

"Where did you learn that?" I said. "It sounds completely . . . it sounds like a real bird."

Rose looked uncomfortable. "Oh, I just . . . practiced." She turned and climbed rapidly up the ladder.

"Why was she suddenly in such a rush?" I asked.

Dina smiled, a very pale, faint smile. "This might not be the first time Rose has been the lookout," she said.

And then I remembered where Rose used to live. Swill Town. The foulest, poorest part of Dunark. Probably half the people there had to pilfer and smuggle to survive, and I bet Rose's bastard of an older brother had not belonged to the honest half. Forcing his sister to act as lookout while he did his illegal "business" would be all in a day's work for him.

"Raise the lantern," I told Dina.

She did. I considered the crate. The slats were about two hands apart, and the beggar was a skinny creature. I didn't think we would need to break more than one. I drew back, balancing on one leg, and kicked as hard as I could. I didn't get much for my pains, apart from a sore heel and a couple of splinters. My boots were still where I had left them in the woodpile at the end of the stable, and right now I missed them.

"Damn!" I clenched my teeth and tried again. Same result.

"This is no good," I said, rubbing my heel. "The only thing that is getting broken here is me."

"Give me your knife," said Dina. "If we can weaken it a bit . . ."

"Get Rose's," I said. "It's sharper."

Dina disappeared up the ladder. I got out my own knife and worked at the slat, shaving curls of wood off it. I wasn't making much headway. The tramp squatted on the floor inside the crate, eyeing my lack of progress with a jaundiced eye. I wished he would find something else to do. Sweat was running into my eyes, even though it was quite chilly in the damp cellar. We had Rose to warn us, but still, if someone saw the light and got to the hatch before we did . . .

Dina came back.

"Here." She handed me Rose's knife—small, rusty, but extremely sharp. She got mine in return, and we both carved away at the slat. Shavings fluttered to the floor.

"Hurry," said Tavis. Apparently we weren't filthy traitors anymore. "Hurry up!"

"I'm going as fast as I can," I said through clenched teeth. My wrist was sore already from the carving, and the back of my neck had become one big anxious knot, almost as if I was expecting someone to seize me by the scruff of it any moment.

"Try again," said Dina. "It's much thinner now."

I tried again. And at my second kick, the wood splintered and cracked. We still had to twist and pull at the slat, but finally we had an opening big enough for the skinny tramp to slip through. And still there were no warning blackbird calls from Rose.

I helped the tramp to his feet. Even in the faint glow of the lamp he kept blinking.

"Humble thanks," he muttered. "Humble thanks to the noble sir."

He looked pitiful. He was absolutely filthy, and even through the stench of decaying beets one could smell his body. There were streaks of crusted blood on his face, and his nose and chin were so swollen that it was little wonder he slurred and snuffled. Clearly he had been beaten—badly beaten. He stood clutching the wall, looking like he would fall over if he let go.

I eyed my little flock of freed prisoners. Small pale Tavis. Dina, hanging her head as if she never wanted to look anyone in the eye again. And the battered scarecrow figure of the tramp. I'd never get that lot through the gate.

"It's no good," I told Dina. "You I might get through the gate somehow. But three! It's hopeless."

Dina shook her head. "No," she said. "I know a place. A secret door."

She hung her head even more. I didn't understand— why should she feel so ashamed?

"Great," I said. "Where?"

"We'll have to go back to the house," she said.

Not exactly the escape route of my choice. A house full of sleeping Dragon soldiers. Or perhaps a house full of Dragon soldiers who were not sleeping quite so heavily anymore.

"Can't we just go around it?"

"No," she said. "We need to get into the Rose Court."

The Rose Court? It made no particular sense to me.

"Are you sure?"

"I found it yesterday," she said in a tired voice. "The door, I mean. When you go through it, you get to a meadow, and on the other side of the meadow lies the wood. No walls, no guards. You can walk right into the forest."

Why didn't you? I thought, but I didn't say it out loud. I suppose the thing with Tavis had stopped her.

"All right," I said. "Let's give it a try."

· · ·

It felt completely crazy to break out of Dracana by breaking into a house. All five of us. I only hoped the half-mad tramp would keep his mouth shut. If he began on his silly rhymes while we were inside the house, I'd clobber him with my boots. I had collected them on the way from behind the woodpile, but I hadn't put them on yet—silence was more important than ever now.

I led the way into the laundry. I had warned everyone about the steps, and this time nobody fell. Behind me, I could hear the snuffling breath of the tramp, quite loud in the silence, but it couldn't be helped. I could hardly tell him not to breathe.

Cautiously, I opened the door to the kitchen, took a few steps—and stiffened. What was that? Not the gentle snoring of the cook, something else . . . I peered around me in the darkened kitchen but could see only the faint red glow of the stove. Whatever it was I had heard, the place was silent now. Maybe it had been only my imagination. My nerves were worn pretty thin by now.

I fumbled behind me until I found Dina's shoulder, and gave it a little push. Stay back, I meant. She touched my hand to show that she understood. Her fingers were so cold it felt like being touched by a ghost.

I crept forward another few steps. In front of me I could just make out the big table I had bumped into earlier. The glow from the woodstove caught the glaze of some large clay bowls. I paused again to listen, but all I could hear was the tramp's snuffling breath. My own bare feet were completely soundless on the stone floor, and the cook didn't seem to be snoring anymore.

All clear, I thought, and turned to wave the others on.

Turning, I bumped into something.

Something large. Something live.

Startled, I leaped back, knocking into the kitchen table once more. The bowls rattled.

"Ssshh!" hissed whatever I had bumped into. "You'll wake her!"

For a brief confused moment I thought it must be one of the others. But none of them were the height of a bear. None of them had a voice that deep and rough. And now that I had my back to the stove, I could see more clearly, and what I saw was a Dragon soldier. Somewhat negligently dressed, to be sure, with his tunic unbuttoned, a large ham in one hand and a knife in the other, but a soldier nonetheless. Why, then, was he shushing me? Why didn't he raise the alarm?

He seemed confused, too. He peered at me searchingly.

"I don't think I know you," he said. "What are you doing here? What's your unit?"

Of course. I was wearing the Dragon uniform myself. Perhaps he thought I too had come to sneak an illicit slice of ham. But I doubted he would think so much longer— and in the laundry waited four others who would definitely not be mistaken for Dragon's men.

I swung a boot and hit him straight on the nose.

"What—" he began, but that was all he had time to say. I got him by the wrist with one hand and by the throat with the other, choking off any cry of alarm he might try to make. He crashed backward with me on top of him, but after that, matters went from bad to worse. There was that knife of his, and I didn't dare let go of his throat; one shout out of him and we were finished. And then he started hitting me with the ham. *Whack!* Pinpoints of light danced in front of my eyes. He kept pounding me with that stupid hunk of dead pig, and my grip started to slip, and in any case he was stronger than I. He twisted free of me and drew a deep breath.

"Guaahh—" he began. But that was as far as he got. There was a curious ringing sound, like someone hitting a gong. And then he collapsed across me like a butchered steer. Only then did I see what Rose held in her hands.

"I told you so," she said a little breathlessly. "A frying pan always comes in handy."

Dina looked down at the fallen Dragon soldier.

"It's Sandor," she said in a low voice, and looked as if she wanted to spit on him. "Valdracu's henchman. Is he dead?"

I touched his neck. He was warm, and I could feel the pulse moving beneath his skin.

"No," I said, "just unconscious."

"Stick him," hissed Tavis. "Stab him with your knife!"

That shook me. What was he—eight? Nine? And here he was, wanting me to stick a knife into an unconscious man. I had no idea Highland children were that blood-thirsty. But I supposed he had his reasons. The cellar we had taken him from had not exactly been pleasant lodgings.

"No," I said. "We'll tie him up. Get a clothesline or something from the laundry and— Is there a pantry or something?" I looked at Dina.

"Here," she said, pointing at a hatch in the floor. "There's a small fruit cellar. It'll take them a while to find him if we put him down there."

The cellar was barely big enough for him to lie flat. I pushed a wrinkled winter apple into his mouth and secured it with one of his own socks. Tavis pinched an apple too and started wolfing it down in big bites. Maybe they hadn't fed him too well, either, in that cellar. A small boy doesn't get that vengeful for no reason.

Outside, the birds had begun to sing, and what we could see of the sky through the kitchen windows was no longer black as night. We had to hurry now.

"Bring the ham," I suggested. "It's a long way home, and we need to eat."

I opened the door to the hall with the staircase. And stood stock-still. In front of me was the prettiest girl I had ever seen.

Her hair was black as night and shone like silk. Her eyes were dark, and yet starry bright. Her face was so delicate that one felt it almost couldn't be real, someone had to have painted it. In one slim hand she held a heavy golden candlestick, and her slender body was wrapped in a gleaming blue-green robe with green-and-gold dragons embroidered on the collar.

For a moment we stared at each other, equally stunned, I think. Then she opened her mouth to scream.

"Sascha, listen," said Dina urgently. "You want to be rid of me, don't you?"

The girl hesitated. Then she closed her mouth, nodded, and listened.

"Just pretend you haven't seen us," said Dina persuasively. "Go back to bed. And tomorrow, I won't be here anymore. Everything will be just the way it was for you before I came."

One could almost see the thoughts grinding around in the girl's head, like the gears of a mill. Finally she nodded.

"Go," she said. "Go away. And never come back."

"I promise," Dina said. "I'm never coming back here, not of my own free will." It was obviously not a promise it was difficult to give.

The girl stepped aside to allow us to pass. She seemed a bit startled when she realized how many we were, but she didn't say anything. She just moved to the stairs and started up them, straight-backed and with the candle raised above her head. She looked like a princess.

I wouldn't have thought the tramp could move that fast. But before I'd even realized what he was doing, he was up the stairs. He caught the girl around the waist with one arm and started dragging her down the stairs again. She dropped the candlestick and the flame snuffed out, leaving the hall suddenly dark, but we could hear her struggles and her muffled attempts to cry out. He must have his hand over her mouth.

"What are you doing?" I hissed. "Let go of her! She was going to let us leave!"

The beggar shook his head and did not ease his grip on the struggling girl.

"Firmly hold the captive snake / Lest you feel the wrath of its fangs," he chanted. "Fool be he who—"

"Stop that rhyming nonsense!" I was about ready to hit him with the ham.

He suddenly smiled, and at that moment looked utterly sane.

"She'll betray us the moment we're out the door," he said. "We have to bring her, at least part of the way."

This was getting completely out of hand. I had set out to free my sister. Now there were enough of us for a family outing. Couldn't we tie her up like the Dragon soldier? But there wouldn't be room for her in the fruit cellar, and time was running out. Already there was much more light in the hall than there had been a moment ago. Dawn was on its way.

"If I let go of her now, she'll scream," said the beggar, still sounding completely normal.

"All right! We bring her too. Now, let us for heaven's sake get out of here!"

Green and White

It was raining. Big fat drops fell from branch to branch. The trees were crowded together in a dense mass of green, and it took a while for the drops to reach the ground. But reach it they did, and we got wet, bit by bit, drop by drop.

In front of me, Tavis slipped on the steep path, and I caught his arm to steady him. He tore himself loose from me with unnecessary force, without looking at me. He clearly wanted no help from a "traitor" like me.

I could hardly believe that I was walking here, underneath the open sky, breathing air that smelled of pine and resin and summer rain. Even getting wet was wonderful, at least at first.

Davin had found me. Davin and Rose. And I was on my way home.

Ahead of me, Davin and the tramp had stopped to untangle Sascha, whose sleeve had caught on a branch. She wanted no more help than Tavis. She tore herself free of the branch with a furious jerk, even though it damaged her silk robe. The tramp carefully removed every single shiny turquoise thread from the branch. She's doing it on purpose, I thought; she is trying to make it easier for them to find us.

"Can't we just leave her here?" I asked. I didn't dare shout. We hadn't heard or seen any sign of pursuit yet, and I thought our escape might still be undiscovered. But that happy state of affairs probably wouldn't last long, and there was no reason to tempt fate. "We could tie her to a tree—they'd be sure to find her quite soon."

The tramp looked as if the plan appealed to him, but Davin seemed more doubtful. And Sascha widened her eyes and put on a terrified expression.

"Oh, no," she moaned, "don't do that. Wolves will eat me!"

I somehow doubted that, this close to Dracana. And most of her terror looked like playacting to me.

"We can't keep dragging her along," I said. "First chance she gets, she'll betray us."

Sascha blinked her big dark eyes, and—was that tears? Yes, a gleaming tear was actually making its way down each smooth cheek.

"Never!" she vowed. "You don't know what horrors you have saved me from. That man"—she heaved a teary sigh—"that man is *evil*."

I didn't doubt that in the least. But the last time I had seen them together, she had called him Lord and gazed at him with adoration.

"Perhaps we don't need to tie her up," Davin said. "We could just let her go, couldn't we?"

Sascha put her hand on his arm and widened her eyes at him.

"*Please* let me come with you. I never want to see that man again."

Surely that was too thick for even my fool of a brother to swallow? Apparently not. He looked as if he wanted to wrap her in cotton wool and carry her away in his arms.

"Davin, we can't. She's lying! Can't you *see* she's lying?"

"We can't send her back to that monster!" he protested. "Not if she doesn't want to. Dina, look at her. If she speaks the truth, then . . . then she's coming with us. All the way to the Highlands, if need be."

He might as well have kicked me in the stomach.

I had almost forgotten about it because I had been so happy to see Davin and Rose, and then there had been all the danger, and finally *freedom*. Now it hit me again. I couldn't look Sascha in the eye. Or rather, I could. Only, nothing would happen. The gift I had inherited from my mother was broken. Gone. Gone like the signet I had lost.

I was not a Shamer anymore.

"Dina. What is it?" He looked at me searchingly. I hung my head.

"Nothing." I simply couldn't tell him. "Davin, she's lying."

"You haven't even looked at her. Not properly. How can you be sure, then?"

I shrugged helplessly. "I can't." I started walking. "Do as you like."

"Dina!" he objected, irritation and confusion warring in his voice.

"Do as you like," I repeated, not looking back.

About an hour later, when we reached the place where Black-Arse was hiding with the horses, Sascha was still with us. She threw me a triumphant sneer when she thought no one was looking.

There were only two horses, so we didn't really travel any quicker. At least we could take turns resting our feet a bit. Much of the time, Sascha somehow managed to get one of the horses to herself. Tavis had short legs and little strength after his many days in the cellar, so he spent most of the day on horseback, too. But even though the tramp was actually in a worse state than any of us, he refused to ride.

"When the woodsman wants to hide / Shank's Mare is the horse to ride," he sang. And despite his limp and his troubled breathing, he was surprisingly quick on his feet. It was not the tramp who slowed us down.

The tramp . . . I couldn't keep calling him that.

"What is your name?" I asked, trotting along next to him.

He smiled—a quick flash of teeth that looked astonishingly white. But that might be only because the rest of him was so weather-darkened and dirty.

"Rover by name and Rover by nature," he chanted.

"Rover? What kind of a name is that? For a man, I mean."

He shrugged.

"It's all the name I have these days," he said.

"Ssshh," hissed Davin. "I think I heard something."

We all stopped. Davin was right. A sound reached us, distant but chilling. The sound of hounds baying.

Without a word we set off again, faster now, and as quietly as possible.

The hunt was on.

Without Rover, we would have been caught a hundred times. I think he may have been part badger, or perhaps part fox. Except foxes don't climb trees, and Rover did.

He laid a dozen false trails. He found us shortcuts and hiding places. He found ways through many a wilderness I would have sworn was impassable. He blocked the way behind us in hundreds of ways—with rocks, with water, with fallen trees. Once he led the hounds astray with a hare he had caught. Another time he flung a wasps' nest into the camp of our pursuers, so that half their horses took off and they had to spend hours catching them.

Yet we still had the Dragon soldiers on our heels. There were so many of them, and they never seemed to sleep. All the time they were there, somewhere behind us or in front of us, and every time we had found a hiding place to get a few hours' sleep, we were torn from our rest and driven onward.

"You get stupid from not sleeping enough," Davin complained, rubbing one eye. "You drop stuff, or you forget to look where you're going."

"Of all the gifts that Nature gave / The boon of sleep we deepest crave," muttered Rover, taking a long swallow of water from one of the two flasks we had left—Black-Arse had lost his the day before, probably while we were crossing a small, fierce river none of us knew the name of.

On the second day, we lost the horses. And Sascha, although I didn't consider that much of a loss.

We were getting closer to the Highlands now, and the ground was growing stonier and steeper. We had to cross a rocky spur with not much cover, and to put a bit of distance between us and our hunters before that, Rover had laid yet another of his false trails. Davin, Black-Arse, and Sascha were to hide with the horses on one side of the trail we hoped our pursuers would choose.

"Keep an eye on her," I told Davin, before Rose and Tavis and I went to our own hiding place, comfortably high above the trail on the opposite side.

"You're so suspicious," said Davin. "Has she done anything to harm us?"

Not if you didn't count being terribly slow and leaving turquoise threads all over the landscape. But I didn't mention that.

"Just be careful," I said, and he sighed in irritation.

"Of course."

So now we were waiting, they in their hiding place and Rose and Tavis and me in ours, all of us hoping that Valdracu's men would pass by without noticing us.

"Here they come," Rose whispered, squeezing my hand. "Listen to the hounds."

Hoouuuuuww. Hoouuuuuwww. Oh, yes, I could hear them clearly now—the peculiar drawn-out howls the Dragon hounds gave when they had the scent of something. And then the first ones appeared, brindled gray rough-coated beasts that could look a child in the eye without rearing. Tavis gave a tiny moan and closed his eyes tightly. He was afraid of the hounds and often dreamed of them, if the starts and cries he made were anything to go by. Rose put a hand on his shoulder—she was much better at comforting him than I was. He still didn't trust me.

I wasn't exactly blissfully calm myself. My palms were clammy with sweat, but the hounds down there had their noses glued to the trail and noticed nothing else. They bounded along, heads low and tails high. After them came the riders—eight, no, nine Dragon soldiers advancing at a brisk trot. I tried to remember to breathe. Being this close to the hunters was an unsettling experience, but they seemed as intent on the trail as the hounds were.

This is going great, I thought. Rover really is a wizard at this game.

And then things stopped going great. Two horses came crashing through the shrubbery on the other side of the trail, one of them with a gleaming blue-green figure on its back.

"Soldier!" screamed Sascha at the top of her lungs. "Soldier, *halt*! The enemies of Lord Valdracu are right here!"

And Davin, the idiot, was running after her.

"Davin," I cried, and meant to rise, but Rose gave an almighty tug at my skirts and pulled me down again.

"Be *quiet*!" she whispered furiously. "What good does it do him if they catch you too?"

The hounds continued, but the riders pulled up sharply. It seemed to occur to Davin that he was running straight into the grasp of the enemy, and that it was far too late to stop Sascha. He turned and dashed off in the opposite direction, zigzagging among the trees. He ran like a deer, but the woods weren't dense enough, they were bound to catch him, and now one of them raised a bow.

"Stay down!" hissed Rose, once more pulling me low. I wasn't even aware that I had tried to get up.

Davin was gone. I didn't know whether he had fallen with an arrow through his chest or whether he had dropped low on purpose. I just couldn't see him anymore. And at that moment, something else was happening on the trail. The dogs were coming back. And they weren't alone. In front of them ran something dark, square, and hunchbacked, a whirlwind of hooves, tusks, and dark fury.

"It's a boar," Rose whispered, awe in her voice. "Where did he get it? I think he really is a wizard. I think he can *talk* to them." She meant Rover, of course.

The riders were forced to forget all about Davin. When a quarter of a ton of raging boar is headed your way, it tends to arrest your attention.

"Come," said Rover quietly, appearing out of nowhere just behind us. "Fools stay to jeer and shout / The wise man runs before his luck runs out."

He had a point. We ran.

It was late afternoon before Rover brought Black-Arse and Davin back to us. Davin looked sheepish.

"She hit me over the head with a branch," he said. "I didn't believe . . . I mean, I didn't think she'd do something like that." He had a bloody furrow at the point of his shoulder where the arrow had grazed him, but apart from that, he was unharmed.

"I wish she had been ugly," I said, pressing a pad of moss against the wound to stanch the bleeding. "If she had been ugly, you never would have trusted her."

"It's got nothing to do with that," Davin protested, embarrassed. But it had, and we both knew it.

My knees hurt. My feet hurt. My lungs hurt. There must have been a time once when I didn't just run, fall, get up, run, run, creep, climb, run again, and fall. There must have been a time when the world had had things in it other than wet pine trees, stony slopes, mud, hoofbeats, fear, and flight. It was just hard to remember right now.

Now that we had lost the horses, all hoofbeats belonged to the enemy. And ever since Sascha's betrayal, they had been breathing down our necks, so close that there had been no chance of sleep, no chance of anything but the briefest of rests. We drank when we could—cold water, at least, was plentiful. I had not eaten anything since we finished the ham the day before.

There was one comfort. The Highlands were near now, and every slope we labored to climb brought us closer to clan lands. It was probably too much to hope for that Valdracu would call off his men and give up once we reached them—he had shown no particular respect for clan rights in the past—but we might find help up there, clansmen who would protect us against Valdracu for Kensie's sake.

"Can you see anyone?" I asked Davin, who was lying on his stomach on an outcrop of rock a bit farther up.

"No," he said. "But I don't think we have lost them yet. That would be too much to hope for."

"Their horses aren't as much use to them anymore."

"No. But then, we don't have as much cover up here."

"Can't we at least rest a bit? Davin, we *have* to rest. Otherwise one of us will drop off the edge from sheer tiredness."

He wormed his way backward, off the skyline, and then sat up. His auburn hair was dark with rain and sweat, and he looked tired and dirty and worried. I wanted to stroke the hair away from his forehead and give him a hug. But I didn't. He wouldn't have wanted me to. Instead I held Rose more tightly. She had put her head on my shoulder a while ago and had promptly fallen asleep. Black-Arse sat with his back against a boulder, just staring into space. He had had to carry Tavis up the last rise, and it had sapped his strength. Rover was nowhere to be seen; as usual, he went his own way.

"I'm hungry," said Tavis. You couldn't say that he was

begging for food, because there was no hope whatsoever in his expression or his voice.

"We haven't got anything," I said.

"I know." He sighed. "But what I'd really like . . . bread and honey, I think. Or a chicken drumstick. Crispy hot roast chicken. Or . . . or a bowl of soup. Aye, soup for sure. With a marrowbone and carrots and meatballs and—"

"Will ye shut up?" moaned Black-Arse. "My belly had just stopped rumbling."

"We have to move on," Davin said. "I don't think they're very far away. If only we can get a little bit farther into the mountains, we might—"

He broke off. We stared at each other, because I heard it too. Hoofbeats. Not from below, but from above us. From the mountain.

Wildly, I looked around me. We had pulled back from the path we had been following, and two big boulders gave us some cover. We were invisible from below, I knew. But from above?

There was nowhere to run to. We could only cower behind the boulders, like leverets in the tall grass. Hide as best we could. Wait. Hope.

The hoofbeats got closer. There were many of them, an entire troop it sounded like. But were they really Valdracu's men? How had they got ahead of us?

They went past. Iron shoes clanged against the rocky path, a horse snorted and jiggled its bit. Cautiously, oh so cautiously, I poked my head around the boulder, close to the ground.

There was about a dozen of them. Tired men. You could see it from the way they sat their horses. Most had spatters of blood on their clothes, and more than one had a dirty bandage around an arm or a hand. But that was not what made my breath catch.

They were wearing clan cloaks. Green-and-white clan cloaks.

"Kensie," I croaked, hardly able to say the word. "Davin, they are Kensie!"

He leaped to his feet, swinging his arms above his head and hollering like a madman.

"Kensie! Hello, there, Kensie!!"

We all got up. The troop of riders halted, turned, and came back to us. The green-and-white cloaks flapped in the wind like banners.

I could hardly believe it. Kensie men. Had they come looking for us, or was it coincidence? What incredibly good luck!

We were safe. We were finally safe.

Soon we were surrounded by tired men and horses.

"Who the hell are you?" asked one of them, a tall red-haired man who reminded me a bit of Callan. "What are ye doin' here?"

"We're Kensie too," Davin said eagerly. "More or less. Some of us. Black-Arse, tell him—"

But Black-Arse was staring at the men. His eyes flickered from one face to the next, as if he were looking for someone.

"Davin," he whispered, "I do not know him. I do not know a single one of them."

Davin's smile faded. "What do you mean?"

"These are not Kensie," said Black-Arse, his voice full of fear and conviction.

It took me a moment to take in what he was saying. That was a moment too much. I whirled and tried to run, but one of the riders seized me by the arm and hauled me halfway up his sweaty horse. My feet left the ground and I dangled in midair like a caught fish.

"Grab them," ordered the man who looked like Callan. "I'm sure Mesire Valdracu can use a few *real* Kensie folk."

Valdracu's Vengeance

"We could have made it," Davin said tonelessly. "We were nearly there. We nearly got away from him."

I didn't say anything. There wasn't much to say.

They weren't in any particular hurry, the false Kensie men. They didn't know that Valdracu was scouring the woods for us a bit farther down the mountain. They had sent a messenger off with the news of their catch, and instead of riding east toward Dracana, they were going almost due south, skirting the edge of the Highlands and heading for some place they just called "headquarters." They didn't know who we were, except that some of us were genuine Kensie. Black-Arse couldn't hide his origins—they were obvious every time he opened his mouth. And Tavis had been foolish enough to tell them that *he* was no lowly Kensie, but Helena Laclan's own grandson. I don't know whether he thought they would then let him go, but if so, he was mistaken—they now watched him even more carefully than the rest of us.

They didn't really ill-treat us apart from tying us up, but they made no efforts to make our lives easier either. We were a nuisance to them, a nuisance they put up with because they hoped for a reward. They allowed us to drink but didn't bother feeding us that night when they made camp. I was so exhausted that I slept at least part of the night, despite the cold ground and the ropes that numbed my hands and arms. The rest of the time I lay huddled against Davin's back, trying to keep warm and trying not to think about what Valdracu would do to us once he had us in his grasp again.

At first I had taken some comfort from the fact that they hadn't caught Rover. Rover the wizard, who would surely think of some way of setting us free. Perhaps he would sneak into camp under cover of darkness and cut us loose. Perhaps he would spook our captors' horses. Perhaps . . . but the night passed, and there was no sign of him or any of his magical stunts. And when I thought about it in the harsh, clear light of the morning, it had been an improbable hope. What was one half-crazed beggar to do against thirteen trained men of war—no matter how good his woodsmanship? He had simply run off, and who could blame him?

Just as the false Kensie were striking camp and getting ready for the day's ride, there were hoofbeats on the mountain path, and a man in Dragon uniform came galloping up to us.

"Message from Valdracu," he called as soon as he was within shouting range. "The captives are to be brought to Hog's Gorge to be delivered there into the hands of Mesire Valdracu himself. Immediately."

"Why the rush?" said the one who looked a bit like Callan—Morlan, they called him. "We have had a hard ride already, and now he wants us to go miles out of our way? If he wants them, he can come get them—at a suitable price, of course."

"Hog's Gorge," repeated the messenger. "At once. And don't worry—he'll pay you a good price. Those are gilded birds you've caught!"

Morlan growled, but the mention of "a good price" had clearly had its effect.

"To horse," he called. "Let's go see what the Dragon will pay for such fancy fowl."

We were quite close to Hog's Gorge when we ran into a small troop of Dragon soldiers—only four men. At the head of our column, Morlan raised his hand and brought his men to a halt. I squirmed and tried to ease my aching back and legs, but the "Kensie" whose horse I was sharing tightened his grips on my waist.

"Sit still," he snapped. "This is hard enough on the nag as it is."

Morlan moved forward a little bit to meet the leader of the Dragon troop.

"Ah, so Morlan has caught them," said the Dragon soldier. "Excellent. I'll take over from here."

"Not so fast," said Morlan. "I already have my orders."

Yes, and you don't want to miss out on your reward, I thought.

"And what are those?"

"To bring the captives to Hog's Gorge. We're headed there now." He pointed forward and to the left, toward a narrow cleft of a valley that we were about to enter.

"Hog's Gorge? I don't know anything about that." The Dragon soldier eyed Morlan and his men suspiciously. "Why there?"

"How should I know?"

"Morlan, I don't know what your game is, but—"

"Do you doubt my word?"

The Dragon soldier looked as if a bad smell had caught his nostrils. "Your word? Why would I doubt your word— just because you bear a false banner and wear a false cloak? Or perhaps it is a turncoat?"

"You cur," snarled Morlan, putting his hand on his sword. "I'll teach ye—"

"I wonder what you'll teach me, once Mesire Valdracu gets here. Give the signal, Horn!" And one of the troopers raised the horn he was carrying and blew a few loud notes that echoed down the gorge.

Morlan let go of his sword hilt. His eyes still blazed, but he spoke no more of curs and lessons.

"I was promised a reward" was all he said.

The Dragon soldier nodded. "To be sure, Morlan. You'll get your wages."

I stared dejectedly down at my hands, which were tied to the saddle horn. Let them quarrel. What did it matter whether Valdracu met us here or farther down the gorge? In the end, the result would be the same.

The four riders were apparently just the outriders. It was only moments before more Dragon soldiers appeared over the ridge above us. Eight men—and Valdracu.

You could tell that he had spent days in the forest, far from the conveniences he liked to surround himself with. Some of the polish had worn off, and his cold rage was almost tangible. His men took pains not to get in his way.

His glare raked over the assembled troops and fixed itself on me.

"So," he said, and there wasn't even triumph in his voice, only coldness, "finally."

He rode Mefisto straight down the crowded trail, and men and horses hastily scattered before him. With a move so fast that I could barely follow it, he freed his chain and raised it. It whistled through the air and would have hit me in the face, except that the horse I was on was no Mefisto. It spooked and sidestepped, and the last few links caught me across the thigh instead. It was bad enough even so, a line of fire that made my eyes sting.

I heard Davin shouting but could see almost nothing for the tears I was trying to blink away.

"Keep that horse steady," ordered Valdracu and once more raised his arm. I couldn't even lift my bound hands, could only turn my face away and duck as best I could. The chain struck the back of my neck, just behind the ear. It was like being cut by thin ice, cold at first, then fiery hot, and I felt the blood well and trickle down my neck.

His knife flashed out. I cowered, half-expecting him to stab me with it, but he cut the rope that tied me to the saddle horn instead, seized my arm, and dragged me off the horse. My legs had no strength in them, and I ended up on my hands and knees on the ground, among the hooves. There was a ringing in my head from the blow, and I dared not raise my eyes, dared not risk looking at him.

He must have dismounted too. The next moment, I felt his grip on my neck, almost in the spot where the chain had hit me. He pulled me to my feet and pushed me against Mefisto's unyielding flank, with my cheek pressed against the saddle flap.

"If you look at me, I'll kill them all," he said, a breath of ice right next to my ear. "All of them. Do you understand?"

I nodded.

"Are you sure you understand?"

"Yes," I whispered, "I understand."

"I have my doubts, you see," he said. "As it seems you did not feel any need to respect our first agreement. Perhaps you think I'm not serious."

A chill spread from the center of my stomach. "Yes," I whispered desperately. "I know you are. I know!"

"Be quiet," he said. Then he raised his voice. "The Laclan boy. Do we have him as well?"

"Yes," said Sandor, who was holding Mefisto's reins.

"Good. Then kill him."

"No," I screamed. "*No!*"

Sandor flung Mefisto's reins to one of the other Dragon soldiers and started toward the horse Tavis was on. I twisted and caught a glimpse of Tavis's frozen white face. One of the other Dragon men, the messenger, beat Sandor to it and dragged Tavis to the ground.

"Let me go!" screamed Tavis, and tried to kick his shin, but the messenger had him by the scruff of the neck and started dragging him into the shrubbery.

I was screaming my head off. I forgot all about Valdracu's threats and so-called agreements.

"Shame on you!" I yelled, trying to catch his eyes. "Shame on you, shame—"

"Shut up, you devil's brat!" he cried with an edge of panic in his voice and tried to get his hand over my mouth. I kept shouting. It just didn't do any good. There was no hint of the Gift in my voice, and this finally dawned on Valdracu. He stopped trying to shut me up and instead turned me so that he could look into my eyes.

"Dear me," he said, sounding as if the whole thing amused him, "my rare bird seems to have lost its claws."

I was sobbing and crying my eyes out and I couldn't stop whispering "Shame on you," even though it did no good whatsoever. From the shrubbery I heard Tavis cry out, a thin terrified thread of a scream. Then all was quiet.

The Dragon soldier came back. His knife and his hands were dark with blood.

"What should I do with the body?" he asked. "Bring it along?"

"No," said Valdracu carelessly. "Leave it. Scavengers have to eat, too."

Hog's Gorge

We started down the mountain, into Hog's Gorge. My head was still buzzing from the blow I had got when I tried to help Dina, but that was nothing compared to the cold feeling of utter shock that made my whole body feel stiff and strange. They had killed Tavis. They had dragged a small freckled boy into the bushes and cut his throat.

I could hear Dina crying. Sometimes there was still a half-choked "Shame on you" from her, but no one paid any attention.

I didn't understand. Why hadn't she been able to stop him? What was wrong with her?

Dina, I thought, how could you let him *kill* a little boy? Valdracu was no Drakan who could look a Shamer in the eye and never blink; that much was obvious from the way he feared her eyes. Or had feared them. Apparently he no longer did.

The trail was steep and difficult. The horse I was on

stumbled and nearly fell. It wasn't easy for it to keep its balance with two people on its back, me and the false Kensie man behind me.

He had realized that too. He cut my hands loose from the saddle horn.

"Get down," he said. "But don't even think about running. I'll put an arrow through you if you try it."

I didn't doubt it. I slid down and tottered stiffly ahead of him, on rubbery legs that would barely obey me. Black-Arse and Rose had been let down as well, I could see. But at the head of the column, Valdracu still held Dina in front of him, and his big dark bay seemed to be able to manage the incline anyway.

It was a wet and stony and narrow place. On both sides of the trail the sides of the gorge rose steeply, and muddy rainwater pooled around my feet, so that it was almost like wading through a stream. Directly in front of me was a dappled gray rump, and if I didn't keep up the pace, I'd likely get trampled from behind; it wasn't easy for a rider to halt his horse here.

There was a whirring sound in the air, and a thud. Suddenly the rider on the horse in front wobbled in the saddle and pitched forward. There was a scream, but not from him. Somewhere else. More whirring. More thuds. Arrows rained down on us, and men and horses were falling and fighting, struggling to keep their footing, to get up, to get away. In moments, the narrow gorge had become a slaughterhouse, and no one in it could even see the attackers that fired the deadly arrows.

I jumped to avoid the panicked charge of the horse behind me and tried to climb a little higher up the side of the gorge. Below, I could see Rose and Black-Arse doing the same thing. We were far better off than the riders, because we were able to clamber up the steep slope, away from the bottom of the gorge, which had become a chaos of fallen bodies and kicking hooves. But Dina? Where was Dina?

At first I could see neither her nor Valdracu. They had been at the point of the column, hadn't they? I couldn't even see that far. I climbed downward, jumped over a dead horse, clambered up the slope again, climbed a boulder . . . there they were. Valdracu had leaped from the saddle and was running downward, away from the slaughter, with the horse at his back and Dina held before him like a living shield.

I quickly stooped to wrest the sword from a wounded Dragon soldier. He looked at me in wide-eyed terror; I think he expected me to finish him off, but I had more important things to do. I edged past a bewildered and riderless horse and ran toward Valdracu as fast as my legs would take me. I began to catch up, too—Dina was no willing shield; she squirmed and kicked and fought him every inch of the way, slowing him down as much as she could.

I got quite close, near enough to actually touch the bay's tail, before Valdracu caught sight of me. For a moment he looked startled. Then he pulled the horse around so that it blocked the trail almost completely. He turned to me with one arm round Dina's throat, and drew his sword with his free hand.

"Stop," he said. "Stay where you are, or I cut her throat."

I stopped. Then I thought better of it and took another slow step forward.

"If you kill her, you won't have any shield," I said. "If I don't get you, the archers will."

An arrow streaked past my shoulder and buried itself in the slope by the horse's muzzle, almost as if to underline my words.

He seemed to consider it for a moment. Then he shook his head.

"You don't quite understand," he said. "You see, I don't care whether she lives or dies. But you do. I even think"—he raised the blade until it rested against Dina's neck—"I even think you might prefer to die, rather than see her killed. Am I right? You *are* her brother, I think?"

I didn't answer. What was I to say? He might be right; I simply didn't know. I only knew that if he used the blade now, against Dina's vulnerable neck, then I might kill him, yes, but I would never again be able to go home.

He smiled. "That's what I thought," he said. "Stay where you are. Don't try to follow me. Your sister wouldn't like it."

He clicked his tongue, and the horse began to move on.

As he turned to follow it, an arrow streaked across the bay's back and grazed Valdracu's right ear. Blood welled from the lobe, and he instinctively put a hand to his neck, letting go of Dina. Instantly, Dina threw herself to the ground, rolled under the horse's belly, and came up on the other side. The horse cow-kicked at her and leaped forward, and Valdracu, who suddenly had neither horse nor girl to shield him, cursed, dropped low, and started worming his way toward Dina like a snake.

There wasn't time to think about it. I raised my stolen sword and struck.

I hit him in the side, just above the hip, but I knew right away that it wasn't enough. He was wearing a mail shirt under his tunic and simply ignored the blow. He didn't even turn to fight, he just reached out, grabbed Dina's ankle, and pulled her down into the mud with him.

I struck again. This time, I aimed for his neck.

A spray of blood spattered over both Dina and me. He made a sound, a sort of bubbling cough. I seized him by the shoulder and dragged him off my sister, tipping him onto his back. He lay there, faceup in the muddy gorge, and I could see that I had killed him even though he wasn't dead yet. The sword had gone halfway through his neck, and he was bleeding like a butchered pig, in quick spurts at first, then more sluggishly. His eyes stared up at

me, but after a while I could tell they weren't seeing anything.

It wasn't like killing a goat or a deer.

It wasn't like killing any animal.

It was like nothing I had ever done before.

I fell to my knees beside the man I had just killed, and
retched until there was nothing left in my stomach.

Unharmed

The fighting was over. After the clamor and the shouting and the struggles of the frantic horses, the gorge was almost silent now. One wounded man was moaning loudly. From both sides the archers began to appear, still with arrows notched in case they met with any resistance. But neither Dragon soldiers nor false Kensies were a danger to them now. Those that were still alive had surrendered, and many were in any case so badly wounded that they couldn't defend themselves, let alone attack.

Davin was on his knees next to Valdracu. He had thrust the point of the sword into the ground and was clutching the hilt as if it was the only thing that kept him from falling.

"Davin . . ."

"Don't look at me," he said. "Not now. Please."

I shook my head. "Don't worry about it," I said. "You can look me in the eye anytime. Nothing will happen."

He made a disbelieving sound, part snort, part sob.

"I mean it," I said. "That's why . . . it was . . . Davin, I couldn't stop him. I couldn't. I'm not a Shamer anymore."

That made him look at me.

"What kind of rubbish is that?" he said angrily. "You don't just stop being a Shamer."

I didn't know what else to say. I just looked at him. And gradually his expression changed.

"Do you mean to say . . . that that was why . . ."

"I couldn't stop him! It didn't work!" And so they dragged away Tavis, they had killed a nine-year-old boy *because* of me, and I had not been able to stop it, any more than I could stop the tears running down my cheeks right now.

"It wasn't really your fault," said Davin, but I imagined I heard a hint of doubt in his voice.

There was a shout from the slope. "Are you hurt?"

I looked up. I wasn't too surprised to see Rover among the archers. But it wasn't he who had shouted. It was the Weapons Master.

For a moment, the world tilted. What was he doing here? I hadn't seen him in nearly a year; he and the Widow lived in Solark . . . and then I remembered some of the guards talking about the fall of Solark. Drakan had taken the fortress that everyone had believed was impregnable. Not so strange, then, that the Master was no longer in Solark. But here?

"No," Davin called back, "we are unharmed."

His voice trembled a bit, and I thought that no, we weren't wounded, at least on the outside, but "unharmed" we were not. Not me, nor Davin.

He got to his feet slowly, and so did I.

"What is the Weapons Master doing here?" I asked, not really expecting an answer. How would he know? But it turned out that he knew more than I did.

"I think he has found a way to fight Drakan," he said. "He and the Widow have been gathering people for some time now. I think Rover must be one of them."

We headed up the gorge, toward the Master and the others. There seemed to be dead people everywhere, but I was almost too tired to take it in. Sandor lay there with an arrow through his eye, and I just thought, Oh, he's dead too, then. Later I would probably *have* to think about it, but right now there really wasn't room inside me.

Not many of Valdracu's men had survived. Morlan was one of them. Two archers were tying his hands behind his back. And behind him was—

I stopped so abruptly that Davin ran into me.

The messenger. The man who had murdered Tavis.

He stood there completely free and unharmed, talking to Rover, and nobody seemed to want to do anything to him.

I didn't even think. I just threw myself at him.

Taken aback, he staggered and fell backward.

"Murderer!" I screamed, going for his eyes. I might not be able to kill him, not with my bare hands anyway, but I would do my best to blind him, and that would be some revenge at least for poor—

Someone seized me from behind and pulled me off him.

"Easy, easy," said the Weapons Master. "Let him be. He is one of ours."

"He is *what*?" I cried, beside myself. "He killed Tavis!"

"No, he didn't," said the Master. "He saved his life."

"Saved his—" I didn't understand. "But I saw—"

"You saw a small boy get dragged into the bushes. And a man returning with bloody hands."

"I had to knock him unconscious," said the messenger. "There wasn't time to explain, and in any case I don't think I could have made him listen. But the blood wasn't his." He pulled up his sleeve and showed me a dark cut on his forearm. "I had to do *something*. Valdracu wasn't meant to come across you until you were well into Hog's Gorge."

"No, we came close to failing completely," growled the Master. "We need more practice at this." He let go of me. "Well? Do you still want to scratch his eyes out?"

"No," I said in a weak voice and had to sit down.

Tavis was alive.

Suddenly, I could breathe again. It was as if I had been tangled in something terrible, cold, and tight that had threatened to strangle me slowly. Now it was gone, and I could breathe. He had *not* died. I had not been the cause of his death.

"Where is he?" I asked. Right now I had the most burning desire to see his hostile little freckled face, even if he was still throwing me dirty looks and calling me a traitor. Maybe I could make him trust me now. Maybe I could explain what happened with Valdracu. At least I could try. You can't explain anything to people if they're dead.

The Weapons Master pointed to the gorge's entrance. "I've just sent a man to get him. If you go up the gorge and turn west, you will find a stream. We were planning on camping there for a bit. You go on ahead."

For the first time in days, I sat by a fire and had something hot to eat and drink. I had stood in the cold water of the brook for a very long time, scrubbing and scouring my hands and my hair and my face until I felt reasonably clean, but the blouse was a hopeless cause. One sleeve was completely soaked in Valdracu's blood, and I couldn't make myself put it back on even though I knew how cold I'd be in just my vest and bodice.

I heard steps and looked about me quickly. It was just Davin. My heart settled again, and I thought that it might be a while before I stopped acting like a hunted animal.

"Here," said my brother, and held out one of the green and white Kensie cloaks. "It's a little muddy round the hem, that's all."

I hesitated, but only for a moment. It was a good cloak of thick wool, and I felt warmer instantly.

"Why were they wearing Kensie cloaks?" I asked.

"The Master is talking to Morlan right now," said Davin. "But he doesn't have much to say for himself."

"Offer him money," I said bitterly. "There isn't much that man won't do if the price is right."

"They had been in a fight," said Davin. "Three of them were wounded. Who do you think they had been fighting?"

"I know that," said Tavis.

He startled both Davin and me. He had been lying close to the fire, so pale and silent that you nearly forgot he was there.

"Who, then?" asked Davin, trying to sound as if it didn't really matter. With Tavis, you never knew when he would turn contrary.

"Skaya," said Tavis. "I heard them talkin' about it. They were laughin' and sayin' that they had taught them Skayas a lesson."

At first I was just relieved that they hadn't attacked Kensie—it would have been so easy, no one would have suspected anything until they were too close. But I could see that relief was not exactly what Davin was feeling.

"Black-Arse," said Davin slowly and quietly, "if a troop of men in Kensie cloaks attack Skaya to—what was it he said?—'teach them a lesson,' what would Skaya do?"

"Strike back," said Black-Arse without hesitation. "But they were not Kensie. Not really."

"Skaya doesn't know that," said Davin, and there was fear in his voice now. "Skaya will attack, then. *Where*, Black-Arse?"

Suddenly, Black-Arse too had gone completely still and frightened.

"Baur Kensie," he said. "They'll attack Baur Kensie."

Scara Vale

I leaned forward over the horse's dark neck, wishing that horses had wings. The Weapons Master had chosen the nine strongest for us among those Valdracu's and Morlan's people had been riding. But they were still only ordinary horses and not fairy-tale creatures with eight legs or fabulous flying skills. And right now we needed miracles.

Two days had passed since the false Kensies had attacked Skaya. And the journey from Hog's Gorge to Baur Kensie could not be done in less than three. Our only hope was that Astor Skaya might choose not to strike back immediately. He had a reputation for planning everything, even a simple hunting trip, down to the last detail. Did it take more than five days to plan an attack on Baur Kensie?

There were nine of us—much against my wishes. I would have ridden alone, but the Weapons Master wouldn't hear of it.

"Too dangerous," he had said. "What if you are

attacked? What if your horse puts its foot in a rabbit hole? No, we ride fast, but we ride together."

"Together" meant Dina, Rose, Black-Arse, and me, the Weapons Master and three of his men—and Morlan.

"We'll need some kind of proof," said the Master. "We cannot expect Skaya to believe our naked word."

So Morlan rode right behind the Master now with his hands tied to the saddle horn and a rope from foot to foot under the horse's belly. If *his* horse put a foot in a rabbit hole, I didn't think much of his chances of escaping unscathed. But then, his well-being was the least of my concerns right now.

It took us the better part of a day and night to reach the Highlands proper. Luckily there was a full moon, but despite that, the Weapons Master commanded a halt shortly after midnight. "Or else we'll kill the horses," he said.

We couldn't gallop or even canter all the time. The climbs were too hard, and the trail too rocky and treacherous, and we had to spare the strength of the horses. I had to fight my impatience and let the Master set the pace, because he knew much better than I did how hard we could press the animals—and ourselves.

"Sometimes you must make haste slowly," he said at one point when I couldn't keep my mouth shut. "Galloping like mad will gain you nothing if your horse breaks down before you are halfway there."

I knew he was right, but in my mind's eye I kept seeing

the same sight over and over again: the blackened lot where our old house had been. The dead animals. The ruined well. Only, now it was our new cottage, and it was not just animals lying there in pools of dried blood. Mama. Melli. Maudi. Nico—I even worried about Nico. If they came to kill him, would he look at them with that cool blue gaze of his and say: "I don't care for swords"?

The second day we made better time, as the worst of the climbs were behind us. But that night the Weapons Master insisted we rest through all the hours of darkness. I lay between Dina and Black-Arse, staring up at the clouded night sky and hearing Black-Arse talk in his sleep. He didn't dream of blueberry pies anymore. "Put out the fire!" he suddenly yelled, and I knew his dreams were like mine.

"Are you asleep?" Dina whispered.

"No," I said.

"I can't," she said. "I'm completely exhausted, but I can't sleep."

"We'll make it," I told her.

"You don't know that," she said. "You just hope so."

"Yes," I murmured. "But what else is there to do?"

Finally I did fall asleep, and I think Dina did too. We were simply too tired to lie sleepless all night. And at dawn we fed our poor horses, brushed them and saddled them, and made ready for another day's hell-ride.

· · ·

We heard it first in the early afternoon. I thought for a moment that it was thunder. But although the wind was fierce and the clouds heavy, there was no lightning. And then I heard the roaring. It hardly sounded human, but I knew now what it was: the sound of men attacking men.

"Ride!" I yelled, for if we were close enough to hear the sounds of battle, there was no longer any reason to save the strength of our horses. So we rode. We were still half a day's ride from Baur Kensie, and I had a faint hope that perhaps it wasn't Skaya and Kensie we were hearing. That hope vanished like a snuffed flame when I kicked my exhausted horse up the final ridge and looked down at Scara Vale.

It was a wide, flat valley normally inhabited only by cows and sheep. A peaceful valley, usually, with a calmly winding stream, green and yellow grasses, a little clover, and a lot more heather.

Now it was filled with men and horses, with battle cries and turmoil, and the sound of blade clashing against blade. I remembered that I had once loved that sound. It seemed a long time ago.

I don't know how many there were, it was impossible to count them. And it didn't matter anyway. They had to stop. I had to stop them. Already there were men on the ground, the wounded and the dead, Skaya and Kensie one among the other.

I put my heels to the horse. It took a few reluctant steps forward and finally stumbled into a last exhausted gallop.

"Stop!" I yelled at the top of my voice. "Kensie! Skaya! Stop! Listen to me!"

I might as well have shouted at the storm. They paid me no notice. Probably they couldn't even hear me through the clamor of the battle. And they were far too busy killing one another.

"HOLD!" It was the Weapons Master, and I had never heard a louder roar from any human throat. But not even his mighty shout could penetrate the tumult. Despair filled me. It was hopeless. No human on earth could get through to them. No ordinary voice would ever—

"STOP."

No ordinary voice, no.

My mother's voice.

No fearsome roar. Not even all that loud. It sounded as if she were standing right next to you.

The men in the valley froze. In the middle of striking, in the middle of leaping, in the middle of killing or dying. It was as if someone had waved a magic wand over them. Even the horses stood still, as if their legs had suddenly turned to wood. The only sound at that moment was the whistle of the wind as it swept through the valley, flattening the grass in great waves.

I knew that my mother had once made thousands of angry people in Dunark's Arsenal Court stand still, be silent, and listen. And a moment ago I myself had been screaming at the fighting men to stop; I had no greater desire than to see them like this, unmoving and silent.

Still it was a frightening thing to watch. So unnatural. Like magic.

I understood why many people were afraid of my mother.

I even understood why some of them called her a witch. But . . .

I shook myself like a dog coming out of water. She had given me this gift, this one moment of silence. If I didn't use it, the silence would be brief indeed, for not even my mother could still the arms and voices of a hundred fighting men for more than a moment.

"Skaya!" I called, as loudly as I could. "Kensie! Both of you stand betrayed. Look! This man wears Kensie's colors on his cloak, and Skaya blood on his hands. But he is no Kensie. His name is Morlan—and he is in the Dragon's pay."

I made my horse take another few steps, and next to me the Weapons Master drew Morlan's horse forward, so that they could all see him. I raked the battleground with my eyes, and was immensely relieved to see a familiar figure still upright.

"Callan!" I called. "Skaya! Astor Skaya! Rest your weapons; come see for yourself whether or not I speak the truth."

Callan was already headed my way—I could see his broad figure cutting through the press. And there, in the middle of the tightest knot of black-and-blue Skaya men, was Astor Skaya, in a shirt of mail so bright it caught the light like a salmon leaping upriver.

"Clan peace!" roared Callan over the heads of men mostly much smaller than himself. "I want clan peace, Skaya, until we get to the bottom of this!"

Nodding reluctantly, Astor Skaya sheathed his sword. "Clan peace," he called back. "But I'm warning ye, Kensie—if this is another betrayal, there will be nothing called Kensie clan or Kensie lands in a year's time!"

My muscles turned to water. I could have fallen off my horse from pure relief.

"Where's Mama?" I asked. "She should help them to talk to each other. She is good at that kind of thing."

"Your mother?" said the Master in a puzzled tone. "Is she here?"

I turned around.

My little sister was sitting on the ground, clutching her head as if she was afraid it might otherwise fall off.

"It hurts," she moaned. "It hurts so much. I'll never do that again, ever!"

Only then did I realize that it was not my mother's voice that had stopped the Battle of Scara Vale.

It was Dina's.

I didn't see my mother until late that evening. And yet another day passed in a whirl of events before we had time to talk properly. She found me by the sheep shed just as I was pushing the sword into the thatch. My new sword that I had stolen by wrenching it from the hands of a wounded man.

"Are you hiding it?" she asked.

I shrugged. "I don't know about hiding," I said. "It just seems like a suitable place to keep it."

"I hear you killed a man," she said.

"Yes. Valdracu. The one who had you shot."

I could feel her behind me, tense and unmoving.

"Can you look at me now?" she asked. "Or are you too ashamed of it?"

I didn't turn around at once. I had to think about it. I remembered the sound he had made. The eyes, growing empty.

"Davin?"

"Yes." I turned. Met her eyes. "I'm not ashamed," I said, "not about that. But I wish it hadn't been necessary."

She nodded.

"Welcome home," she said, putting her arms around me very carefully, as if she wasn't sure that I wanted it. But I did.

Silky

The sun was setting. It had been a hot day, and Beastie lay in the tall grass by the woodpile with his tongue hanging out like a pink ribbon. In the middle of our yard stood Ivain Laclan with a small, dappled gray mountain horse, much finer than Debbi Herbs's gray pony.

"There is a letter," he said, "from Helena."

I took it, and read it carefully. She had written to me, not to my mother. She thanked me and my family for bringing back her grandchild. And she wrote how happy she was that the clan war between Kensie and Skaya had been averted with so little loss of life. It was a very grown-up letter. Not the kind you would normally write to a girl my age. And at the end it said:

"Tavis sends his warmest greetings." That was probably a polite lie, I thought. I didn't think he would ever feel any warmth for me. "And I send you Silky, who will serve you faithfully and well. You will have need of her when you follow your mother in her craft."

"It's a very fine gift," I said awkwardly and didn't quite know what to do with my hands. "Will you thank Helena Laclan for me, many times?"

"Aye," he said, "that I will. Where is that hotheaded brother of yours?"

"Out somewhere with Black-Ar—I mean, with Allin Kensie. I don't know where they are."

"Ah, well," said Ivain. "Perhaps it's just as well. I had a mind to shake his hand, but he might not want to shake mine."

"You are welcome to stay the night," I said. "He'll be back before dark."

He shook his head. "Thank ye kindly, but I have already made my arrangements with Maudi Kensie. Shall I put up the nag for ye?"

"I can do that," I said.

"Right, then. Good luck with Silky. She's a fine little mare—a real lady's horse."

Smiling, I thanked him once more, and did not ask the question that was on my mind: did Silky know how to haul timber? If she didn't, she would have to learn. That kind of thing could save your life.

Ivain Laclan disappeared over the hill in the direction of Maudi's farm. I led Silky into the stable and let her get acquainted with Falk. He was of course completely

delighted to have company at last. He pranced and whin-
nied and pawed the ground, probably telling Silky what a
glorious male animal he was. Silky snorted and drew back
from all his antics and pretended to prefer my company to
his. She blew softly on my neck and nibbled at my hair,
and when you touched that soft dark gray muzzle, it
wasn't hard to tell how she had got her name.

I fed both of them some hay, gave them fresh water,
and then went back to the house.

Mama was sitting by the kitchen table, shelling peas. I
showed her the letter.

"That is a grand and generous gift," said Mama.
"Laclan breeds very fine horses."

I nodded. Mama looked at me.

"Why aren't you pleased?" she asked.

"I am."

"No," she said, "not really. What's wrong?"

For a while I just sat there, shredding empty pea pods
into green slivers. In the end the words came bursting out
of me on their own:

"I didn't deserve it!"

"Why not?"

"She writes . . . she writes that I'll need Silky when I
follow you in your craft. But I'm not sure . . . I don't think
I can ever *be* a Shamer."

I had tried. Rose had helped me. Davin too. But no
matter how hard I strained, I had been able to say nothing

whatsoever in the Shamer's voice, not since that one word in Scara Vale. I had so wanted to look Davin in the eye again, and now I had my wish—but not quite the way I had imagined.

Mama suddenly got up. She went to the alcove I slept in and slipped her hand under my pillow.

"Is that why you don't wear this anymore?" she said, holding out the Shamer's signet.

Miserable, I nodded.

"I'm so sorry, Mama—but I don't think I can be your apprentice anymore."

"Why ever not?"

"Because . . . you know why! I can't do it anymore. Most of the time I couldn't even shame a mouse. I . . . I'm not a Shamer. Not anymore."

"Oh?" Mama smiled, but there was a touch of sharpness in her voice. "Perhaps you should ask Callan about that. Or Astor Skaya. Or any one of the men who were in Scara Vale and suddenly lost the desire to fight. Many a full-grown Shamer would be hard put to do as much."

"But that was . . ." I almost said "an accident," but those weren't quite the words. "That was something I did without thinking. And my head hurt so much afterward that I was nearly blind. When I *try* to do it, nothing happens."

"Sweetie"—Mama sat down next to me on the kitchen bench—"it will come back. Sooner or later. You haven't lost your gift. It has just gone into hiding, because an evil man made you abuse it. Don't try to force it; it will come back on its own. When you are ready."

She put the signet on the table in front of me and stroked my hair.

"I'm so glad to have you back," she said.

"Do you want me to put it on again?" I asked.

"That's up to you," she said.

"When they took it away from me, it felt like I was no longer your daughter."

She laughed. "That is the stupidest thing you have said in a good long while. Isn't Melli my daughter? Isn't Davin my son? Do you think you stop being mine just because you can't always shame people?"

"No," I said tentatively, "I suppose not."

That night I lay with my hand under the pillow, holding the Shamer's Signet. I couldn't sleep. I could hear Rose's quiet breathing, and Melli's. I was thinking about everything that had happened. It was so incredibly lucky that Tavis was still alive. Actually I was lucky to be alive, too, and Davin, and Rose. It was lucky that I was lying here, with our new roof over my head, and that there was peace among the clans for now.

In the Lowlands, Drakan hunted down Shamers and burned them at the stake. Davin had told me that.

"Mama says he is spreading shamelessness around him," he had said, "like some kind of infectious disease."

My fingers slid across the cool pewter circle, tracing the edge of the enamel. It had become a dangerous emblem to wear. Particularly for someone like me who could no longer defend myself. But perhaps, tomorrow, I'd put it on again.

Maybe.